BRIA

SUCH BRIGHT DISGUISES

BRIAN FLYNN was born in 1885 in Leyton, Essex. He won a scholarship to the City Of London School, and from there went into the civil service. In World War I he served as Special Constable on the Home Front, also teaching "Accountancy, Languages, Maths and Elocution to men, women, boys and girls" in the evenings, and acting in his spare time.

It was a seaside family holiday that inspired Brian Flynn to turn his hand to writing in the mid-twenties. Finding most mystery novels of the time "mediocre in the extreme", he decided to compose his own. Edith, the author's wife, encouraged its completion, and after a protracted period finding a publisher, it was eventually released in 1927 by John Hamilton in the UK and Macrae Smith in the U.S. as *The Billiard-Room Mystery*.

The author died in 1958. In all, he wrote and published 57 mysteries, the vast majority featuring the super-sleuth Antony Bathurst.

BRIAN FLYNN

SUCH BRIGHT DISGUISES

With an introduction by
Steve Barge

DEAN STREET PRESS

"Men put such bright disguises on their Lust."

JOHN MASEFIELD

INTRODUCTION

"I believe that the primary function of the mystery story is to entertain; to stimulate the imagination and even, at times, to supply humour. But it pleases the connoisseur most when it presents – and reveals – genuine mystery. To reach its full height, it has to offer an intellectual problem for the reader to consider, measure and solve."

Brian Flynn, *Crime Book* magazine, 1948

BRIAN Flynn began his writing career with *The Billiard Room Mystery* in 1927, primarily at the prompting of his wife Edith who had grown tired of hearing him say how he could write a better mystery novel than the ones he had been reading. Four more books followed under his original publisher, John Hamilton, before he moved to John Long, who would go on to publish the remaining forty-eight of his Anthony Bathurst mysteries, along with his three Sebastian Stole titles, released under the pseudonym Charles Wogan. Some of the early books were released in the US, and there were also a small number of translations of his mysteries into Swedish and German. In the article from which the above quote is taken from, Brian also claims that there were also French and Danish translations but to date, I have not found a single piece of evidence for their existence. The only translations that I have been able to find evidence of are *War Es Der Zahnarzt?* and *Bathurst Greift Ein* in German – *The Mystery of the Peacock's Eye*, retitled to the less dramatic "Was It The Dentist?", and *The Horn* becoming "Bathurst Takes Action" – and, in Swedish, *De 22 Svarta*, a more direct translation of *The Case of the Black Twenty-Two*. There may well be more work to be done finding these, but tracking down all of his books written in the original English has been challenging enough!

Reprints of Brian's books were rare. Four titles were released as paperbacks as part of John Long's Four Square Thriller range in the late 1930s, four more re-appeared during the war from Cherry Tree Books and Mellifont Press, albeit abridged by at least a third, and two others that I am aware of, *Such Bright Disguises* (1941) and *Reverse the Charges* (1943), received a paperback release as part of John Long's Pocket Edition range in the early 1950s – these were also possibly abridged, but only by about 10%. They were the exceptions, rather than the rule, however, and it was not until 2019, when Dean Street Press released his first ten titles, that his work was generally available again.

The question still persists as to why his work disappeared from the awareness of all but the most ardent collectors. As you may expect, when a title was only released once, back in the early 1930s, finding copies of the original text is not a straightforward matter – not even Brian's estate has a copy of every title. We are particularly grateful to one particular collector for providing *The Edge of Terror*, Brian's first serial killer tale, and another for *The Ebony Stag* and *The Grim Maiden*. With these, the reader can breathe a sigh of relief as a copy of every one of Brian's books has now been located – it only took about five years . . .

One of Brian's strengths was the variety of stories that he was willing to tell. Despite, under his own name at least, never straying from involving Anthony Bathurst in his novels – technically he doesn't appear in the non-series *Tragedy at Trinket*, although he gets a name-check from the sleuth of that tale who happens to be his nephew – it is fair to say that it was rare that two consecutive books ever followed the same structure. Some stories are narrated by a Watson-esque character, although never the same person twice, and others are written by Bathurst's "chronicler". The books sometimes focus on just Bathurst and his investigation but sometimes we get to see the events occurring to the whole cast of characters. On occasion, Bathurst himself will "write" the final chapter, just to make sure his chronicler has got the details correct. The murderer may be an opportunist or they may have a convoluted (and, on occasion, a somewhat over-the-top) plan. They may be working for personal gain or as part of a criminal enterprise or society. Compare for example, *The League of Matthias* and *The Horn* – consecutive releases but were it not for Bathurst's involvement, and a similar sense of humour underlying Brian's writing, you could easily believe that they were from the pen of different writers.

Brian seems to have been determined to keep stretching himself with his writing as he continued Bathurst's adventures, and the ten books starting with *Cold Evil* show him still trying new things. Two of the books are inverted mysteries – where we know who the killer is, and we follow their attempts to commit the crime and/or escape justice and also, in some cases, the detective's attempt to bring them to justice. That description doesn't do justice to either *Black Edged* or *Such Bright Disguises*, as there is more revealed in the finale than the reader might expect . . . There is one particular innovation in *The Grim Maiden*, namely the introduction of a female officer at Scotland Yard.

Helen Repton, an officer from "the woman's side of the Yard" is recruited in that book, as Bathurst's plan require an undercover officer in a cinema. This is her first appearance, despite the text implying that Bathurst has met her before, but it is notable as the narrative spends a little time apart from Bathurst. It follows Helen Repton's investigations based on superb initiative, which generates some leads in the case. At this point in crime fiction, there have been few, if any, serious depictions of a female police detective – the primary example would be Mrs Pym from the pen of Nigel Morland, but she (not just the only female detective at the Yard, but the Assistant Deputy Commissioner no less) would seem to be something of a caricature. Helen would go on to become a semi-regular character in the series, and there are certainly hints of a romantic connection between her and Bathurst.

It is often interesting to see how crime writers tackled the Second World War in their writing. Some brought the ongoing conflict into their writing – John Rhode (and his pseudonym Miles Burton) wrote several titles set in England during the conflict, as did others such as E.C.R. Lorac, Christopher Bush, Gladys Mitchell and many others. Other writers chose not to include the War in their tales – Agatha Christie had ten books published in the war years, yet only *N or M?* uses it as a subject.

Brian only uses the war as a backdrop in one title, *Glittering Prizes*, the story of a possible plan to undermine the Empire. It illustrates the problem of writing when the outcome of the conflict was unknown – it was written presumably in 1941 – where there seems little sign of life in England of the war going on, one character states that he has fought in the conflict, but messages are sent from Nazi conspirators, ending *"Heil Hitler!"*. Brian had good reason for not wanting to write about the conflict in detail, though, as he had immediate family involved in the fighting and it is quite understandable to see writing as a distraction from that.

While Brian had until recently been all but forgotten, there are some mentions for Brian's work in some studies of the genre – Sutherland Scott in *Blood in their Ink* praises *The Mystery of the Peacock's Eye* as containing "one of the ablest pieces of misdirection" before promptly spoiling that misdirection a few pages later, and John Dickson Carr similarly spoils the ending of *The Billiard Room Mystery* in his famous essay "The Grandest Game In The World". One should also include in this list Barzun and Taylor's entry in their *Catalog of Crime* where they attempted to cover Brian by looking at a single title – the somewhat odd *Conspiracy at Angel* (1947) – and summarising it as "Straight tripe and savorless. It is doubtful, on the evidence, if any of his others would be different." Judging an author based on a single title seems desperately unfair – how many people have given up on Agatha Christie after only reading *Postern Of Fate*, for example – but at least that misjudgement is being rectified now.

Contemporary reviews of Brian's work were much more favourable, although as John Long were publishing his work for a library market, not all of his titles garnered attention. At this point in his writing career – 1938 to 1944 – a number of his books won reviews in the national press, most of which were positive. Maurice Richardson in the *Observer* commented that "Brian Flynn balances his ingredients with considerable skill" when reviewing *The Ebony Stag* and praised *Such Bright Disguises* as a "suburban horror melodrama" with an "ingenious final solution". "Suspense is well maintained until the end" in *The Case of the Faithful Heart*, and the protagonist's narration in *Black Edged* in "impressively nightmarish".

It is quite possible that Brian's harshest critic, though, was himself. In the *Crime Book* magazine, he wrote about how, when reading the current output of detective fiction "I delight in the dazzling erudition that has come to grace and decorate the craft of the *'roman policier'*." He then goes on to say "At the same time, however, I feel my own comparative unworthiness for the fire and burden of the competition." Such a feeling may well be the reason why he never made significant inroads into the social side of crime-writing, such as the Detection Club or the Crime Writers Association. Thankfully, he uses this sense of unworthiness as inspiration, concluding "The stars, though, have always been the most desired of all goals, so I allow exultation and determination to take the place of that but temporary dismay."

In Anthony Bathurst, Flynn created a sleuth that shared a number of traits with Holmes but was hardly a carbon-copy. Bathurst is a polymath and gentleman sleuth, a man of contradictions whose background is never made clear to the reader. He clearly has money, as he has his own rooms in London with a pair of servants on call and went to public school (Uppingham) and university (Oxford). He is a follower of all things that fall under the banner of sport, in particular horse racing and cricket, the latter being a sport that he could, allegedly, have represented England at. He is also a bit of a show-off, littering his speech (at times) with classical quotes, the obscurer the better, provided by the copies of the *Oxford Dictionary of Quotations* and *Brewer's Dictionary of Phrase & Fable* that Flynn kept by his writing desk, although Bathurst generally restrains himself to only doing this with people who would appreciate it or to annoy the local constabulary. He is fond of amateur dramatics (as was Flynn, a well-regarded amateur thespian who appeared in at least one self-penned play, *Blue Murder*), having been a member of OUDS, the Oxford University Dramatic Society. General information about his background is light on the ground. His parents were Irish, but he doesn't have an accent – see *The Spiked Lion* (1933) – and his eyes are grey. Despite the fact that he is an incredibly charming and handsome individual, we learn in *The Orange Axe* that he doesn't pursue romantic relationships due to a bad experience in his first romance. We find out more about that relationship and the woman involved in *The Edge of Terror*, and soon thereafter he falls head over heels in love in *Fear and Trembling*, although we never hear of that young lady again. After that, there are eventual hints of an attraction between Helen Repton, but nothing more. That doesn't stop women falling head over heels for Bathurst – as he departs her company in *The Padded Door*, one character muses "What other man could she ever love . . . after this secret idolatry?"

As we reach the halfway point in Anthony's career, his companions have somewhat stablised, with Chief Inspector Andrew MacMorran now his near-constant junior partner in investigation. The friendship with MacMorran is a highlight (despite MacMorran always calling him "Mr. Bathurst") with the sparring between them always a delight to read. MacMorran's junior officers, notably Superintendent Hemingway and Sergeant Chatterton, are frequently recurring characters. The notion of the local constabulary calling in help from Scotland Yard enables cases to be set around the country while still maintaining the same central cast (along with a local bobby or two).

Cold Evil (1938), the twenty-first Bathurst mystery, finally pins down Bathurst's age, and we find that in *The Billiard Room Mystery* (1927), his first outing, he was a fresh-faced Bright Young Thing of twenty-two. How he can survive with his own rooms, at least two servants, and no noticeable source of income remains a mystery. One can also ask at what point in his life he travelled the world, as he has, at least, been to Bangkok at some point. It is, perhaps, best not to analyse Bathurst's past too carefully . . .

"Judging from the correspondence my books have excited it seems I have managed to achieve some measure of success, for my faithful readers comprise a circle in which high dignitaries of the Church rub shoulders with their brothers and sisters of the common touch."

For someone who wrote to entertain, such correspondence would have delighted Brian, and I wish he were around to see how many people have enjoyed the reprints of his work so far. *The Mystery of the Peacock's Eye* (1928) won Cross Examining Crime's Reprint Of The Year award for 2019, with *Tread Softly* garnering second place the following year. His family are delighted with the reactions that people have passed on, and I hope that this set of books will delight just as much.

Steve Barge

BOOK ONE
HUBERT

CHAPTER I

THE time was four o'clock in the afternoon of Friday, the twenty-first of December. The Friday before Christmas. It was cold in the extreme. The sky was dark grey with the chill promise of snow that must fall before long. People who stamped their feet and swung their arms remarked sagely that it would be warmer after the snow had fallen. But despite the rigours of the weather, they hurried upon their business and upon their errands with cheerfulness. The great festival of Christmas was but four days ahead. There would be a welcome break from work. For almost everybody there would be an abundance of food. There would be more than the usual quantity of drink. It was true that in some circumstances unpleasant relatives would have to be suffered in closer proximity than usual, but the conditions of this suffering would help to alleviate matters. Flesh and wine are great healers. Since noon the wind had increased in severity and by now had acquired an edge like a razor. It was going to be a good night to be indoors.

Dorothy Grant went to the window of her dining-room and, lifting the casement-curtain, looked out into the dusky chillness. She was annoyed because she was waiting for something which should have already arrived. Her husband's hamper, which he ordered annually from Pegram and Manson's. That is to say *she* actually ordered the hamper, but Hubert always selected the various items which made it up. This selection was made with a meticulous care and precision, seasoned with the anticipation of delight. The turkey, the brace of pheasants, the ribs of Scotch beef (from the King's farm), the York ham, the Melton Mowbray pork-pie (large size), the ox tongue, the various cheeses which tickled Hubert's palate, Cheddar, Camembert, Stilton, Port du Salut, and Gouda, the confectioneries and sweetmeats and, lastly, the different wines and spirits. Champagne, whisky, port (Old Rich Tawny), sherry (Amontillado), beaune, gin, Hollands (Bols—not De Kuypers—Hubert was dignifiedly insistent on the distinction), rum, brandy and the various liqueurs which appealed to him. Hubert's especial favourites were Green Chartreuse and Kümmel.

During the week that followed the despatch of this annual order, Hubert invariably lived in a malaria of delightful anticipation. Until the day when the consignment arrived. On the evening of the day that happened, Hubert decanted the wines, put the spirits in the different bottles of the tantalus and generally made himself a nuisance who got in Dorothy's way. The birds would be hung up, the meat placed in the refrigerator, the other parcels and packages emptied and their contents arranged and all the time this was going on Hubert would fuss and bustle and perspire and knock things over and pick them up until Dorothy seethed with indignation in the thought that food and drink were her husband's almost only source of inspiration.

He was forty-two and already showing the flaccid signs of middle-age deterioration. She was eleven years his junior and had been but twenty when she had married him. Their only child, Frances, was ten. Dorothy Grant herself was still nearly beautiful. Almost miraculously, she looked scarcely a day older than when Hubert had married her. She had kept her figure, her intelligence had matured, her eyes were as darkly blue as they had been when she had first turned them on to Hubert, her hair had retained its sheen and lustre and her poise and balance and vivacity had developed with the years.

On this twenty-first of December, Dorothy was looking her demure best. She had been for some time. There was a reason for this. Six months ago, to her own utter surprise and astonishment, she had taken a lover. When she looked back on this amazing occurrence, as she frequently did, calmly and dispassionately, she had come to the conclusion that such a happening was inevitable. That it was simply a question of time when it took place. Now she counted herself fortunate. Fortunate to have discovered what so many of her friends and acquaintances had so obviously failed to discover. What life could mean, as compared with what life had usually meant. There were disadvantages, of course. Certain nightly scenes with Hubert that were increasing in acuteness which shamed and shocked her and hurt her. For it was now physically impossible for her to go on in every way as she had been accustomed. Up to the moment, neither she nor Laurence had faced up seriously to the full contemplation of their future. Sufficient for the day was the ecstasy thereof! The future would have to be faced—in time— but why worry? She had Frances whom she loved devotedly, she had Laurence Weston whom she loved passionately, she would see him before Christmas (that arrangement had already been made between them), why, therefore, should she wear forebodings on her brow and meet trouble before trouble came to meet her?

Dorothy craned her neck to see if the carrier's cart were turning the corner into Ridgway Gardens. Hubert would be more intolerable than ever that evening if the Christmas fare upon which he had set his heart were still delayed. Christmas! If only she and Laurence could spend it together—alone! Even without Frances. She admitted to herself, quite calmly and dispassionately and altogether without turning a hair, that were she forced to choose between Frances and Laurence she would choose this man, this complete stranger of but six months since, before her own daughter and that the choice, moreover, would be made without the slightest hesitation. Dorothy shrugged her shoulders.

She had begun by loving Christmas, then she had learned to endure it, now she hated it! All because of her love for Laurence. It was strange how one's outlook changed. How things *made* one change it.

On Christmas Day she would be hostess to the usual crowd of people who received their invitations to the house. Hubert's mother and father (her own parents were dead), Dick and Ella Fanshawe (Dick Fanshawe was an office colleague of Hubert's), Ethel and Roy Thornhill (before Ethel Thornhill had married she had worked with Dorothy), Maureen Townsend and Gervaise Chard. Maureen Townsend was her own friend whose marriage had turned out disastrously and who was now separated from her husband. Chard was a freelance journalist just beginning to make his way up the rungs of the ladder. Dorothy and Hubert had met him on a holiday three years before. He was always good company. A short year ago, this

Christmas gathering might have attracted her, contemplatively, but now she hated and loathed even the idea of it.

As she watched by the curtain for the hamper that hadn't come, with her rioting thoughts disturbing her mind, the long-awaited van turned into the road, and Dorothy saw it approach and then, at last, draw up outside "Red Roofs". The house, needless to say, had been given its name by Hubert. She heard Alice, her maid, go to the front door. There came the usual accompanying noises. The man's hoarse cough, the dumping of the packing-case in the porch and Alice's interested treble as she took the stump of pencil and scrawled her initials on the line indicated to her. Dorothy heard the man's voice.

"I'll give you a 'and with it into the 'all, miss. It's on the 'eavy side for you."

Shuffling sounds followed. Dorothy called out:

"Alice, come here a minute." Alice obeyed. Dorothy handed coins to her. "Give this to the man—and ask him whether he'd like a cup of tea. I expect he's cold."

"Yes, ma'am. I know he's cold. He's blowing on his hands and his breath's all steaming."

Dorothy smiled. Her well-shaped mouth was sensitive and attractive. When the man had gone, she went into the kitchen. Hubert's case had been placed on the table. The carrier, his enthusiasm stimulated, evidently had carried it right through to the kitchen from the front door.

"Shall we open it, ma'am?" inquired Alice.

Again Dorothy smiled. Alice had been with her but ten months. "I don't think we will, Alice. We'll leave that job to the master. He enjoys opening packing-cases at Christmas. It would be a shame to disappoint him."

Alice nodded vigorously. It was clear that on the last count she was in agreement with her mistress. Dorothy looked at her wristwatch. Dully she comprehended that Hubert would be home and with her in less than a quarter of an hour. He held the position of Deputy Treasurer and Accountant to the neighbouring Borough of Tudor. Although he constantly worked late in attendance on various Committees, things were more or less quiet for him at this time of the year from the business standpoint and he arrived home these nights comparatively early. Frances, on the other hand, would be in late. She was at the breaking-up concert of the Tudor High School for Girls.

Dorothy wondered where Laurence was at that particular moment. Laurence worked in the city—thirty miles away. Just as well—she had always thought. There wasn't a soul in Bullen who could connect him with her. Or in Tudor. Both ends were sealed. That was right. As it should be. Both ends in an affair of this kind should be sealed. Then there was but little danger. Possibilities of disaster were minimized. Brought to zero point. She wasn't at all concerned that she was in any way deceiving Hubert. She had given herself to Laurence and she guarded herself, and that exalted secret, night and day, lest she should be unworthy of him or unfaithful to him. Every one of her present loyalties was to Laurence. That was all that mattered to her.

She went back to the dining-room after telling Alice to start laying the tea. This had been one of the days when Hubert had dined at midday. Usually they had dinner when he came in. "Poach two eggs for Mr. Grant and put them on toast. And there's a pot of new cherry jam in the cupboard—bring it in."

"Yes, ma'am."

Dorothy sat in an armchair and turned on the radio. As she looked at the time again, she realized that Hubert would be with her in less than five minutes.

CHAPTER II

PUNCTUALLY to the minute Hubert entered—complacent, self-satisfied and smiling. Although Dorothy had taken Laurence Weston into her life and heart six months ago, to the entire and eternal exclusion of Hubert, Hubert was supremely unaware of the fact. Even the bare bones of the idea, if presented to him, would have astounded him and he would have rejected them instantaneously. Damn it all—what reason could there be for such a grotesque absurdity! As he came into the dining-room he bent over his wife and kissed her.

Dorothy submitted to the intimacy as an act of supreme resignation. Hubert performed the duty in exactly the same manner as he signed an official letter. Just as though that particular letter was exalted amongst all other letters in that its fate was to be approved by Hubert.

"'Evening, my dear. What's for tea?" Hubert took off his horn-rimmed glasses and polished them assiduously. He had evidently temporarily forgotten the matter of the delayed hamper. When he had gone out that morning, it had filled his horizon.

"Alice is poaching you two eggs." Her voice was cold and flat. So much so that Hubert glanced shrewdly at her. She looked all right, however. To his eyes.

"Where's Frances?"

"I told you yesterday evening that she'd be late. She's staying for the School Concert—with Molly Neame. They'll come home together."

Suddenly, as she spoke, Dorothy felt a twinge of mischief. "Where's your memory going, Hubert? Don't tell me you're losing grip."

The particular phrase was one that he was inordinately fond of using. Hubert frowned.

"A merely domestic matter of that kind is hardly comparable with—" He hesitated.

"With what, Hubert?"

Hubert's frown deepened. He evaded the direct issue. "I have many more, and, if I may say so, many more *important* matters to remember than where Frances has tea. Actually, I should have thought there was no need to remind you of the fact."

His eyes brightened as Alice came in with his poached eggs on toast. "Ah," said Hubert, "that's better."

At the sight of his tea, his mood of momentary irritation passed. More truthfully, it had suffered a process of engulfment by one of his strongest emotions. Dorothy poured out his tea for him. He took his cup and a warm feeling of greater satisfaction began to spread all over him.

"What have you been doing today, my dear? Reading?"

"I read a little. After lunch. Not a lot."

"Book not too interesting—eh?"

"Yes. The book was all right. It's a play, as a matter of fact. Expect I wasn't in the mood."

Hubert shook his head as his teeth crunched a generously buttered portion of toast. "Don't agree! You should read the best stuff. Confine yourself to the best stuff. Er—Priestley and . . . Wells . . . and—er—Dickens. You don't pick and choose enough."

"I certainly don't read the books that I'm told to read—if that's what you're trying to say. I read because I love reading. Just as you yourself enjoy . . . say . . . eating."

Hubert affected indignation. "Here, I say—that's a bit spiteful. Not like you. Can't compare the two things. One's a necessity. The engine won't go, you know, unless you stoke it up."

For some reason which she would have been unable to explain, Dorothy felt that she wanted to argue fiercely. To tear Hubert's smugness and complacency to pieces! This feeling had been coming over her for weeks now.

"That applies to the brain as well as to the body."

"The brain's part of the body," countered Hubert.

"That's difficult to realize—in a good many people."

Then the desire to cross swords with him suddenly vanished. His dull, municipal "parish-pump" mind wasn't worth her powder and shot, she thought, and then smiled inwardly at her mixture of metaphors. With a half-sense of relief she knew that she could adroitly change the subject. She would do! As he passed his cup up for re-filling she said quietly, "oh—by the way—the hamper's come from Pegram and Manson's."

Hubert's rather protuberant blue eyes gleamed with pleasure. "Good! About time, too! Did you open it?"

Dorothy shook her head. "No. It hasn't been here long and I've left that job to you. I know how you always enjoy doing it."

Hubert simulated disinterest. "Oh—I don't know. I don't mind, really. In a way it might have been more business-like if you had seen to it. You could have checked the delivery then, with the order. It's always as well to do that. You know how careless people are."

Dorothy pushed the pot of cherry jam towards him. "Try some of this, It's new. The last time I was in Tudor, old man Wallace strongly recommended it. I fell to the temptation."

She spoke as a mother might to a recalcitrant child. As though she were offering a new toy to lure him from the shades of sulkiness. Hubert clutched the pot avidly.

"Jolly good. I'll pass judgment on his recommendation. There's one thing you must admit—old Wallace certainly stocks the right stuff."

He helped himself generously to the jam. Dorothy found herself thinking of Laurence. Hubert chose the moment to expand.

"Spoke to Linklater today with regard to the Christmas break. We're closing Tuesday, Wednesday and Thursday. For most of the staff, that is."

Hubert's mouth being uncomfortably full, he hesitated for a moment. "But we must have some in on Thursday for the preparation of the wages sheets, so those who have to come in on the Thursday will be allowed to take the Monday. That's the Christmas Eve."

Dorothy began to listen. She was vitally concerned in this matter, although Hubert didn't know it. Linklater was Hubert's chief. Usually it was Linklater's habit to keep Hubert guessing. Indeed, the only certainty that Hubert ever felt about Linklater was that how much better he could do Linklater's work if he were in Linklater's position. With an edge of nonchalance sharpened specially for the occasion, Dorothy made an attempt to discover what she so badly wanted to know. She asked an indirect question.

"Which day is Linklater taking himself?"

"The Monday. That's Christmas Eve. So I shall be off on the Thursday. Not so bad, old girl. That means three successive days for us. Suits me down to the ground."

"Holiday for *you*, Hubert. 'You' is truer than 'us'." Dorothy assumed an air of annoyance. Secretly, however, she was delighted. With Hubert at the office on Monday until fairly late in the afternoon, the way was clear for her and Laurence Weston.

Hubert bridled. "Oh—I say—come off it. What's scaring you? The cooking, as usual? Don't tell me that the effort isn't worth it! Good Lord—the Christmas dinner too! Christmas only comes once a year, you know, and when it does come, we can't make too much of it. That's where we owe such a debt to Charles Dickens." (Hubert had read this somewhere). "By Jove—yes—those words of his. Marvellous! What are they now? We don't get writing like it nowadays. My old dad used to quote them every Christmas dinner—'"God bless us all," said Tiny Tim'."

Hubert made a clucking noise that denoted supreme satisfaction. Dorothy searched her heart. She wondered at herself. How had she endured him all these years?

"I suppose you'll close early on Monday?" she ventured. At the same moment she poured hot water into the teapot.

"The rank and file may—I doubt whether I shall be able to. Must be there, you see, with Linklater away. You never know what may turn up and, of course, there are always the letters to be signed. Anyhow—what does it matter? All the presents have been bought and you say the grub's come. We can sit pretty, my dear."

Hubert pushed away his plate and made for his armchair by the fire. "Jolly good that cherry jam and you can tell old Wallace I say so." He patted his pocket and produced his pipe and pouch. Hubert smoked a pipe. Not for the reason that he particularly liked it but because he had always held the idea that the man who smoked a pipe was eminently sound and always to be relied upon. It was, he considered, like the fundamental difference between "Rugger" and "Soccer". All the best people played "Rugger". Cigarettes were frankly—suspect. A cigarette-smoker might well be the forger of cheques. Hubert regarded himself as an influence—especially amongst the junior members of his staff and on that account he had to watch himself carefully so that he always did the right thing.

Dorothy rang for Alice. "Clear away, please, Alice."

Hubert lay back in his chair. He felt serenely easy and content. Suddenly he caught sight of Alice as she stacked cups and saucers on the tray. "When you've washed up, Alice, get a hammer and a screw-driver and some clean paper out of the garage and put them on the kitchen table. Let me know when you're ready and I'll come out and open that case."

"Yes, sir," Alice smirked. "'E don't 'arf like 'imself," she muttered when out of earshot. "Diggin' his grave with 'is teeth—if ever a man was. 'Ammer and screw-driver indeed"—Alice sniffed contemptuously.

Dorothy went back to her reading. She was reading Charles Morgan's *Flashing Stream* and Karen's arguments were holding and interesting her. Hubert coughed and spat and occasionally smoked. Eventually Alice gave the summons for which he had been waiting. Hubert rose and removed his coat—his black badge of office. He donned a vividly striped blazer. It was the blazer worn by the Ridgway Methodist Tennis Club and Hubert prided himself that he looked a fine figure of a man in it. Nobody shared the opinion with him, but of this latter fact Hubert was blissfully ignorant. He made his way into the kitchen and attacked the Christmas case with screw-driver and hammer. Hubert began to split the wood. The noise, or rather the significance of the noise, pleased him. He also began to sing. Now Hubert was very nearly the worst singer in the world. Surprisingly he was very modest with regard to this distinction. Hubert sang "You are my Heart's Delight". He hoped Dorothy could hear him—but the truth of the matter was that he was really singing to his Christmas hamper.

When the time came, he lifted the lid of the case and began to take out the various articles in order that he might check them against his purchase list. "Method," he muttered—"method in everything. Pity Dorothy hasn't more. If she had, things would go a great deal more smoothly here. I'll deal with the big stuff first." He noted the bright red comb of the turkey, looked at its eyes with almost pontifical approval, held the York ham reverently and made obeisance to its paper frill, fondled the pheasants and carefully appraised the ribs of Scotch beef (from the King's farm).

Then came the bottles. Hubert liked to get to them quickly. The magnums of champagne in their bass coverings . . . they felt grand . . . Hubert checked the bottles one by one as a High Priest might tell the number of his chalices as he took them from his acolytes. He would open some of them later . . . it was chilly . . . a drop of Scotch would do him a world of good tonight. He came to the smaller things. The Melton Mowbray pie (large size), the tongue and the many cheeses. Yes . . . they were all there . . . good!

Now for the confectioneries . . . more for Dorothy's department than for his own . . . still—you had to have them at Christmas. Muscatels and almonds, figs and dates, Turkish delight, chocolates, mixed sweets, crystallized fruits, candies . . . where were the Elvas plums? Hubert scrabbled at the packages. Of all the wretched nuisances! He adored Elvas plums . . . liked them better than any of this other stuff! Of course—Elvas plums *would* be the one commodity not delivered. Might almost be a piece of carefully calculated spite against himself! Now if Dorothy had only the intelligence—the common sense—to check the stuff in, when the carrier had brought it—this frightful contretemps could have been reported immediately to the firm responsible. Now—it would be almost too late. Absolute carelessness! Why should people's Christmasses be ruined by reason of other people's sheer ineptitude? The country was decadent. Not a doubt of it. Democracy, eh? Misapplied Democracy! Here was a crowning example. He appealed to Dorothy. Went to the kitchen door and called out to her.

"Dorothy! Come here a moment, will you?"

Dorothy put down the *Flashing Stream* and came. She saw that Hubert was flushed with annoyance. "What is it?" she inquired quietly.

"I'm most annoyed. These wretched people have forgotten the Elvas plums. Of all the contents of the case, they *must* forget the Elvas plums. Can you beat it?" Hubert embraced self-pity. He continued. "Of all the unlucky people in the world I think I'm the unluckiest. When anything goes wrong it's always a dig at me. I'm fed to the teeth with it all."

Dorothy knew that argument with him would be futile. "Does it matter so very much?"

"Matter? I should say it matters. Don't you realize it's the apparently insignificant things in life that make all the difference."

Dorothy intimated that she did. But she didn't mean what Hubert had meant. Then she walked to the table, put her hand into a heap of straw-packing that she had observed there and took out a square wooden box.

"What are these, Hubert? Aren't they your missing plums? I rather fancy they are."

Hubert took them with a gesture of delight. "Oh—good. Dorothy, I feel a different man. I'm sorry, but I can't help kicking up a shindy over a thing like that just now. It's because I'm such a stickler for what's right . . . I suppose. I simply *must* have things right. If they're not—I feel as though I just can't go on. It makes me see red."

He completed his unpacking. "Cranberry jelly . . . brandy sauce . . . salted almonds . . . the little jar of caviare . . . *foie gras* . . . yes, I think that's the lot." He arranged the bottles at the back of the table and stacked the other things in front of them. Turning to Dorothy, he rubbed his somewhat soiled hands.

"Good show—eh? Nobody can say that old Hubert Grant doesn't do his guests well at Christmas. Not even his worst enemies." He touched her lightly on the shoulder. "Now take Linklater," he said acidly, "Bernard T. Linklater, Esquire, F.I.M.T.A. . . . . do you think he's got a Christmas show like this on his kitchen table? Not he, my dear. Too blasted mean. A bottle of cooking sherry and a bunch of bananas." Hubert chuckled and became reminiscent. "Did I ever tell you a yarn I heard about him once? It was the year of the depression—the slump—you remember—when we all had our screws cut and the teachers moaned like hell about it. Linklater told the Borough Engineer that year that his wife wasn't going to make any Christmas puddings. The fruit was too dear! In addition to that—and here's the scream of it all—he actually had the effrontery to tell Horsfall that the Linklater kids—and they're all boys, mind you—*preferred* a nice milky rice pudding to a Christmas pudding! What do you think of that, Dorothy? A milky rice!"

Hubert's tones conveyed utter and supreme disgust. Dorothy smiled. Thank God he went to business most days of the year. But Hubert was by now thoroughly into his stride regarding the parsimony of his chief, Linklater.

"I'll tell you something else about Linklater. *Mr.* Linklater with his fifteen hundred per annum plus extras! Mrs. Linklater lost her 'char' the other day—I believe the old girl moved down into the West country to spend her remaining days with her daughter or son or something—I'm not sure which but it's immaterial to my story—so Linklater fixed up with Godbold, the cashier, to have Mrs. Godbold's 'char' for a couple of days in the week. So far so good. But what do you think Godbold told me? The 'char' told Mrs. Godbold and Mrs. Godbold told him."

Hubert paused. Expectant for Dorothy's reply.

"I've no idea. Shall I be interested? I've seen the wives of most of your colleagues—and judging by their faces and the clothes they wear I don't think that I—"

Hubert's impatience to finish his story mastered him. He interrupted. "Well—when lunch-time came at the Linklaters' the day the Godbold 'char' was there—the *pièce de résistance* was beef sausages! My God, Dorothy! They're about eightpence a pound, if that. And Mrs. Peddar—that's the name of Godbold's woman—was carefully measured out with *one and a half* as her portion! Mrs. L. did the measuring, I believe, with a ruler they pinched from the Town Hall. It's God's truth, my dear. Godbold swears to it. Fancy cutting a beef sausage to get two portions out of it."

Dorothy shuddered appropriately and edged away.

Hubert demanded the applause that was his by right. "Well— what do you think of that?"

"I don't know that I'm very surprised. As far as I've been able to judge, the god of the Linklater household has always been money. Anyhow—need we talk about it?—it's not very important."

Hubert glared at her through his glasses. "I know it isn't. But it's significant! Little straws show the way the wind blows. It's those little matters—unimportant as they may seem to you—which are indicative of a man's real character."

"Very true, Hubert, and now, if you don't mind, I'll get back to my book."

Hubert shook his head as Dorothy disappeared. She had disappointed him. For some time now it had seemed to please her to disagree with him. He heard her putting coal on the fire. Then draw her chair up to it. Reading! She was always reading! Fiction at that! Never seemed interested in the Local Government literature that he sometimes brought home with him for week-end consumption. He didn't know why she had no time for it. Some jolly interesting things in those publications sometimes! Good jokes about people like Town Clerks and Rate Collectors. Important people. Hubert took a bottle of Scotch liqueur whisky—one of his Christmas consignment—and proceeded to open it. Alice had dutifully washed the several spirit-bottles and the various decanters—there they were on the table at his elbow. Good girl! His eyes glistened. He poured the spirit into the big bottle. The noise it made was as music in his ears. He took a glass from a cupboard and poured himself a good stiff "three fingers". Holding the glass in his hand he went to the kitchen door and called Dorothy.

"Come and have a drink, old girl. I've got a jolly good drop of 'Scotch' here. The real McCoy."

He waited for her reply to the invitation. At Hubert's request, Dorothy's blue eyes had clouded with apprehension. She knew what the inevitable sequel would be. When Hubert drank spirits, even modestly, the process invariably had the effect of rousing his amorous qualities. Dorothy knew only too well what Hubert would demand of her before the morning. From mere dislike she had come to hate the idea. Worse than that even—she had begun to hate Hubert for his association with the idea. She called out her refusal of his invitation. To her surprise, her husband took it good-temperedly. The liqueur evidently had already commenced to do its work.

"All right," he cried, "but you don't know what you're missing."

Dorothy made no answer. She sat prim-lipped and defiant with a cold anger clutching at her heart. The anger increased because she knew that she had no one but herself to blame. She had made her bed. The bed on which she had to lie. Now she was trying to unmake it. Which was manifestly absurd if she desired conditions of comfort. She took herself to task. But only one thing emerged with clarity from this effort of introspection. That she loved Laurence Weston! This love had brought beauty into her life. Beauty that her life had never held before. She couldn't help about Hubert—she couldn't worry about even Frances—Frances whom she loved so devotedly. When Laurence called to her she knew that she would be compelled to answer that call. That meant losing Frances? Losing her for almost always? She recoiled at the thought. Why couldn't she have Laurence *and* Frances? But if Hubert divorced her the Courts would almost certainly give Frances to him. Again she shuddered. She would be what is known as the guilty party. She and Laurence. How ghastly! All the fragrant charm and beauty of their romance made sordid and horrible by cheapness and publicity. Why couldn't people who fell in love with each other go off somewhere quietly and privately and be divorced? Like they could in Russia. It was all wrong.

Suddenly she shut the book and went to the oval mirror which hung over the mantelpiece in the dining-room. She examined her face critically. But what she saw could only please her. The fingers of the years had indeed touched her lightly. She was thirty-one, but she could pass easily—before the most critical of onlookers—for a mere twenty-two or twenty-three. Her heart exulted in the triumph of this knowledge. The exultation was on behalf of Laurence. It had no real part with herself. With him pleased—she was pleased. He was her life, her strength, her joy. She came away from the mirror and switched on the radio. A song came over. "My Hero" from *The Chocolate Soldier*. Dorothy's eyes filled with tears. Laurence! Her hero! And Hubert fuddling himself with whisky in the kitchen. She wondered if Laurence and Hubert would ever meet. She prayed that they would not. Laurence belonged to a different place. He didn't belong here. She didn't want his world to touch her world as it was here. With a half-smile and a shake of her head, she went back to her book. Frances would be home soon. She would come with Molly Neame, who lived but a few doors away. The two girls would be perfectly safe together. It was nice Molly and Frances living so close to each other. Nice for both of them.

Again she closed her book. This time with impatience. She wasn't being fair to the author. She wasn't concentrating. What was Hubert doing in the kitchen now? Surely he had finished his unpacking by this time. She decided to go to see for herself. She walked quietly along the hall to the kitchen. Hubert was seated at the table reading something. She was unable to see, from where she stood, what it was. As she came through the doorway towards him, he looked up from what he was reading and caught her eye. She saw that he looked unusually grave and serious. For a moment an unexplained fear clutched and held her. Could she have possibly dropped . . . ? Then Hubert spoke.

"I've been thinking, Dorothy! Something which has been on my mind for some little time now. The stuffing for the turkey on Christmas Day." His eyes were fixed and staring.

"What about the stuffing?"

"Well, I've been giving that matter a lot of thought lately. What stuffing did you intend to serve with the turkey?"

"Well, *I* haven't given it *any* thought. But veal stuffing, I suppose. Why do you ask?"

"I'll tell you why. We ought to have chestnut stuffing. We really ought. It's damned important. It's been one of my ambitions for a long time. For one thing it's correct. With cranberry sauce we should have chestnut stuffing. See to it, my dear, will you?"

For once in a while Dorothy could think of no adequate reply. Her eager, vivid, combative, unflagging spirit was submerged. She nodded to him. The nod was weak and non-committal. Then she walked away mechanically. She would go to bed early. Then there would be a good chance of her being asleep when Hubert came to bed. She was learning a new technique—but how long would she be able to maintain it? More than that—how long would she be able to stay with Hubert? Even as it was now, but for Frances . . .

CHAPTER III

THE next morning brought Saturday. By dint of calmness and supreme coolness of nerve, Dorothy had been successful in evading Hubert's amorous intentions just before midnight. She had feigned sleep when his clumsy caresses had begun to serve as the emissaries of his desires. It had not been too easy, because Hubert had persisted. He was not easily put off. She had moaned a little (an artistic touch, this, she thought) and had breathed deeper and more heavily. After a time, Hubert abandoned his attempts. But once, she knew by an activity of mere instinct, that Hubert was scrutinizing her sleeping features as deliberately and as searchingly as he would scrutinize a petty cash voucher which he regarded as suspect. She had triumphed, it was true, but she was by no means sure that Hubert had been thoroughly satisfied that her slumbers were genuine. Dorothy made another mental note. This was yet another avenue of life where she would have to watch her step and take the utmost care. It would be dreadful if Hubert were to find out about her faithlessness, through the medium of his own desires. When he did know, it must be through her telling him.

She looked at her wrist-watch. The time was a quarter past eleven. Christmas cards had been dropping through the letter-box on to the mat with constant regularity. "Wishing you and yours", "to Hubert and Dorothy", "to Dorothy and Hubert", "to Mr. and Mrs. H. M. Grant—" the different combinations mocked her and made her heart ache. Why didn't they read "to Laurence and Dorothy" or "to Mr. and Mrs. Laurence Weston"? She wanted the world to know of her love for Laurence and of his for her. She wanted to do everything for *him*, not for Hubert. She hated all this subterfuge with its environment so inevitably clandestine. She looked at the time again. In a few minutes Laurence would telephone her. He always 'phoned to her from the city. She never 'phoned to him. To "Red Roofs"—always an inward call. Another obeisance to safety. When he came through she had a code for warning him if his conversation were to be eminently discreet and a second code which meant that he must ring off immediately. In addition to these precautions she also had a code word which told him at once that it was she who was answering him and that the domestic coast was clear. So impatient was she to hear his voice on this particular Saturday morning that she went and stood by her telephone and deliberately waited for it to ring. She would have invoked it, had she possessed the power. As it happened, she was forced to wait some minutes before her eagerly expected call came through. Her hands trembled and she breathed more quickly as she picked up the receiver.

"Hallo?" Yes, it was Laurence all right.

"Is that you, Semiramis?"

She answered him in code. "Semiramis lies in her rose-red Tomb." She heard his delighted chuckle. His freshness, his gaiety and his radiant enthusiasm engulfed her.

"Well, darling, how are you?"

"Not so bad, Laurence lovely, but wanting you terribly. Tell me you're the same and I shall feel better."

"That's easy," he answered. "Whatever love pangs you're enduring, mine are worse. But listen. Strict business. The order of the day. Pay meticulous attention so that not a syllable is lost. What about Monday? For the love of Mike tell me everything's all right."

"It is, my angel! He's going in to work. Says he won't be able to leave early. Usual place, usual time. I can manage everything comfortably."

"Everything?"

She detected the mischief in his voice. "Don't be rude, sir. And be thankful for the favours that *do* come your way."

"I am—believe me. Good-bye, darling, *toujours*."

She replied, "*Toujours*, my angel. Till Monday then—and I'll—"

The pips came through, intimating that the time-limit of the call was up. Dorothy hung up. Her cheeks were flushed, her eyes sparkled. She was alive—and in love! Laurence's voice never failed to stir her. His mood never failed to infect her. His love never failed to inspire her. Christmas was near—with all its appalling infidelities, as far as she herself was concerned—but Laurence was between her and the mockery of the festival. She would see him on Monday. He would hold her in his arms. They would exchange presents. They would use the ways that lovers use. They would travel together *dans le pays du tendre*. It was all so beautiful to her. If only she had met Laurence before she had met Hubert. Idle wishing. If she weren't sure of seeing Laurence, the prospect of Christmas would be intolerable! Her meetings with him were milestones. Milestones on the journey through Life. Without them, without the certainty of them, she would be unable to go on. She had no doubts at all with regard to that. She jerked herself out of these moods and dreams. It would soon be lunch-time. If things went as she wanted them to, she and Frances would go to a "flick" in Tudor. This project would enable her to avoid going out with Hubert. She had never really cared for walks with Hubert, but during the last six months—since June—she had come to loathe every minute of them. Now, of companionship, he brought her none.

She heard Frances coming in by the side-entrance. She had been into Tudor to buy some of her own personal Christmas presents. "Hallo—child," said Dorothy, "good hunting?"

"Not so bad, Mumsie. When you consider how limited the child's income is. I've managed to get most of what I wanted." Frances was ten. But, the only child of her parents, she was grave and wise beyond her age. Accustomed to spending a great deal of time with her mother she talked much more on level terms, as it were, with her mother, than the ordinary child of ordinary parents, and her mental development had reached a standard far beyond the average for her age. Frances had taken as her heritage much of her mother's beauty. Her face was sensitive, her brow broad, her eyes grey and her expression gravely, if pensively, intelligent. Most of her school work came all too easily to her, which fact, perhaps, had not proved to be entirely for her own good. Still, that notwithstanding—Frances was a charming girl with an attractive personality that showed signs of rapid development. Often, as she thought things over, Dorothy wanted Laurence to meet Frances. Equally often—she didn't. On the whole, she did not want her two worlds to make any contact. She had a feeling that if they ever did, something (she didn't know what exactly) would be spoiled—and so spoiled, that nothing or nobody could ever make it right and whole again.

"What are you doing this afternoon, child?" asked Dorothy. "Made up your little mind?"

"No. I think though it would be nice of you to take me to the 'Esmeralda'. Molly's mother saw the film there last Tuesday evening and told Molly it was wizard. The best for ages. I'd love to see it. That is, of course, if you haven't already promised to go out with Daddy."

Dorothy shook her head. "No, I haven't promised anything. What's the title of the picture at the 'Esmeralda'?"

"*The Lonely Queen*. It's historical—Mumsie. I love history. And I'm sure you'd like it from what Mrs. Neame told Molly."

Dorothy smiled at her daughter's eager enthusiasm. Laurence, despite his years, had the same quality to an advanced degree. She fell to wondering what Frances would have been like if Laurence had been her father. "All right," she replied as she came back to earth at the sight of the child's inquiring face, "I'll come with you, Frances. And Daddy can stop by himself and have forty winks in the armchair. I expect he'll be tired and won't mind particularly."

Frances nodded brightly. "Good. It'll make a perfectly lovely start for the Christmas hols. Just right! A wizard film along with you, Mumsie—I enjoy films ever so much better when you're with me. Better than when I'm alone or even with anybody else. I don't know why it is. But I think having you with me—you help me to understand them properly. Just by being close to me."

"Darling," said Dorothy impulsively, "that's very sweet of you and I appreciate it. But run away now for a little while. If I'm not careful, Daddy will be in to lunch and lunch won't be ready for him. Then what would he say?"

Frances curled her sensitive lip. "He thinks too much about things like lunch! I'd like a father who was more artistic."

"We can't all be alike," said Dorothy reprovingly. "It wouldn't be well for us, if we were."

"Why not?" demanded Frances. "I think it would be rather nice. We should all be so even minded. None of us would want to quarrel—if we all liked the same things."

"Well—that's all very well—but supposing all the gentlemen wanted to marry the same lady—and vice versa—all the ladies fell in love with the same gentleman? I can imagine that growing into a very big quarrel indeed. Can't you, Frances?"

"I suppose it might. I never thought of it quite like that. What does vice versa mean, Mumsie? You said it just now."

"For you—this morning—'turned round the other way'. Now buzz off and amuse yourself somehow—I must help Alice with the lunch."

When Hubert came in Dorothy felt the first real shock that had ever come her way. She told him that she was taking Frances to the pictures. Hubert had simply nodded acquiescence. Suddenly, when he seemed thoroughly engrossed in his steak and kidney pudding, he looked up and asked Dorothy a question.

"Who 'phoned here this morning?"

Although her pulse accelerated and she knew it, Dorothy answered quite calmly, "Nobody that I know of. Why?"

"Well—that's curious—I wanted to get through to you and I couldn't. Our operator told me that this line was engaged. I'll give her a piece of my mind on Monday morning."

Then Dorothy made a mistake. Directly she had done so, she was conscious of the fact and her cheeks flaunted the red banners of self-consciousness. She retreated over the piece of ground she had already covered.

"Oh yes, I remember now. The time was about half past eleven. Some idiot had been given a wrong number. Wanted ANN 2436 and they gave him 2346 by mistake. Having no real conversation with anybody there was no impression left on my memory'."

Hubert grunted. "Damned funny I should pick out just that very second to 'phone you. The arm of coincidence must have been pretty long."

To Dorothy's intense relief, Frances intervened.

"I know what it was, Daddy. Pure cussedness. Miss Lyall was telling us about it the other day at school. Everybody suffers from it at some time or another in their life."

"Very extraordinary," muttered Hubert, "say what you like about it."

He considered that he was receiving an unusually full cup of vexation on this particular Saturday. So far, on his plate, despite the most vigilant search, he had been unable to detect more than one small piece of kidney. He felt a strong sense of flagrant injustice. It was all very well but . . . Dorothy saw him frowning into his plate. She was feeling terribly annoyed with herself. Hubert's 'phoning at the same time as Laurence's call was just a stroke of bad luck. Nothing less and nothing more—but she had, to a certain extent, played into his hands by lying about it when he had first mentioned it to her. She was ashamed of herself. Primarily because she looked at her misdemeanour from the point of view of having let Laurence down. Hubert passed up his plate for a second helping.

"Is this a steak pudding," he inquired with heavy sarcasm, "or is it a steak and kidney?"

"I'm sorry," returned Dorothy, raging inwardly, "I'll try to serve you better this time."

Hubert growled an unintelligible reply. Frances looked at him indignantly. Then suddenly Hubert threw off his mood and approximated the jovial.

"I suppose we've plenty of stuff in for over Christmas, haven't we?"

"I should imagine we had. Why do you ask?"

"I've asked another couple for Christmas Day. We can fit 'em in all right I've no doubt."

Dorothy was interested. "Whom have you asked? Anybody I know?"

"As a matter of fact, I think you do know the man. It's Kennerley. The assistant M.O.H. An exceedingly nice chap. I met him in the corridor of the Town Hall this morning. In the course of our conversation he informed me that he's just had a Christmas disappointment. He and his sister were to have spent their Christmas with a married brother over at Chiswick somewhere. But the kids over there have contracted scarlet fever or something and the do's off. On the spur of the moment, I invited them here. His sister lives at Castle Hedingham, in Essex, and has come up especially for the holidays. You don't mind, do you, Dorothy?"

She smiled. She welcomed the change that had come over Hubert. "All the same if I do—considering that you've already pushed out the invitation. But candidly—I do know Dr. Kennerley. I danced with him, as it happened, at the last two Mayoral receptions. And I thought him a very charming man. So, my dear Hubert, all things considered—you're forgiven."

Mentally she patted herself on the back. She had emerged from that neo-crisis a great deal more comfortably than she had originally anticipated. If only— At that moment the voice of Frances intervened.

"If you ask me, Daddy—you've done a very silly thing."

Hubert stared aggressively at his precocious daughter.

"How do you mean, child?"

"Think," retorted Frances with demure insistence. A vague look of misgiving took possession of her mother's features.

"I know what Frances means," she contributed quietly.

"What?" demanded Hubert—"what's all the damned mystery about?"

Dorothy gave him the explanation that was eluding him. "We shall be thirteen at table on Christmas Day. Count the people with me. We three, your mother and father, Dick and Ella, Ethel and Roy, Eileen and Gervaise Chard—that's eleven, and now you've asked the two Kennerleys. There's your thirteen." She shook her head as she concluded, "I don't like it. I'm not foolishly superstitious, I hope, but I definitely don't like to sit thirteen at table."

Hubert affected intolerance of Dorothy's point. "Oh—rubbish! Who said so? Lot of antediluvian nonsense only fit for old women. I'm really surprised at you." Then a look of triumph darted into his eyes. "I know. You've forgotten something, haven't you? What about Alice where art thou? She makes your number up to fourteen. So what have you got to worry about? Your devil is therefore exorcised."

Dorothy dismissed his contention with a shake of the head. "Alice doesn't sit here at this table. You know very well she has her meals in the kitchen."

"It's the same thing," grumbled Hubert, "we shall all be under the same roof. That's what matters."

"No, it doesn't," countered Frances fiercely, "it's sitting at the same *table* that counts. It's because of Judas Iscariot. You ought to know that. Mumsie's quite right and I agree with her."

"Oh, well," conceded Hubert with ill grace, "have it your own way. The mischief's done now. It's all my fault. I asked the Kennerleys without thinking. Blame me for it."

"Whom else is there we could ask?" said Dorothy thoughtfully. All the time her thoughts were centred on Laurence Weston. It would be, though, criminal negligence on her part to suggest him even. Negligence? Well—negligence of that care she had always taken to seal up both ends. Her reverie was summarily cut short.

"Nobody," snapped Hubert. "I never listened to such ridiculous rubbish in all my life. What do you expect me to do? Go out into the highways and hedges and select a particularly unsavoury tramp, with the seat out of his trousers, to eat his Christmas dinner with us? Not on your life. We'll behave like sane and sensible people and chance your thirteen at table 'joke'. For once I'll put my foot down."

Alice came in to clear away. Dorothy spoke quietly to Frances. "Put your things on, my child. We'll be off to the 'Esmeralda'. We don't want to be too late getting home."

Frances darted out to obey her mother. The thought of the afternoon that lay just in front of her completely dispelled all the irritation that her father had caused in her. She so thoroughly detested him when he argued with her adored mother as he had during that dinner-time. A few minutes and Frances with eager eyes was ready to accompany Dorothy on their journey. When the door shut behind them, Hubert pulled up his armchair to the fire. Methodically he found tobacco and filled his pipe. Try as he would, he could not divert his thoughts from the incident of the telephone. Dorothy had looked so damned uncomfortable all the time they had discussed it. Why was that? It was so unlike her. Was it because she had made a mistake, forgetting that she had been called to answer a wrong number inquiry? Yes—that was probably the reason. She hated anything in the nature of inefficiency or incompetence. And, because of that quality of hers, she had been the victim of acute annoyance. Hubert settled himself more comfortably in the armchair and accepted the warm benison of the burning logs. After all—Life was good. He puffed complacently at his pipe. Life was very good. Before many minutes had passed, Hubert Grant was asleep.

CHAPTER IV

PUNCTUALLY at two o'clock in the afternoon of Christmas Eve, Dorothy set out to meet Laurence. Frances had gone to tea with Molly Neame. Dorothy attired herself to the accompaniment of quickened pulses, a fluttering heart and all the delightful and delicious thrills which bless the girl who is on the way to meet her lover. It was as though Hubert had never even existed for her. That she had never met him, that he had never courted her, that they had never married, that she had never surrendered her virginity to him, that Frances was not, that there was in fact nothing—before or beyond herself and Laurence. Before leaving the house she looked at herself in the mirror. She knew that her love-affair had given her an added beauty. "I'm certainly no hag," she said to herself thankfully. "Laurence darling—I love and live for you."

She caught the bus outside the Roman Catholic church and booked to Cleves. On the railway, Cleves was two stations beyond Tudor—in the London direction. Bullen, Tudor, Seymour, Cleves. Cleves was a tiny place by the river. There was little call for anybody to visit it, for either business or social reasons. And anybody who was compelled to enter Cleves was always desperately anxious to get away from it as speedily as possible. The bus journey from Bullen to Cleves took forty minutes. At least that was the scheduled time. To Dorothy, it always seemed like forty days. She would repeat to herself ceaselessly as the wheels of the bus rolled along, "forty days and forty nights". The repetition of these five words had become part of her Laurence meeting routine. To her, Cleves, during the journey, was as far distant as Samarkand.

The streets, naturally, seeing the day that it was, were thronged with people. She had deliberately selected this route for many reasons. The bus avoided both the towns of Tudor and Seymour. Its destination was Wolsey and it ran round the back of Seymour and Tudor before making Cleves. She knew nobody in Cleves and her one risk was a stray encounter there with somebody who had gone in from either Bullen or Tudor. A most unlikely contingency. When she met Laurence in Cleves, the programme was already mapped out and had the merit of being always the same. So far, she had met him on something like ten occasions and not once, so far as she knew, had she had the slightest reason for apprehension.

One of the many things that positively delighted her about Laurence was his absolute reliability. He had said to her once, half-mockingly, half-seriously, that his telephonic address was "'Reliability, London'—it'll find me anywhere". She appreciated and approved this quality—because she was always so reliable herself. Everybody with whom she came in contact knew that. In six dear months, Laurence had never once let her down. By such a matter as a minute even! He telephoned to her and he met her, exactly as he told her he would. Dorothy looked at her watch. Twenty-five minutes past two! Half the journey had been accomplished. Only another twenty minutes and she would see Laurence waiting for her outside the cinema at Cleves. A much the worse for wear, old-fashioned building that rather vaingloriously announced itself to the world at large as the "Luxuriant". The films it showed were all hopelessly out of date, and its afternoon audiences were sparse—which facts suited Dorothy and Laurence from every standpoint.

Dorothy scrutinized the features of everybody inside the bus and of everybody who entered at the various stopping-places. She snuggled herself into her corner seat to do so. On this Christmas Eve everybody looked pleased and contented. Mothers with laden baskets, children clutching parcels of all shapes and sizes, all looking forward to something lurking just round the corner. The magic of the manger in Royal David's city. Glory be to God on High and in earth. Peace—*to all men of Goodwill*. Dorothy knew the accuracy of the Latin. Even though the festival was one mainly of eating and drinking, nearly all the men and women *did* put bickerings and selfishness aside for a few hours and approximated love for their neighbours. A band at the corner of a street struck up a Christmas carol. "Good King Wenceslas looked out . . ."

Dorothy felt beautifully and supremely happy. Her parting with Laurence, but another two hours ahead, might have been due in a thousand years' time for all the consciousness that she had of its imminence. Sufficient for her hours was the joy thereof. She sought meanings from herself. She knew that she intended to get, to possess, all things that she desired. She was not predatory. Not acquisitive. Not even possessive. Just resolute and determined to know what she wanted of life and in life, and to obtain them. Only a few moments now and Laurence would be with her in the flesh.

The "Luxuriant" cinema at Cleves lay tucked away inconspicuously in the main street. It was a low-lying building which had originally belonged to the Wesleyan movement. At that time, it had been principally used for Sunday School concerts. When pictures were first mooted as an addition to the social life of Cleves, the Wesleyan interest had seized the opportunity which had come its way and sold well. On the corner of the block which contained the cinema was the general post-office. Then came various other shops of the usual kind, about five of them, and next the cinema itself. Laurence usually waited on the corner by the post-office as Dorothy's bus came down the hill into view. Then he would turn and walk in the same direction as the bus until it pulled up outside the cinema.

This afternoon, Dorothy watched eagerly for Laurence's tall figure as the bus began the descent into the main street of Cleves. While she was so certain of his utter reliability the fear was always present in her mind that Laurence might be ill. That he might have 'phoned to her at "Red Roofs" cancelling the appointment, and have got through to the house a few seconds, say, after she had left it on her way to meet him. Suddenly, her heart gave a great leap—for there was Laurence, her loving, faithful Laurence, waiting on the corner in the exact attitude that she had been picturing all the way along. Laurence was tall and slim and dark. His face was thin and lean and eager. His features were sensitive and clean cut. He had a habit of thrusting his head well forward and looking intently at the person to whom he spoke. His eyes were dark and quick moving, and for ever questing. His brain was well stocked, his memory prodigious and he had learnt to speak on most subjects in such a way as to interest most people. He was a charming conversationalist— for the main reason that he knew something about everything and everything about something. When he and Dorothy had met in the June of the year, at the little seaside resort of Tristram, he had fallen in love with her almost instantaneously. Dorothy, who for once had gone away alone, had put up but little fight, and she was his almost as soon as he was hers.

Dorothy rose quickly, darted to the pavement, looked love from her eyes into his, caught his hand, and then hurried with him into the cinema. Laurence paid for their two seats, at the back of the house—there was no circle—and still holding hands, they were ushered into them by the torch-bearing attendant. Laurence took off his hat, scarf and overcoat and as Dorothy turned to him impulsively and eagerly, he took her into his arms. They kissed passionately. The row of seats where they were was unoccupied but for themselves. Then Laurence held her away from him just a few inches, and looking into her eyes said "how long since I did that?"

"Exactly seventeen days, my darling," replied Dorothy in a whisper—"December 7th, as you know as well as I do." Her eyes swam with delight.

"Days," he said incredulously and then: "'Tears are in my eyes and in my ears, the murmur of a thousand years.' That seems more like it to me."

"Who wrote that?" she whispered, and put her head on his shoulder.

"Keats—or almost that. I changed the pronoun for your benefit—that was all."

"How are you—well—darling?"

"Ever so. Never felt better. And you, dearest?"

"Yes. But desperately wanting you—every day and all the day. I have the harder part of the two of us—I have to live with Hubert and do things for him. Things I crave with all my heart to do for you. Some of them are ordinary, commonplace things. You live alone—you are better off because of that, my darling."

Laurence frowned. What she had said had touched the red rawness of his jealousy. "Has he been bothering you again?"

Dorothy hid her face on his shoulder. "Once or twice. Not a lot."

"I hate him," declared Laurence intensely, and then quickly, "You refused him, of course? You promised me last time you'd finished with him as far as that sort of thing was concerned."

"I didn't refuse him. I avoided him."

Laurence pressed for further details. "How do you mean exactly? Tell me."

"What does it matter, darling? Why probe for all these details? You only torture yourself by asking me all these questions."

"But, darling, I want to know! I must know. I love you so. I can't bear to think of him even laying a finger on you—let alone . . . It makes me see red."

"I pretended to be asleep. I always do that now."

"Always?" he frowned again. "How often, then, are you pestered by him?"

"I told you—not often. Since I promised you—I haven't given in to him once."

Laurence, mollified, held her tightly in his arms. "I'm sorry, sweetheart, if I appear tyrannous. I can't help it. You're mine. He doesn't *possess* you and he's got to be made to understand that. Marriage is a sacrament of wills. Mutual. Of the spirit. Your ring doesn't mean a thing. Directly you don't want him, your marriage ceases."

Dorothy put her fingers on his cheek and caressed it. "I know. And I understand. We've agreed on that so many times before."

"How long have you got this afternoon?"

"I must say good-bye at a quarter to five. It'll be dark when we go away from here. Is that all right for you?"

"Yes. I can catch the 5.27 back to town. Gets me in to Waterloo about half past six."

"What's the time now?"

Laurence screwed his eyes down to his wrist-watch. "Almost exactly three o'clock. Which means that we've less than two hours. Two hours a fortnight! If we're lucky! God—what a ration for devout lovers."

"Before we knew each other—we had none."

Laurence bent over and kissed her lips. "True—my darling. Still my clear-thinking Dorothy—steel true? Blade straight? How I love you for it! What are we going to do about it all? That's what's worrying me."

"Just go on loving each other. That's all that matters. Don't worry about possibilities this afternoon."

He looked at her full breasts and voluptuous lips and then gave himself up entirely to her mood. After the first fierceness of his kisses had been spent, she withdrew from his arms a little.

"What's the matter?" he asked anxiously.

"Let me alone for a little while, Laurence. You take my breath away."

"You took mine away the first time that I ever saw you. So I'm only getting my own back."

She put her hand to her hair to straighten it. "God knows what I look like after the mauling you usually give me."

He chuckled at her description. "I know—as well as God."

She came back to Life for a moment or so. "What's the name of the film we're supposed to be looking at?"

"Haven't the foggiest. Not interested. Only want to look at you. Every time I look at you, I feel that I ought to blush."

"Why, Laurence?" She put her head close on his shoulder again. She was able to see him well now. Her eyes had grown accustomed to the darkness. He furrowed his brows at her question.

"Why? Well—it's difficult to explain—rather. I know how I feel— but I'm not absolutely certain as to why I feel like it." He shook his head as though impatient with himself and his indecision. Then his brow cleared and the doubt seemed to pass from his eyes. "I think I *can* explain—now that I've thought it over. Do you know Dryden at all?"

"No. Not well. Tell me."

He bent down and kissed her again before continuing. "Dryden wrote a perfectly lovely poem on the marriage feast at Cana in Galilee. You remember—when Christ turned the water into wine."

Dorothy nodded that she did remember.

"Well—one of Dryden's lines after the miracle has been per- formed is 'the modest water blushed to see its Lord'. Isn't it an absolutely marvellous line? You couldn't presume to argue about its merits, could you?"

Dorothy half-whispered the line to herself. "It is beautiful," she said—"yes—and wonderful."

Laurence brushed a piece of his unruly hair with the back of his hand. "Well—that's something like how I feel when I look at you— and we kiss each other."

"I am glad," she said simply. "Glad and thankful to have lived and have such love come to me. Now make a fuss of me again."

She put her lips up to his once more. The minutes passed. Dor- othy lay happily in her lover's arms. Laurence whispered to her again.

"The old sundials used to say 'I only count the hours that are serene'. I'll give those words a revised version—'I only count the hours I spend with you'."

"That's sweet of you. Is it nearly time to go?"

"Very nearly, my Dorothy. I shall soon see the gates of Paradise closing behind me."

She whispered. "It'll be quite dark when we go out. And I shouldn't be surprised if it hasn't turned a bit foggy. That won't worry us, will it? If we leave here at half past four, we might turn down that avenue with the trees. I think it's the next turning but one from here. That would give us another quarter of an hour together. How does the idea commend itself to his Majesty?"

He nodded and kissed her again. "It's just half past four now. Get ready to slip out sharp. You first. Then I'll follow you."

Outside the cinema, on the pavement, there were many people. Cleves was far busier on Christmas Eve than on any other day of the year. But as Dorothy had said, the weather was benevolently dark and she and Laurence, turning quickly, were soon walking down the avenue of trees which she had mentioned to him. Laurence slipped his arm round her waist. She nestled against him as they walked. After a little while she caught his arm.

"Here," she said, "let's stay here for a few minutes. It's beautifully dark."

Laurence pulled her to him under the big tree. The trunk was broad. They kissed again—fiercely and passionately.

His hands trespassed over her body, fondling and caressing her. Dorothy knew ecstasy for a few brief seconds. Then she disengaged herself.

"I must go, darling. My bus won't wait for me. Or will your train wait for you. Kiss me—and here's your Christmas gift from me. I do hope you'll like it. Don't open it until you're in the train." She slipped a packet into his overcoat pocket.

Laurence Weston pressed a similar something into her hand. "And there's my present to you. With all my love."

She kissed him and held him fiercely. "Think of me at Christmas."

"All the time. Every minute that passes. Every second. Will you think of me?"

"You know I will. What are you going to do?"

Laurence laughed rather bitterly. "As I don't particularly fancy my landlady's grub—I shall probably have my Christmas dinner in a low Italian restaurant. But I shall be with you all the time— *really*—all the best of me. I'll make a bargain with you, carissima. Every time the clock strikes the hour—all over the holiday—I'll say 'I love you, my Dorothy'. You do the same. Say 'I love you, my Laurence'. Then we shall have sweet communion every hour. Yes?"

"That's lovely. I promise as you have promised. Goodbye, darling, till next time. Kiss me—I must fly."

She pulled his mouth down to hers with a fierce pride of possession, kissed him ardently, turned and ran. He knew that she must if she were to be sure of catching the bus.

He heard the sound of her running footsteps die away in the distance. He looked at his watch. It was just a quarter to five. It was all right. That was the time she had said. She would catch the bus she wanted. He had ample time in which to stroll to the station for his train. The two hours he had longed for had come and gone. They had passed like lightning. He would not be able to see Dorothy again for at least a fortnight. He was able to obtain an afternoon's leave from time to time as compensation time for certain late work he did in the evening. He worked for a firm of accountants and auditors, whose professional staff put in a good deal of overtime. But he had to wait for his occasional leave and was far from being his own master as to when he might be allowed to be off duty. As he walked slowly to the railway-station of Cleves, through the throng of shopping housewives, past the shop windows advertising their fare and good cheer, Laurence surrendered himself entirely to the reminiscence of the fragrance of Dorothy and to the anticipation of a nebulous prospect ahead of him somewhere when Dorothy should be all his and the two of them live together in tranquil happiness with vivid patches of superb ecstasy, all the days of their life.

While Laurence was musing thus, Dorothy had been running for the bus which was to return her to her own district of Bullen. She had hurried past the cinema and past the post-office on the corner, until she had come to the stopping-place. The bus to Bullen was due at Cleves at 4.50. This meant that she was able to be indoors soon after half past five. Hubert usually came in about a quarter to six. To find a calm unruffled Dorothy awaiting him. Unless he thought to ask her the direct question, she need not say that she had been out at all. Very often Hubert did not ask her. He took it for granted that she had been in all the afternoon. So far, on all the occasions when she had met Laurence in Cleves, things had gone quite smoothly for her and not once had she been called upon to answer any awkward questions. If Hubert ever did take it into his head to question her, she was perfectly confident of her ability to keep her head and in her answers steer clear of any trouble that might be inclined to rear its ugly head to threaten her.

Dorothy waited at the bus stop for the bus to come. She had a good minute to spare. In all her experience, it was never early. Occasionally it arrived a little late. Her feelings, as she waited, were a curious mixture of happiness and sorrow. She was happy because she had just been with Laurence for two magic hours, and she suffered because he had gone out of her real life again, back to that shadowy, indistinct place where he belonged and she would not see him again for many days. Dorothy herself knew, that as she stood there, she was smiling through her tears. Her eyes were moist and misty as the bus drew up by the kerb in front of her. Behind the bus there came a private car. It was a Vauxhall. The fact that the bus had stopped, caused the car to stop also, just as Dorothy stepped on to the conductor's platform. As she did so, she caught sight of the car away to her right . . . and of a man's face within it. It seemed to her, although she could not be certain of it, that this man who was driving the car was looking at her. That he saw her . . . plainly. And it seemed to her, too, though again without absolute certainty, that the man's face was familiar to her. Dorothy passed into the interior of the bus, and sat down in her customary corner. As she seated herself, her mind was groping as to the identity of the man. Who *was* the man?

By the time that she was seated comfortably, she knew who she thought it was. It was Linklater, the Borough Treasurer of Tudor. The man who was Hubert's chief. The man who had been absent from the office today and whose absence had been the main reason for Hubert, her husband, to be on duty. But she wasn't absolutely sure. The glimpse she had caught of his face had been but a momentary one. And, of course, it was dark. But there had been a fairly powerful street light close to the bus stopping-place. She mustn't forget that. She was pretty certain that it *had* been Linklater. He did run a car. She remembered hearing about it from Hubert. Was it a Vauxhall? She tried to think. Had Hubert ever told her any details? Again she wasn't sure if Hubert had. If it *were* Linklater, had he seen her clearly enough to recognize her? Well enough and plainly enough to have recognized her beyond any doubt? On the whole she considered that this was improbable. She reassembled the scene. She had stood there, though, right in the full glare of that light . . . there was a strong chance that he *had* seen her. Dorothy began to reassure herself. After all—why worry? It didn't matter a great deal. She had been alone. He hadn't seen her in any compromising circumstances. He might even refrain from telling Hubert. Such a triviality—he might regard it as not worth mentioning. In her heart, though, right down at the cold corners of it, Dorothy knew that if it were Linklater who had just seen her, he *would* tell Hubert. Linklater was exactly a man of that type. Her thoughts began to riot—and then Dorothy realized that she was getting on edge and actually inclined to panic. She, Dorothy Grant, of all people! She must take firm hold of herself. This was the second time now within a few days. There had been that wretched incident of the telephone-call, when she had blundered, just because she hadn't taken care to keep reasonably cool and collected.

The conductor came for her fare. Dorothy showed him her return ticket. He looked at her as though he recognized her. As though he had seen her before. He probably has, thought Dorothy, but I'm not going to encourage the idea. The more I remain in obscurity, the better, from my point of view. So she ignored the conductor's gesture and turned her head away. Back darted Linklater into her thoughts. If only she were certain of what had happened. It was this devil doubt which was assailing her. Until she knew if it *were* Linklater, and whether he had seen her and recognized her, she would have no peace within her heart. She would soon know!

Then another fear clutched at her and held her. Hubert would not be going to the office again until Friday. He wouldn't meet Linklater until Friday! She wouldn't know anything at all until Hubert returned from the Town Hall at Tudor on Friday evening. Or, in terms that were more tangible, until four whole days from now. Dorothy felt sick at heart at this realization. She would have to go all through Christmas with this horrible uncertainty tugging and tearing at her heart. For the first time in her life that she could remember, Dorothy felt afraid. She attempted to analyse her feelings. To find out what it was exactly that she feared. She decided after a time that it was the sordidity of it all. Any scandal must inevitably mean sordidity. Frances would be implicated. Dirty-minded people would talk about her and include Frances in their salacious sniggerings. Experience had taught her that. Her love for Laurence, if it were discovered and published as illicit, would be raked over on the public muck-heap. Dorothy shuddered. That would be simply awful. She could face anything in preference to that. But she couldn't go back now. And there was nothing she could do with regard to this afternoon's incident. The milk was spilt and tears were of no avail. She would pluck courage from somewhere and over her shoulder would go the Linklater care.

The bus was almost into Bullen now. It was passing the row of shops just before the Roman Catholic church. In a couple of minutes she would be getting out. She gathered up her belongings and slipped Laurence's Christmas present into the pocket of her coat. She would open the packet later. At a time and in a place of safety. She got out of the bus. As she crossed the road to Ridgway Gardens, she considered her plan of campaign. She must have one and she must keep to it. After some, moments' consideration, she decided to wait and see. To let it depend upon what Hubert did. If she plunged she might plunge in the wrong part of the sea. It would really hinge on what questions Hubert asked her. If he did question her she would not say anything that would cause her to be vulnerable at any point.

She came to her house and rang the bell. Alice answered the door and let her in. As the door opened, Dorothy listened. The house was quiet. Hubert was not in yet.

"Tea's all laid, ma'am," announced Alice.

"Thank you, Alice."

Dorothy put her clothes away and went into the dining-room. She sat down and waited quietly for Hubert. It had turned six o'clock before he arrived. At her first glance, Dorothy knew that Hubert was a trifle "merry". She knew what had been happening. She felt reassured at what she had seen. Confident that she could easily deal with Hubert in this condition. He had been celebrating Christmas Eve. It was his habit. She smiled as he sat down.

"Had a thick day?" she asked him.

He shook his head a little foolishly. "No! Christmas Eve? What do you take me for? Tell you what I did do! Put in a good session with the boys. At midday. Horsfall, Godbold, Dick Fanshawe, Bill Munden and I. And who do you think turned up about half past one? Said he couldn't keep away."

"I've no idea."

"Guess. Give you six guesses."

"I really haven't a notion. So it's no use my trying to guess. Tell me who it was."

Hubert goggled at her. "Little Bertie Wiggins. Used to be on the Internal Audit Staff."

"How thrilling."

Hubert regarded her with suspicion. "What do you mean exactly by that?"

"Oh, nothing! Don't be so querulous." She felt that she would almost welcome a quarrel. Wanted to get both her feet planted firmly in Laurence's camp. Let Hubert know where she stood. But Hubert wasn't having any. His good nature, well fortified by alcohol, was uppermost. And it was Christmas Eve. In Hubert's philosophy, everybody should be merry and bright on Christmas Eve.

"Little Bertie's one of the best. A character! Might have walked straight out of the pages of a book. It's a treat to see him knock back a Guinness."

"It must be. And I suppose you believe all he tells you."

Hubert grinned. "What does that matter?"

Dorothy endeavoured to change the subject. "Well—shall I ask Alice to bring in the tea—or don't you want any?"

"Of course I want some. What are you hinting at? That I'm too full up to eat? Don't you believe it, my dear. On with the motley. Tell Alice to bring in tea. I'll put the decorations up after tea. Up so high—nobody'll ever be able to take the bloody things down!"

Hubert rubbed his hands at the prospect. "Holly and mistletoe, streamers and silver bells . . . and . . . er . . . cockleshells all in a row."

"Give master his tea, Alice, please," said Dorothy Grant, curtly.

Alice obeyed, and Hubert fell upon it. The clock on the mantelpiece chimed the first quarter past six.

CHAPTER V

Not once during the evening that followed did Hubert allude in any way to Dorothy's afternoon. Not a single question emerged from Hubert's lips as to the manner in which she had spent it. Frances came in at half past seven and Mrs. Neame, who brought her, stayed, at Hubert's request, to drink a glass of wine with them and to be the first that Christmas to be regaled with the hospitality that was so inseparable from "Red Roofs". Hubert beamed on Mrs. Neame, as he asked her what she was going to have.

"Well—that's very nice of you, Mr. Grant. If I may ask the question, what have you to offer me?"

Hubert puffed out his cheeks and became grandiloquent. "In the shape of liquid refreshment, Mrs. Neame . . . say the word and it's yours."

"Do you mean—"

"Anything, Mrs. Neame." Hubert became stark pride. "Anything. I don't think you can name any . . . er . . . beverage which 'Red Roofs' would find it impossible to produce. That's so, isn't it, Dorothy?"

Dorothy intimated that, for once, Hubert was speaking the truth. Hubert began to recite his catalogue. "Port, sherry—"

Mrs. Neame soon stopped him. "I'll have a nice glass of port, Mr. Grant, if it's all the same to you."

Hubert prepared to dispense largesse. "Port it is," he said, as though pronouncing a benediction. He went to the sideboard, found glasses and the appropriate decanter. "Drop of port for you, Dorothy?"

"I don't think so, Hubert—thank you."

"Why not? Can't you join me when I'm drinking a guest's health?" Hubert was annoyed.

"I don't really want anything—thank you. I haven't long had my tea." Dorothy turned and smiled apologetically at Mrs. Neame. "I'm sure Mrs. Neame won't mind if I don't join you—will you, Mrs. Neame?"

Mrs. Neame smiled back. "Of course not, Mrs. Grant."

But Hubert looked a little sulky as he filled two wine glasses with the port. "Well—here you are, Mrs. Grant—Merry Christmas."

"Same to you, Mr. Grant. And many of 'em."

Hubert nodded at her benignly. Dorothy thought for the first time in her life how like an owl he looked. Hubert rolled the wine round his palate with the air of a connoisseur.

"Rich old Tawny," he declared.

"And very nice, too, Mr. Grant. This drop of wine didn't come from the grocer's round the corner, I'll be bound."

Hubert smiled sapiently. "You're right there, Mrs. Neame. Only the best is good enough for me."

"There's a compliment to you, Mrs. Grant. The nice things your husband does say."

"I think," said Dorothy acidly, "that my husband was referring to matters of food and drink."

"Oh, come, come—I'm sure he wasn't. Were you, Mr. Grant?"

Hubert avoided giving Mrs. Neame a direct answer. "Have another glass of port, Mrs. Neame. We don't often see each other."

"I won't say no. But I hope it won't get to my head. Or I shan't be able to walk home straight."

Hubert poured out the second helping. He and Mrs. Neame drank up. "Now I'll run along," she said, "and between you and me I think I've had quite enough."

She waved a hand comprehensively. "Merry Christmas all! Be sure and enjoy yourselves tomorrow."

Dorothy murmured her thanks. Frances came into the dining-room. "Daddy—are all the competitions done for tomorrow? We don't want any muck up, you know, at the last moment."

Hubert checked an inclination to burp. "Frances, my child. The various competitions *are* done. Your father is an organizer! And there are, if I may say so, very few of us about."

Frances giggled. "Hark at him, Mumsie! Does he put on side?"

"The programme for tomorrow," continued Hubert sententiously, "is complete. Completely . . . er . . . complete. And will, I hope, be carried out without the slightest hitch. There will be 'Ghosts', 'Re-Actions', 'Potted Personalities', 'Alibis', a 'Treasure Hunt' and—of course 'Murder'."

At the sound of the last-named, Frances clapped her hands and gurgled with joy. "Oh—wizard! I love it. And I love Christmas. And I love you, Daddy. And I love Mumsie too. Now, Daddy, I'm going to help you put the decorations up in here, in the hall and in the lounge. Where are they, Mumsie?"

"On the table in the kitchen. Alice will let you have them if you ask her."

Hubert took a stand. "I don't think, Dorothy, that you're being very sociable. Seeing that it's Christmas Eve."

Dorothy was suddenly conscience-stricken. "I'm sorry, Hubert. I'm tired, I think. I've had a bit of a headache nearly all day."

Hubert looked as though he weren't thoroughly satisfied with her explanation. He was beginning to see new Dorothys. Beginning to contact Dorothys that were alien to him and foreign to his own memories. Damn it all—what did she want of Life that she hadn't got? That he hadn't already given her? Why weren't women more reasonable? Up to now he had always prided himself upon the fact that *his* wife *was* reasonable! He had chosen her carefully. And, of course, she had profited by his training. How could she help doing so? She certainly didn't lack intelligence. As he went to the kitchen with Frances, he couldn't resist a parting shot at Dorothy. "Sure it's your head and not your temper?"

Dorothy gasped. She couldn't remember that Hubert had ever spoken to her quite like this. Whatever had been his failings—he had always been courteous and polite. This was too much. After all—he had no reason to . . . Then Dorothy's thoughts were arrested. Yes—there was a reason. Even though Hubert didn't know it, she knew it! Laurence Weston was standing between her and Hubert. He had separated them. He must do so! It couldn't be otherwise. And she wouldn't have it otherwise. Laurence and she loved each other. Then an awful thought struck her. A thought from which she recoiled! She was beginning to hate Hubert. The man with whom she lived. The father of her child. She could hear him in the other rooms now. With Frances. Frances was laughing. It was Christmas Eve, as Hubert had said. There was every reason why Frances *should* laugh.

When Dorothy went to bed a feeling of sickness came over her. With the faintness that accompanies nausea. It seemed to her that she was frightened of something. Something which lay ahead. She didn't know what it was. As she undressed the waits started to sing outside the house. They sang the "Adeste". "O come let us adore Him . . . Christ the Lord". Frances was already in bed. Dorothy wondered if the singing would awaken her. She hoped it wouldn't. Before Frances woke up, she and Hubert had to go in her bedroom and fill the gaping pillow-case. Frances always hoped that it would be filled with books. Frances liked books best. Dorothy went to sleep hoping that Frances would find unalloyed happiness. She herself had found happiness, but there were so many barriers between. In the morning her first duty would be to undo Laurence's packet and to find out what he had given her. This she would do while Hubert was still in bed. What a mockery it all was! Dorothy slept.

CHAPTER VI

THE first incident of Christmas Day was the arrival of Frances into the parental bedroom. Frances, of course, having emptied her pillow-case of its contents, was in the seventh heaven of delight. The muster of books she had received had exceeded her wildest expectations. She had, in fact, done better than at any previous Christmas. Frances danced in, kissed both her parents effusively and pranced out. As far as she was concerned, it was going to be the loveliest of all lovely days. When Frances had retreated to her own bedroom, Dorothy made haste to look at Laurence's present. She camouflaged it to the bathroom in her dressing-gown. The little loving note which accompanied it, she destroyed at once, having committed it to memory. She looked at the book which she had taken from the parcel. Her heart thrilled to it immediately. It was a delightful edition of Fitzgerald's translation of *The Rubáiyát*. Dorothy fluttered the pages. "Ah, Love, could thou and I with Fate conspire . . . would we not shatter it and then . . . nearer to our Heart's Desire."

Dear Laurence! As her mind registered the thought, Dorothy heard the lounge clock chime the hour and, triumphantly remembering, she sent her first message of the day to Laurence. This pleased her. She had been true to the promise she had made to Laurence. She had been afraid that she might forget. She *knew*, without the shred of a doubt, that Laurence would not forget. Even once during the entire day! Laurence never forgot. Whatever he undertook to do—he did. Always!

Dorothy put her book in the pocket of her dressing-gown and returned to the bedroom. Alice was already getting breakfast. Dorothy heard the familiar sounds coming from the kitchen. The real day was about to start. She dressed without enthusiasm. Hubert was still asleep. With him, the wages of drink was slumber. She looked at his face on the pillow. It was flushed and entirely unattractive. Hubert was ageing rapidly. His physical descent was going to be absolutely easy. The best of him had already been left far behind. He would wake before very long and come down to breakfast.

Dorothy went to the kitchen. She began to help Alice. So it would be all day—butchered to make a Hubert holiday. Fancy being alone with Laurence Weston somewhere! "There would be such wonderful things to do." Dorothy pushed the thought away. Hubert came down to breakfast. He was quiet and subdued. Dorothy knew that he would mellow as the morning went on. As the time drew nearer for the various guests to arrive. After breakfast, Dorothy went back to Alice to superintend the cooking of the Christmas dinner. Hubert amused himself by arranging the Christmas cards. He rather prided himself on what he called his artistic touches. This morning, however, his comments on the various cards were few and far between. Hubert was certainly not himself. After a time, he presented himself to Dorothy in the kitchen.

"I think I'll go and dress. What time's dinner?"

"As near to three o'clock as I can manage."

Hubert nodded. "Right-o. When I'm ready, I'll come down and do the glasses for you."

"Thank you, Hubert."

Somehow, at that moment, for no reason that she could explain, Dorothy thought of Linklater. If he had seen her in Cleves and he told Hubert—Dorothy shivered inwardly. She saw Hubert disappear upstairs to the bathroom. In due time, she heard him descend again. She heard the chink of the glasses. Hubert was most meticulous with regard to this department of his Christmas dinner. Champagne glasses, claret glasses, spirit glasses, wine glasses, and liqueur glasses were all appropriately prepared and placed in the correct positions on the dining-table. Hubert sorted them out with scrupulous care. At times, Dorothy admired him for the trouble he took. There were certain tasks that he had always refused to delegate. He was a firm believer in the adage "if you want anything done well, do it yourself". He often quoted this to juniors in the office at Tudor.

Dorothy looked at the clock and saw that time was getting on. Hubert was ready. She must get ready herself and, in addition, put the finishing touches to Frances. That was the worst of having "too much to do". You had no time to do anything properly. She thought, however, that she could now safely leave the kitchen front to the industrious Alice. Everything was well forward. Up to now she had not forgotten Laurence *once* on the occasions when the clock had chimed. Laurence would *know* that she was not failing him. Laurence knew everything.

Dorothy began to turn herself into the hostess of "Red Roofs". Bedroom, bathroom and bedroom. When she was ready, her mirror told her that she was looking at her best. She smiled sadly at her reflection. "Not with you, Laurence darling," she whispered—"but *for* you all the time."

When Dorothy went downstairs again, she heard Hubert talking on the telephone. She was rather surprised. She hadn't heard the ring. Strange—because as a rule when she was upstairs and the telephone rang, she heard it. Was it a guest who wasn't able to come? Or—and again the chill thought of Linklater invaded her heart. Was it Linklater, by any chance, ringing Hubert? As she stood in the hall she strained her ears in the hope that she might hear a snatch of a sentence, or catch a phrase from the conversation. The telephone was in the dining-room, and the door was shut. She decided to go in. Hubert was still talking. He had his back to her. As she entered the room, she heard Hubert finish the conversation.

"All right," she heard him say, "I'll discuss it further with you next time I see you. On Friday. Thanks for letting me know—and the compliments of the season. Good of you to ring me."

Her curiosity, conscience-fanned, made her ask him a question. Affecting nonchalance, she said quietly, "Can't they let you alone on Christmas Day? Of all days? If you ask me you're a fool to put up with it."

Hubert showed signs of surprise. "Who?" he asked rather sharply.

"The office. I suppose it *was* the office."

"What made you think that?"

Dorothy shrugged her shoulders. "I don't know. I suppose it just occurred to me. I've got used to it. It doesn't matter. I don't mind. I was thinking of you—that was all."

"Well—as a matter of fact," went on Hubert, "you're partly right. Though how you guessed, I don't know."

"What have you got to do now? Attend a Committee meeting this afternoon? Or this evening? It would be quite in keeping with their usual policy."

Hubert grinned. As the hour for dinner grew appreciably nearer, his normal geniality was returning. "No—it's not as bad as that. It wasn't an *official* call—although an official made it. If you want to know, it concerned an entirely private matter."

Dorothy wasn't sure of the genesis of Hubert's grin. Another day she might have been, but today was different. She had been disturbed. The thought of Linklater was by this time almost obsessing her. She would never have believed such a thing of herself. She took control of herself, however, by means of a supreme effort.

"My dear Hubert, I don't want to know. If it were nothing important, as you have already indicated, I'm perfectly satisfied."

Hubert's grin grew. "It was Horsfall—the Borough Engineer. He promised to ring me up yesterday afternoon and it slipped his memory. Wants the insurance cover increased on the big greenhouse in Arragon Park. He was really apologizing this morning for letting me down, as he put it, yesterday afternoon. Very decent of him."

Dorothy breathed again. She even smiled at her husband as he gave her the explanation. "The table looks very charming, Hubert," she said.

"Not so bad. Glad you think so. The tinted paper in the bowl shades the light beautifully. Watch the effect."

Hubert switched on the electric light. It was as he had said. The room was lit with a soft, shaded radiance.

"When the pudding comes in, we'll turn out this light and burn the candles. Jolly fine! Talk about filling the flowing bowl—that'll be well-filled all right." Hubert chuckled.

He looked at the clock. "Getting on. Some of 'em ought to be here in a few minutes." Then he added, almost malevolently, "Making up the dread thirteen."

Dorothy remembered. The remembrance almost shocked her. She had been so much taken up with thoughts of Linklater that the matter of the number of their Christmas dinner-party had escaped from her mind. "We won't go into that again, Hubert," she said firmly. "Because it won't get us anywhere. All that's to be said on the subject has already been said. Where's Frances?"

"In the lounge—reading. Lying full length on the rug in front of the fire."

Dorothy smiled. This had always been her own favourite attitude and Frances, doubtless, had inherited the inclination. She went in to her.

"What are you reading, child?"

Frances exhibited her book triumphantly. "*The Wind in the Willows*, Mumsie. It's a present from Auntie Ethel."

This was Mrs. Thornhill. Frances was prodigal in the bestowal of the title of "Aunt".

"I'm glad you like it. I thought you would. It used to be one of my own favourites."

As Dorothy spoke, the bell rang. Frances literally leapt from the rug. "They're coming. That's the first guest. Hooray for Christmas—I think it's *lovely*."

Dorothy went into the hall to welcome the arriving guest. It turned out to be Maureen Townsend, looking rather beautifully fragile behind her furs. Sometimes, thought Dorothy, as they kissed each other, Maureen looks really beautiful. I know that if I were a man, I'd soon fall for her.

"Do you like my hat, Dorothy?" asked Maureen. "I'm anxious to have your opinion. Personally, I'm a trifle doubtful about it."

"I can put your mind at rest. It's wizard—as Frances would say."

"So glad. When I looked in the glass just now I didn't feel at all sure."

"Here's Hubert," said Dorothy.

"Hallo, Maureen! Compliments of the season, old girl."

"Thank you, Hubert. And the same to you. Very sporting of you to have us all here again. I don't think I know any other married couple who would go to all the trouble you two do."

"Thanks, Hubert. I'll have a short one as dinner isn't too far away."

"You shall. When they've seen to your things. I'll have it ready for you. What shall it be?"

"Make it a Dry Martini, Hubert."

"Delighted, Maureen."

Hubert watched Maureen Townsend as Dorothy bore her away. "Damned attractive woman—and no mistake. Pity she's made a mess of things. Can't think what Townsend's doing, not to pull smoothly with a fine woman like Maureen." Come to think of it, what a number of couples there were knocking about who couldn't see eye to eye with each other in the matter of their marriage lives. Several of them in his own circle. Dash it all—nobody could apply that to him and Dorothy. No trouble there. Only a matter of common sense after all. Give and take. That's what marriage was—give and take. Simple enough formula! Why didn't more people realize it? Why—what it came to in Maureen's case was this—she was wasted! No real home. No kids. Damned shame. Got a lovely mouth too. Glorious eyes. Not as nice as Dorothy's—but grand for all that. A mouth like she had wanted kissing.

Thus Hubert philosophized as he prepared Maureen's drink. What was the trouble between her and Townsend? Another woman? Most probably. It wouldn't be another man. He would no more associate that sort of thing with Maureen than he would with his own Dorothy. You could always tell when a girl was straight. Something about them. Showed in their eyes. Just as you could tell when a man was straight. Take his own case to prove his point. Tarts never accosted him in Tudor High Street. They knew it was no good. Would be wasting their time. Could tell they were, directly they as much as glanced in his direction. Funny, really, how they told. Still, say what you like, it was a compliment to him. Hubert Grant. Deputy Borough Treasurer of Tudor. Shame some people had all the luck. Poor old Maureen. Married a wrong 'un. A bad egg. Dorothy was lucky. He heard them outside. Then other voices. Many of them—

merging in a medley. The Thornhills, the Fanshawes and his own father and mother.

Hubert called to Maureen to take her Martini and then projected himself towards his other guests. Laughter and merriment were everywhere as the honoured greetings of the season were mutually exchanged. Frances danced in and out, Dorothy was looking a picture, and Hubert felt damned good. He was the host for the day and going to see that all of them had a real good time. Hubert shook hands all round, kissed his mother, all the girls kissed one another, everybody kissed Frances and Frances kissed them all in return. Ethel Thornhill, who was demure, blonde and placid, linked arms with Dorothy and Ella Fanshawe as the three of them made their way upstairs. Ella Fanshawe was dark, slim and rather fascinating. Fanshawe, her husband, was chief clerk in the Town Clerk's Department of Tudor and an old friend of Hubert's. Unkind people were inclined to say that Ella always took advantage of the position which occurred when her husband's back was turned. Dick Fanshawe was short, lean and wiry. Looked like a man who'd spent the better part of his life out East. Roy Thornhill was mentally indolent but physically competent. He ran a prosperous motor engineer's business in one of the busiest parts of Tudor. Ethel, his wife, was supremely content with her lot. She had plenty of money to spend and ample comfort after she had spent it. Neither the Fanshawes nor the Thornhills had any children. This condition suited Ella Fanshawe, but Ethel often thought that children, had she been blessed with them, would have brought her another kind of happiness. A different kind from the one she had. At the same time, she never hankered for them or approximated a state which in any way could have been construed as discontent.

Hubert's parents deserve special mention. They were, truly, a remarkable couple. Constance Grant was seventy-seven, Ralph Grant was seventy-four. He was small and spare, she was tall and amply made. In most respects that counted, the grey mare was the better horse! Strange to relate when we recall Hubert, who was their only child, Ralph Grant was a total abstainer. He advertised this melancholy fact by wearing a small piece of blue ribbon in the buttonhole of his left lapel. But—as he constantly asserted—*"he was no bigot"*.

Constance looked down upon him benignly, called him "father" to everybody and in her heart regarded him as a funny little object whom it was her duty to protect and look after. This duty was in no way irksome to her but one, on the other hand, which she thoroughly enjoyed. Indeed, she would have strongly resented the idea of anyone else in the world doing it. When she spoke to him or about him to others, she always smiled. They were both fond of Hubert, but not as proud of him as Hubert himself would have liked them to be. Hubert treated them well and was invariably mindful of their welfare and their comfort. More than once he had been heard to say "I don't hide my people when they're in my house. Like some people do! I'm not ashamed of them or afraid the old man may drop an 'h'. Or the old lady pour her tea into her saucer to cool it before she drinks it. I believe in the promise of the fifth commandment, and I try to live up to it. I've got my faults, no doubt, but being secretly ashamed of my parents isn't one of 'em—and I don't care who hears me say it, either."

"Well, my boy," said the old man, "here's another Christmas round. Can hardly believe it, you know! Time flies when you get on in years. I was saying to your mother only this morning—it seems only like a week ago that we were picking the June roses."

Hubert dispensed many drinks. Dorothy came and looked after old Mrs. Grant.

"Who is there to come?" cried Hubert above the din and merriment.

"Gervaise," replied Dorothy, "and the Kennerleys. Dr. Kennerley and his sister. Gervaise is bound to be late. I've never known him not to be."

Hubert thought how glorious Dorothy was looking. At her best absolutely. And it wanted whacking! His wife, too! Mrs. Hubert Grant. His! There must be dozens of fellows who envied him his possession of her. Possession? Was that the right word? Yes—of course it was. What did the commandment say with regard to covetousness? "Thou shalt not covet thy neighbour's wife . . . nor his ox . . . nor his ass." Funny—putting a chap's wife with his ox and his ass! Still—there it was—you couldn't argue about it! What was that? He listened. Gervaise Chard's voice and also young Dr. Kennerley's. Hubert hustled along the hall so that he might meet and greet them.

"Hallo there, Gervaise! And you, Doctor. Come in, old man! Your sister? Good. Delighted to think you've brought her along. Mrs. Grant shares my feelings. Come right along, Miss Kennerley, and make yourself at home. You can do what you like, you know, at 'Red Roofs'."

Kennerley was tall, clean-shaven and debonair. With slightly mocking eyes. Especially when he looked at a woman. His nose was distinctly large, his hair dark, and his mouth rather attractively predatory. Elizabeth Kennerley, his sister, had brown hair, nice eyes and a prim air of propriety that sat well upon her and gave her a certain quality of winsomeness.

After the necessary introductions, the guests began to mix and Dorothy, who was quick to sense the slightest suggestion of anything in the nature of an atmosphere, was satisfied that all was well in this respect. She went into a corner and had a quiet cocktail with Gervaise Chard. She liked Gervaise. Gervaise liked her. He was short and tubby, with an unruly mop of flaxen hair that fell absurdly over his forehead.

"Who mixed the cocktails, Dorothy? That old war-horse, Hubert?" He ate his impaled cherry.

"M'm," nodded Dorothy. "Hubert's an indefatigable cocktail mixer. He shakes and rolls with an almost barbaric relish. His face grows uglier as he does it. His ancestors were probably cannibals."

Chard glanced at her sharply. He wasn't quite sure of the note in her voice which he fancied he detected. What was in the wind? He wouldn't like to feel that there was anything which might . . . He endeavoured to pass it off with a flippancy.

"Why—has he been biting you in an excess of passion or—"

Dorothy cut into his speech. "Don't talk utter rubbish, Gervaise. Please! I don't care for that sort of remark at all! Don't ever say anything like that again. Promise me, Gervaise."

Gervaise Chard remained cool and collected under the barrage. Whereas another man who had committed the *faux pas* might have been flustered beyond measure at its unhappy reception, Gervaise was made of "sterner stuff".

"Frightfully sorry, old girl," he said quietly. "No idea you felt like that about things. Forget it! And out of your old natural goodness of heart, accept my sincere apologies."

"That's all right, Gervaise." Dorothy smiled at him bewitchingly; "there's Frances. She's been with her grandmother. I must speak to her. Help yourself to anything you want—won't you?"

Without another word, Dorothy slipped away. Chard watched her go and whistled softly under his breath. "Phew!" he muttered. "I nearly made a mess of things with that remark. But who'd ha' thought it, laddie, who'd ha' thought it? Dorothy's not sweet seventeen! She's thirty odd—without a doubt—and the mother of a long-legged daughter. What's been brewing in this house of Hubert to bring such ultra modesty to a matron's cheek? Begin to wish I hadn't been in such a hurry to come."

Chard watched the guests as they mingled. He knew all of them except the Kennerleys. As he looked, he saw Dr. Kennerley approach Dorothy. Kennerley put his hand on her arm. Gervaise Chard caught the look in his eyes. It was certainly a look of admiration—if nothing more than that. Chard began to feel interested. He looked carefully to see whether Dorothy returned the glance. He couldn't see too well, but he thought that she didn't. As an interested spectator of human problems, Gervaise Chard made up his mind to watch one or two points on this Christmas Day that ever was.

As he moved towards the main group of people, he heard the sound of the dinner-gong. Produced by the hand of Alice. The guests filed into the dining-room. They took their seats as indicated to them by the table plan conspicuously exhibited. More of Hubert's work! Hubert looked at the clock on the mantelpiece. He nodded approvingly at what he saw. He gave a sign to an already impatient Frances. Hubert went round the table, took orders and filled glasses. There came a moment of eager expectancy, the voice of the announcer came over the air, clear and distinct. "Ladies and Gentlemen . . . His Majesty the King." Hubert lifted his glass. His guests did likewise. "The King." As Alice helped Dorothy to bring in the soup, they listened quietly to the royal and Empire broadcast. It was soon over. Christmas dinner had begun at "Red Roofs". For all thirteen of them! Or for fourteen, including Alice.

CHAPTER VII

A FEW minutes before nine o'clock in the evening of Christmas Day, Hubert Grant opened his front door and looked out into the road. Cars were in his run-way and parked by the kerb, for some distance past his house. Hubert felt gratified to see them there. They afforded a complete sense of opulence. So far, everything had gone splendidly. Dorothy had seen to everything most efficiently. Hubert felt that he himself was the ideal host. It was the label that everybody would instinctively apply to him were they asked for a quick epitome of his character. Not such a bad one—either! Hubert came in and closed the door. The house was being prepared for "the games". The games which delighted Frances so intensely. Of course, it was inevitable that they should start with "Murder". Everybody joined in this—including Hubert's mother and father. His mother was a rare old sport. "As young as I feel" was one of her husband's sayings. It was true, too.

Frances and Dick Fanshawe had drawn the two slips marked "detective". Frances was a wee bit disappointed at this trick of Fate, but naturally. If it had been possible to see closely into the child's mind; it would have been found that she would have liked to have combined the rôles of detective, murderer and murderee! To Alice had been delegated the highly important work on the electric-light control.

Hubert went back from his journey to the front door to the chattering congregation of his Christmas guests. There they were, clustered in doorways and passages, awaiting the signal for the first stages of the crime. Dick and Frances were alone in the centre of the lounge, preparing themselves for the inquisition that was shortly to come from them. Suddenly, Hubert caught sight of Julian Kennerley. In Hubert's opinion, Dr. Kennerley was regarding Dorothy in a most strange manner. Hubert didn't like it! It wasn't at all the kind of way a man should look at another chap's wife. Not playing the game! Then Hubert grinned. Inwardly. It was as though he hugged the grin to himself. Of all the consummate silly asses, he was one. Revelation had come to him. The explanation of Kennerley's look was as simple as possible. He had drawn the assassin's ticket and had already marked Dorothy down as his victim! Hubert chuckled to himself. If only he'd been cast as a detective. His brilliant deductions would have earned him a halo of personal glory. The clock struck nine. He saw Dorothy glance towards it and a peculiar rapt expression take possession of her face. She couldn't see him—although he could see her. There were too many people in between them. Hubert couldn't account for this look on the face of his wife. Dorothy didn't know that Kennerley had murderous designs on her. Unless—Hubert licked his dry lips. Unless—Hubert's lips became dryer. Unless Kennerley and Dorothy had made the arrangement in advance. Which indicated some sort of understanding between them.

His brain raced round to consider and to assess possibilities. Dorothy had met Kennerley at the Mayoral reception in the early part of the year. She had admitted that. Supposing—supposing Kennerley had deliberately engineered this invitation for Christmas Day? That Dorothy all the time had been party to the intrigue? It might explain one or two rather intimate domestic conditions which had been puzzling him and causing him some concern lately. Hubert set his teeth and decided there and then to keep both his eyes open! Alice was a hell of a time over that light. Why the blazes didn't she give the signal that everybody was waiting for? Snap! At last it came. The entire house was plunged into darkness.

Hubert knew where Kennerley was and Dorothy's relative position with regard to him. There was a biggish space in the hall between the foot of the staircase and the doors of the lounge and the dining-room and Hubert flattened himself against the wall between the foot of the stairs and the front door. Vague forms of men and women passed near him. He heard whispers and barely concealed laughter. Some of the forms he heard go into the dining-room which was in the front of the house. Others turned when they were close to him and crept up the stairs to the bedrooms or the bathroom. Hubert felt certain that one of these was Julian Kennerley. The sounds of many different treadings came to his ears. He heard, too, the unmistakable swish of frocks on the stairs. Resentment and suspicion flared in Hubert's heart.

When the first noises of the human procession subsided, Hubert crept up his own staircase in the wake of them who had gone that way before. On the wide, spacious landing he paused. At the turn of the staircase, in the wall, stood the statue of a goddess who held a pink lamp in her raised hand. The light in the lamp, of course, had been extinguished. Hubert stood on the landing, for the space of a few seconds, and, from his coign of vantage, looked down upon the lamp-carrying lady. He couldn't hear a sound. But all the bedroom doors were closed. He felt, certain of that fact, by the temperature. In all, there were five doors. Four bedrooms and a bathroom. He and Dorothy used the big bedroom in the front of the house. Frances had the room which overlooked the back garden and the remaining two were spare. They were used, naturally, for guests who from time to time stayed the night. On this Christmas night, Mr. and Mrs. Grant senior were using one of the two and the Thornhills the other.

Hubert listened hard as he stood there, but not the slightest sound came to his ears. Hubert frowned. His experience of the world and of previous games of murder which had been played at "Red Roofs" told him that there were, in all probability, eight people in these rooms. Certainly eight—perhaps ten. He stood there in the darkness, irresolute and undecided. Eight people. Kennerley and Dorothy. Ella Fanshawe and anybody, Thornhill and somebody and probably Chard and Maureen Townsend. He made nine. His father and mother eleven . . . that was right. Dick and Frances downstairs made up the complement. His parents would be downstairs—that was a certainty. Well—he'd put something to the test—he'd go quietly and carefully and—Hubert's plans were thwarted. A scream rang out from downstairs somewhere and Hubert, for reasons well known to himself, darted for the open door of the bathroom. He made it just as the lights came back. Much to his surprise, there, seated nonchalantly on the edge of the bath itself, was Elizabeth Kennerley. Hubert was just a trifle taken aback at the unexpected sight of her. She put her fingers to her lips to enjoin silence upon him. Hubert smiled and nodded his understanding. What he specially wanted to see was the various people behind those various bedroom doors. He heard the deep voice of Dick Fanshawe and the treble of Frances as they made their way upstairs for their investigation. Under the rules of the game—and Hubert wouldn't have dreamed of cheating at any game he played—he must not move until Dick and Frances had noted his position. If any severely punctilious person had confronted him with the charge that he had already been guilty of cheating—that he had moved after the victim's scream—Hubert would have compounded with his conscience and argued forcibly that this was *not* so. He would have asserted that he had moved simultaneously with the scream—and then merely for private reasons of his own which had absolutely nothing to do with either the game or the rules of the game.

So he awaited the entrance of Dick Fanshawe and Frances with the serenest equanimity. He was annoyed that he hadn't been able to find out what he had wanted to know. That he had not been able to allay the doubt which had brought him upstairs in the first place. But there would be at least one more game played which would present him with another chance. Unhappily the bathroom door did not command a view of all the bedrooms. So that when Hubert came from his temporary lair, the others were already gathered on the landing. There were Kennerley, Ella, Gervaise Chard and . . . wonderful to relate, his own father! Hubert realized that his first reckonings must have been unsound. That he had made a miscalculation. Still, as he knew from past games—some people could move with astounding quickness and agility. He trooped downstairs with the five others. Dick Fanshawe, aided by much intelligence from Frances, proved slick with the interrogations. He deduced with commendable speed that Ethel Thornhill had been "murdered" by Mrs. Grant senior.

After spirited applause, the necessary tickets were prepared and drawn for the second time. Frances, much to her disgust, again drew the comparatively unexciting rôle of detective. On this occasion she was companioned by her grandfather.

Hubert at once arranged his plans. He made—sidled would be the better word—for the staircase, before Alice put the lights out. Directly the lights were off, Hubert made straight for one of the spare bedrooms. It was his house and he knew every inch of it— even in the darkness. Hubert chose the bedroom from which he thought Julian Kennerley must have come on the occasion of the previous game. He made it with many seconds in hand. There was a small table in the angle of the wall by the window. Hubert pulled the table out, made a place for himself and crouched down in the corner behind the table. He hadn't long to wait. He heard people come into the room. But for the life of him he was unable to identify them. Hubert listened until his eardrums were near to bursting point. He could hear whispers. A shuffle of feet. More whispers. A voice that he would swear belonged to Julian Kennerley. A light laugh. Then silence. Almost immediately broken by the unmistakable sound of kissing.

Hubert, like Gilbert's kettles, boiled with rage. These people would look sick and sorry when they saw him there when the time came for the lights to go up. More kisses and quick moving—then absolute quietness. Hubert swallowed hard. He waited for other sounds of amorousness, but he was disappointed. A scream came from somewhere not too far away, and after a brief interval the lights came again. Hubert dashed from his uncomfortable corner by the wall. Seated on the bed, smoking a cigarette, was Julian Kennerley. He was even more nonchalant than his sister had been on the occasion of the previous game. But to Hubert's intense chagrin and disgust Kennerley was alone.

"You shouldn't move, you know, Grant," he said reprovingly. "It isn't done. It doesn't give the sleuths a fair chance."

"I've been here all the time," muttered Hubert rather truculently.

"So have I," said the doctor, "and as one sportsman to another, I think I ought to tell you I heard those kisses of yours. I must hand it to you, Grant. Pretty sound technique! Where's the lady?"

Hubert opened his mouth to reply, but the words stuck in his throat. At that moment, Frances and her grandfather came in. Frances, fortified by experience, went about her work with the assurance of the "old hand". Assuming the rôle of principal detective, she preceded her grandfather into the bedroom which housed her father and Dr. Kennerley and duly noted their respective positions to the manner born.

"Who's been murdered, Frances?" inquired Kennerley.

"Uncle Gervaise," replied Frances—"Mr. Chard. 'E's come to an 'orrible Hend. You and Daddy must come downstairs now."

They accepted the advice and went to the usual inquisition in the lounge. Hubert, a prey to conflicting thoughts, watched the various people like a hawk. Who was the girl who had been with Kennerley in the bedroom? That there had been a girl in there with him—Hubert *knew*. He had knowledge now—not mere suspicions. The people, one by one, some in pairs, came back to the lounge. Frances, true to the Fanshawe tradition, began her investigation. Her grandfather, it seemed, had been relegated to the rôle of a very silent Watson. Hubert could pay little attention to the questions and answers. He heard them, but that is the most that can be said. He had his own problem to solve. A most pressing problem too. As unobtrusively as he was able, he noted the looks on the various faces. The clock struck ten. Dorothy looked supremely happy, he thought. Curse Kennerley! He started to attack his problem. The girl with Kennerley in the bedroom had *not* spoken—this, in Hubert's carefully considered opinion. He could have sworn he heard Kennerley's voice, but no more than that. The girl, feeling guilty, might have decided purposely not to use her voice in such a manner that it might be heard, in the event of a third person being in the room. That was feasible. Upon second thoughts, Hubert came to the conclusion that this desire for silence would be the policy of all the girls in the house. Even of Maureen. They were all married, and with the exception of Maureen all their respective husbands were in the house with them at the time. So that this theory of his had established little or nothing for him. But if he—He was suddenly aware that Frances had shot a question at him.

"Were you and Dr. Kennerley alone all the time in that bedroom?"

Hubert gaped.

"Please, Daddy, answer up as quickly as possible."

"Have you any idea who was with you?"

"Not really."

"Was it a lady or a gentleman?"

"A lady, I think."

"What makes you think that?"

Hubert hesitated. Where was this going to finish? He knew Frances's passion for detail. He saw, also, the face of Julian Kennerley smiling at him. The face was bland, cynical and obviously on the best of terms with its owner. Kennerley was waiting upon his answer. Hubert burnt his boats.

"I don't *think*! I *know* that it was a lady."

"How do you know, Daddy?"

This was awkward. Frances in full cry. There would be no shaking her off now that she had got as far as this. "By her movements. A lady's movements are not so heavy as a gentleman's."

"When did she leave the—when did she go out of the room?" Frances coloured. She had very nearly uttered a *faux pas*.

"I don't know."

"You don't know?"

"I haven't the slightest idea. I didn't hear her go out of the room so I can give no opinion on the point."

"H'm." Frances looked thoughtful and sucked the point of her "Uncle Dick's" silver pencil. With true feminine instinct she had snaffled this at the first opportunity. Then, to Hubert's infinite relief she turned from grilling him to an examination of Ella Fanshawe. Hubert at once returned to his own individual problem. He became aware that Dorothy was watching him intently. Was she suspicious that he had discovered something? Had Kennerley been able to warn her? The whole thing was assuming the most alarming proportions. It was monstrous! In his own house! His wife! A man he had befriended! Gone out of his way to help. He had pitied him. Sympathized with him in his bad luck. Invited him *and* his sister to a Christmas party. In an hour or so's time he supposed Dorothy and this scoundrel would be dancing together. When they rolled the carpet back and the dance-band came on the radio. Would they? He'd see they didn't! Never mind if there was a scene! Some things were going a bit too far. If they thought he was some sort of a tame cat, they'd jolly well find out their mistake. Hubert then heard without emotion that Frances had failed in her search to find the murderer. He heard Ella Fanshawe confess to the crime. Dorothy was still watching him. He wondered what she was thinking. . . .

This is what Dorothy had been and was thinking. Her thoughts were of three men. Laurence Weston, Julian Kennerley and Hubert Grant, her husband and the father of Frances. Her thoughts were a turmoil of triumph, anger, shame and resentment. She had known earlier on in the evening that Kennerley had already consumed quite enough alcohol to make him mischievous, and that she herself would probably be the object of his amorous intentions. When she looked towards him, she observed that he was almost invariably looking at her and that the hint of mockery his eyes carried was always turned full on when he caught her looking at him.

When the first game of murder had started, she had found him close at her side, and had made up her mind to go to her own bedroom in order to avoid him. She reckoned, however, without her Kennerley. He had been clever enough to follow her and eventually, to her dismay, she had discovered him in the room with her. When he tried to kiss her, she had resisted him. It seemed that this resistance on her part surprised him. Evidently, in similar circumstances, he was unused to resistance. During the exchanges he had whispered something to her which obviously had a relationship to her husband. She desired with all her heart to tell this wretched man that she was not concerned with her husband *or* with her husband's point of view. Her faithfulness, the loyalty which was prompting her and burning up her very soul, was to Laurence. She twisted herself violently out of Kennerley's grasp and broke right away from him. He muttered the semblance of an apology to her.

She thought to herself bitterly and indignantly that if ever a day did come when she should leave Hubert for Laurence and the vitriol of the world's opinion were flung over her in consequence, this man, whom she had just repulsed, would doubtless stand amongst her most abusive accusers. This treacherous hound, who couldn't keep his hands off the wife of a man who had been his friend. To him, her love for Laurence would be "a nasty business, old man—wife went off the rails", something about which dirty-minded people sniggered, whereas he would regard this evening's episode as something in the nature of "why shouldn't you and I have a little fun, my dear". Beastly! Revolting! She had heard all these expressions before, but they had always been used with regard to other people.

Dorothy shuddered as she left Julian Kennerley to the devices and desires of his own nasty heart. As she darted across the threshold, there had come the cry of the stricken Ethel, the lights had come on again, and she had managed to mingle with the crowd that was met by Frances and Dick Fanshawe. From thence onwards, she had avoided the amorous doctor who, to judge by the rather sullen expression on his face, had not taken his rebuff at all sportingly.

When the second "murder" game had begun, Dorothy had hoped she would be fortunate enough to draw one of the tickets marked "detective". Her hope had been unrealized. At the same time, when the lights went out for the second time, she had kept a wary eye on Kennerley so that she might be able to avoid the circumstances of the previous game. But she had seen Hubert do his rapid vanishing act. She had noted his lightning dash up the stairs and had guessed, knowing Hubert as she did, that he had a special plan in view to deal with something which was occasioning him anxiety. The result was that after Hubert had gone she kept *behind* Kennerley and arranged matters so that he went upstairs in advance of her.

Watching him as she had been, she came to the opinion that he had already fitted a second string to his bow. Dorothy thought that this second string was Ella Fanshawe. She knew Ella well. She liked her immensely. But she knew, nevertheless, that Ella had a heel of Achilles. She knew that Ella was vulnerable where a good-looking man was concerned. She was not doing Ella any injustice. Ella had as good as admitted it to her. Many times more than once. In other words, given Dick Fanshawe out of the way, Dorothy was sorely afraid that Ella's weakness would be very successfully exploited. She feared for Ella. Feared that Ella would cheapen herself, let herself down, let her sex down. It never occurred to Dorothy that these or similar charges might have been levelled against her. Such a contingency never entered her mind. If such charges had been made against her—she would have derided them—laughed them to scorn! You couldn't compare her glorious love for Laurence Weston and his for her with the nasty, fumbling, furtive, clandestine cuddling of Ella and Kennerley in the dark. Such an idea would be absurd. Nobody with the slightest degree of understanding could entertain it for a matter of two seconds.

When she reached the top of the staircase she lost sight of Kennerley and Ella. But when the first part of the game finished and she saw them again at the re-assembly in the lounge, she felt convinced that her suspicions had not been ill-founded. Kennerley looked distinctly less sullen. There was a look, too, in Ella's eyes which Dorothy had seen in them before. She rather thought that she knew what it betokened. She would show Madam Ella what she thought of her. She would be quite safe in doing that. She frowned at Ella, therefore, and enjoyed doing it. Ella seemed oblivious of the frown, however. This *confirmed* Dorothy's suspicions.

Frances was doing her stuff when the clock struck ten and Dorothy lay on her magic carpet and translated herself to Laurence. When she came back, she saw Hubert glaring at her. Dorothy wasn't slow. She knew what his glare portended. Hubert had noticed something with that nasty "municipal" mind of his, had positively leapt to conclusions, and was now throwing a "peeve" all over the place. Yes—she couldn't help saying it to herself—she said it every day and every night now—"hateful Hubert". Then she thought again of his vanishing act—and a little sick at heart—understood what had lain behind it. Hubert had been sleuthing. Sleuthing after her and Kennerley. And had caught nothing!

Stay, though—she remembered the darkness and the general conditions. What the room had been like on the occasion when she and Kennerley had been alone together in it. Supposing Hubert *had* heard something and had connected *her* with it? Had noticed something of what had happened earlier and had associated her with the kissing during the second performance. She was certain that a second performance *had* taken place. Ella was flushed now. With a pink spot burning in each of her cheeks. Ella was *not* the best of dissemblers. And if Linklater *had* seen her on Christmas Eve and told Hubert about it when he met him—Dorothy bit her under-lip with conscious vexation. She hated Hubert, she hated Kennerley, she hated Christmas, she hated this wretched party which Hubert always had to have, she hated everybody! Yes—everything and everybody—with the exception of Laurence and Frances.

"Dorothy darling." She looked up, to hear her mother-in-law addressing her . . . "Hubert has just told me that you have a surprise in store for us . . . and he refuses to give me the slightest indication as to what that surprise is. He insists that I must ask you."

Sick at heart, Dorothy realized that Christmas at "Red Roofs" had still several hours to go. She answered Mrs. Grant mechanically. That lady smiled . . . more mechanically. Yes . . . there were still several hours to go.

CHAPTER VIII

DOROTHY Grant's first serious clash with her husband occurred on the evening of the Thursday—that is to say, the day after Boxing Day. There were reasons, probably, why it was delayed until then. The Christmas Day party had gone well into Boxing Day, as it always did. The senior Grants and the Thornhills had stayed over Boxing Day. They departed, two by two, on the Thursday afternoon. After they had gone, Dorothy took Frances to a "flick" in Tudor. All this time Hubert had seemed quiet. Subdued was the word which Dorothy Grant used to herself with regard both to him and this dominant mood. His mood of quietness had persisted when she and Frances had returned from their outing somewhere about the middle of the evening. His replies to Dorothy and even his conversations with Frances had been mainly monosyllabic. Dorothy read the portents and braced herself for the breaking of the inevitable storm. As far as she herself was concerned, the sooner it came, the better. Frances said "good night", made a grimace to her mother *at* her father, but unseen by him, and went to bed. Not overlong after, Dorothy announced herself of a similar intention.

"I'm tired, Hubert. I haven't had much rest these last few days. I think I'll go to bed."

"Very well," returned Hubert.

"Alice will get you anything you want."

"No doubt," replied Hubert.

"I'll go up then."

"Do."

Dorothy smiled a hard, unfriendly smile as she went upstairs to bed. He wouldn't hurt her like that, if he thought he could. As she patted a skin cream into her cheeks, she flew away to Laurence. This was her nightly habit. She wasn't going to hurry herself in any way because of Hubert—she didn't intend to put herself out—but she hoped to be in bed and well asleep before he arrived. She wasn't going to run away from a rough house but she loathed rows and always did her best, therefore, to avoid one. At the same time, if Hubert insisted on one she still thought, as she had thought before—"the sooner the better".

Eventually she got into bed and composed herself for sleep. Her statement to Hubert concerning her tiredness was only too true. Dorothy closed her eyes for slumber. She was fated, however, on this twenty-seventh of December, to be disappointed. Before she could get thoroughly off, she heard Hubert's step on the staircase. He must have either refused Alice's hospitality or made martyred shift with his own. This was a Hubert whom Dorothy had encountered before. You can't live eleven years with a man without getting to know quite a lot about him. She heard his hand on the handle of the door. Dorothy threw pretence to the winds. She was awake . . . She would remain awake. Her conscience was clear—well—as regards Kennerley it was—and Hubert knew nothing about Laurence Weston. Yet! If Hubert went for her, she'd give him as good as he gave. Felt just in the mood for him now. Hubert took certain articles of toilet and marched off into the bathroom. So far he hadn't spoken a word. She waited, grim and hard-hearted, for his return. He had washed and cleaned his teeth. He took off some of his clothes. He carefully brushed his hair. Suddenly, hairbrush poised over his head, and his eyes gazing straight into a looking-glass, he appeared to come to a decision. When he spoke, his voice was unusually dry and harsh.

"I want a word with you. On a somewhat serious matter."

She replied in the same vein. "What is it? The turkey done too much—or were the pheasants below their usual standard?"

"I said it was a *serious* matter."

Dorothy put scorn into her laugh. "Don't tell me such things aren't serious to you! I know you too well, my dear Hubert."

He flared into temper. "Don't play at words with me. Because you know perfectly well what I'm alluding to."

"I assure you that I don't."

"I think you do."

"My dear Hubert, I haven't the slightest idea. And please don't look at me so ferociously. You look like an infuriated owl."

"Very well, then—I won't beat about the bush any longer. I'm referring to a little matter connected with your friend Kennerley."

"Pardon me, Hubert, *your* friend Kennerley! *You* invited him—not *I*."

"You won't put me off like that—even if you think you will." Hubert was raising his voice. Almost beginning to shout. Dorothy found pleasure in this.

"I don't understand you, Hubert." Dorothy grew quieter.

"Oh yes, you do, my lady! I watched you. You didn't know that, did you? I spotted your little games and if you want to know, I was a bit too smart for you. You thought you got away with it, but I kept my eye on you all the time."

"How charming of you." Dorothy put up a really good specimen of a yawn. "And now that this interesting accusation against me has been made with such dramatic fervour, perhaps, in justice to me, you will be good enough to define it a little more closely. Do you mind, Hubert?"

Hubert banged the hairbrush on the dressing-table. "If you want to know, I was in that bedroom. All the time."

"And what bedroom was that, may I ask?"

"The room where you and Kennerley were! Kissing! Cuddling! Laughing together! A petting party in one of your own bedrooms. And I was there. Listening! That takes the smile off your face, my girl."

"I have no doubt that if you were anywhere—you'd be listening. I have no doubt of that, whatever. But as it happens, you're barking up the wrong tree. As I said to you just now, I haven't the slightest idea what you're talking about. I have neither kissed your friend Kennerley, nor, as you put it rather vulgarly, 'cuddled him'! What is more—and I don't know whether this will interest you or otherwise—I haven't the slightest desire to do either."

Dorothy turned over on her side so that all Hubert could see of her was her back. To say that Hubert was dumbfounded is beside the point. He had been so sure of his ground. Even now, he was unable to persuade himself thoroughly that Dorothy was telling the truth. Some seconds passed before he could find an answer.

"I don't believe you," he muttered. Dorothy completely ignored the remark. Hubert approached close to the bedside. He would endeavour to bluff her into confession.

"I saw you."

Dorothy's reply was curt and directly to the point. "You're a liar, Hubert."

Hubert stepped back a pace and gasped. There was no *finesse* here. It sounded like the positive condition of unchallengeable innocence. Suddenly, Dorothy propped herself up in bed on an elbow. She was determined to take the war into Hubert's camp with as little delay as possible. She spoke cutting words. "And before you go any further with this rather disgusting subject, Hubert, I should like an apology from you. Please understand that."

Hubert stood by the bed, his hands thrust deep into his trousers pockets. His face was ugly with vexation and bad temper. He said nothing. His interview with Dorothy had gone very differently from his intentions. Dorothy struck harder at him.

"I might, my dear Hubert, it seems to me, bring an accusation against *you*. With certainly no less justification."

Hubert glared at her. "What's that?" he demanded. His voice was thick.

"Think," said Dorothy persuasively.

"I don't know what you mean! *My* conscience is perfectly clear." He was careful to place the accent on the personal pronoun.

Dorothy toyed with him. "I'm surprised you can't remember."

"For goodness' sake, shut up talking in enigmas."

"Please don't raise your voice so. It doesn't worry me. Don't think that. But I was thinking of Frances. I should hate to think that she could hear you talking to me as you've been doing. What I alluded to was this. I saw you on one occasion in the bathroom with the Kennerley girl. You were alone, what's more. I admit that I didn't listen to your conversation. But still—"

Dorothy, lying down, did her best to shrug her shoulders.

"I might have imagined things—and I *might* equally have hurled accusations in *your* direction. After all, you had provided me with evidence—it was *you* who insisted on inviting the Kennerleys."

This, to Hubert, was the last straw. "You'll regret that! And you'll take it back. You know that I'm not that sort of man. If you don't—all I can say is—that it's about time you did."

In the shadow Dorothy smiled. "Nevertheless, *I*, in your estimation apparently, am that sort of woman! Thank you, Hubert. Thanks for the compliment! That's very charming and quite typical of you. Well—there's one thing—we now know where we stand."

She spoke in a tone which suggested that she had made her final contribution on the subject.

"Right," said Hubert—"then I'll sleep in the spare room."

He spoke almost savagely. Gathering up the necessary clothes, Hubert walked to the bedroom door.

"Do," said Dorothy sleepily. "I for one shall thoroughly appreciate it."

Hubert banged the door.

CHAPTER IX

WHEN Hubert returned home from Tudor on the Friday evening, Dorothy, silent and defensive, awaited events with supreme coolness. Since the scene in the bedroom of the night before, no conversation whatever had passed between them. At breakfast, Hubert had been sullen and silent. He had almost completely ignored her presence and she had taken her cue from him and said nothing. This condition suited her prevailing mood. It assisted to magnify Laurence and the things that were Laurence's. It amplified her sense of loyalty. When, however, Hubert came in to dinner, Dorothy was determined to make the first move towards *rapprochement*. Her paramount thought concerned Linklater and what Linklater might have said to Hubert. And she resolved, too, to tell the truth right up to that point where she was able to tell the truth without damaging her position, either her own or where it was relative to Laurence. That is to say if she found it necessary!

Hubert seated himself at the table and Alice served the soup. Dorothy could tell from his manner that eventually he would forsake his silence. This put her even more on her guard. Hubert started the ball with one or two short commonplace questions. He avoided all reference, either direct or indirect, to the altercation of the previous night. Dorothy replied to his questions coldly and with a severe economy of phrase. So far, he had given her no clue with regard to Linklater and Christmas Eve. But she *thought*, after a time, that it was coming. The meal proceeded. Dorothy had again arranged that Frances should be out. Such arrangements were easy during the school holidays. The meal reached the sweet course. Suddenly Hubert came to his sticking-point.

"I've been thinking," he said with affected nonchalance, "where did you get to on Christmas Eve?"

"Good," thought Dorothy. "Linklater has opened his mouth. Scandal-mongering old woman!" She simulated surprise.

"Why? What on earth takes us back to Christmas Eve?"

Hubert stiffened and shrugged his shoulders. He was a poor dissembler. "It's true that I had a reason for asking."

"What was the reason, Hubert? I confess I'm intrigued to hear. After an interval of five days—is it? Such a strange question?"

"Perhaps it is. Perhaps it isn't. You aren't going to tell me, I suppose, that you can't remember?"

Dorothy decided that she had delayed her answer long enough. She would now strengthen her position, probably, by telling him what he was anxious to know. "Christmas Eve? Let me see now—oh, I know, I took the bus into Cleves." She paused to see the effect her statement had had upon him. "There you are—now you know."

"Whatever took you into Cleves of all places? Of all the one-eyed—"

"Do I understand that you object to my going into Cleves?"

"Not exactly. But what on earth you want to—"

"Am I to understand that you desire to draw up a list of places to which you will allow me to go? Is that the idea?"

Hubert looked decidedly unpleasant. His eyes gleamed dangerously behind his glasses. "Please don't be absurd and . . . er . . . ridiculous. I never hinted at such a procedure. I merely wondered why you went there."

"Why does one go anywhere? Of all the grotesque insinuations this one is about the—"

"I have made no insinuation. All I said was that I couldn't understand you going into Cleves. On Christmas Eve, too! And I *can't* understand it now."

Dorothy smiled mockingly. "Oh—I see. I'm beginning to get a little light on the matter. Sorry I was so dense before. Your point, of course, is that I went into Cleves to see your friend Kennerley! Please accept my sincere apologies for being so slow in the uptake."

"I said nothing of the kind."

"No—you didn't say it. But I knew! Well, well—what a reputation I'm getting."

"Why didn't you tell me you'd been to Cleves?"

Dorothy was curt. "Don't be foolish, Hubert. Since when have I had to account to you for my daily minutes? But tell me—who told you I was in Cleves? Somebody must have. That's obvious. Don't waste time in denying it."

Hubert, brought to bay, surrendered. "As a matter of fact it was Linklater. Linklater told me."

"Dear me. Chatter over the tea-cups, eh? Hope the typists don't hear you discussing your wives' movements. So dignified and all that. And Linklater was in Cleves—just fancy that. Cleves of all places! It appears to me then, Hubert, that despite what you said, people *do* go to Cleves. How do you account for that?"

Hubert turned sullen again. "Linklater passed through Cleves on his way home. He had been up to town."

"I don't care where he'd been. I find myself wishing almost that I *had* been with Kennerley. That *would* have given him something to chow about. Don't ever accuse my sex of gossiping! After this!" Dorothy laughed scornfully.

Hubert looked at her suspiciously. He chanced his arm. "Supposing I told you that Linklater did see Kennerley with you in Cleves? What would you say to that?"

It was the venture of the desperately jealous man. Dorothy's laugh of scorn changed immediately to one of delicious merriment. "I should have but one answer, Hubert. But an extremely adequate answer! I should say that Mr. Linklater was a liar. Does that satisfy you or must I go even further?"

Hubert rose from the table. He had finished his dinner for one thing. For another, he had been ignominiously defeated in a most undignified verbal encounter. "I have nothing more to say," he announced. As he stood there, pompous and self-sufficient, Dorothy marvelled at what could happen in six short months. At what had happened! From a mild affection to toleration, from toleration to passive dislike, from passive dislike to the active, from there to something perilously akin to hatred. The road which she herself had travelled. The road which but a short time ago she would not have believed she could ever have travelled. She made no sign. The breach was widening. She was content that it should widen.

CHAPTER X

THINGS were uneventful for Dorothy Grant during the next few days. She had no definite understanding with Laurence as to when she would see him again. She contented herself with waiting for the usual sign. That sign would be transmitted to her by telephone. All she had to do was to wait for it. She knew the exact time of day when it would come. The week-end passed with but little incident. Hubert gradually thawed. On Old Year's Night he was almost his old self. He and Dorothy saw the Old Year out with the usual acclamations and the rather absurd ritual. Dorothy, quiet and restrained, held herself well in hand. Silently she drank a toast to her absent lover. She knew that Hubert watched her intently. When she had drunk her wine and the disturbing noises of the night were dying down, she turned quietly away from all of it and went upstairs to bed. Hubert stayed downstairs to listen to the special radio programme. She was half afraid, when she got into bed, that Hubert would select the occasion for a reconciliation. A reconciliation which would, of course, if she became party to it, be celebrated by her surrender to Hubert for the full exercise of what she had heard him describe as his connubial privileges.

But to her unspeakable relief she was spared the ordeal. Hubert stayed downstairs for considerably longer than she had expected he would, and came to bed much more tired than usual. He had resumed sleeping with her on the second night after the quarrel, but apart from the sharing of the bed had left her severely alone. This Old Year's Night proved no exception to this condition. Dorothy slept and greeted the first morning of the New Year feeling well and, when she thought of Laurence, happy!

That evening, it was a Tuesday, Hubert was late coming home from the office. So far as she knew, there was no Committee meeting that evening, which he was compelled to attend, and he had not warned her when he went out in the morning that he might be late home. When he came in, he was over an hour late. The dinner was cold. In addition to being late, Hubert was annoyed. Try as he would to conceal his annoyance, he signally failed. Dorothy made no comment. She was adhering to her decided plan to show no curiosity and even little interest in the matter of Hubert's comings and goings. It seemed to her that on this particular evening Hubert was pleased rather than otherwise with this absence of curiosity and lack of interest on her part. The evening passed off quietly. Dorothy read. Hubert smoked, spat and coughed and generally tinkered about with the radiogram.

On the following Thursday evening, however, Hubert was late again. By approximately the same time. Again he was in a far from good temper when he arrived. Again Dorothy showed herself as completely unconcerned. And again it was obvious that Hubert welcomed this mood of hers. The same thing happened on the Friday evening. Dorothy began to exercise her wits. But outwardly she still refrained from making the slightest sign to Hubert that she was in the slightest degree interested. Another week-end passed entirely like its immediate predecessor.

On the next Monday afternoon, Dorothy decided to throw a cast. She 'phoned to the Town Hall at Tudor and asked for Hubert. The time was almost exactly four o'clock. Dorothy had chosen it with a certain amount of care. She was some time getting through. When she did get on to the Treasurer's Department, she was informed that Mr. Grant was out. Inquiring further, she was told that Mr. Grant had left the office for the day. Dorothy put down the receiver and thoughtfully caressed her cheek. Hubert was undoubtedly up to something. She systematically thought things over. What was it that he was up to? After a period of intensive thought, she came to the conclusion that he was putting in a little job of sleuthing. She chuckled. Sleuthing her and Julian Kennerley! What a farce! All the same, though, on second thoughts, she didn't like it. It didn't please her. It didn't help her. It didn't suit her to be watched. It didn't help her and Laurence. That was the point. It was just possible that Hubert, searching for Kennerley, might find Laurence. She donned her thinking cap. There was one thing. She knew where she was. She had been put on her guard.

On the whole her luck was in. She had *seen* Linklater when he had seen her. She might have missed him and then, when Hubert had questioned her, might have made the cardinal mistake of lying to him. The main point was, as she saw it, where was Hubert sleuthing her? She must find that out. She would return the coin with interest. She would sleuth him. She had received no sign from Laurence, although it was a full fortnight since she had seen him. He might 'phone towards the end of the week. Perhaps on Thursday but more probably, she thought, on Friday. Before she saw Laurence again, she would find out for certain where Hubert was doing his stuff. Meanwhile, she would keep her eyes wide open when Hubert returned home that evening. He was careless in some matters. Matters he regarded as trivial. She might be able to find out something if she played her cards skilfully. She waited in patience for Hubert's homecoming.

When he arrived they followed their now normal procedure. Little conversation was exchanged over the meal. When it was finished, Alice came in and cleared away. Hubert filled his pipe and betook himself to the radiogram, as he had done for several evenings. Frances went to bed. She had been extremely quiet since Christmas. Dorothy felt that the child knew more than either she or Hubert had imagined.

When Hubert had removed himself, Dorothy went quietly to the clothes-cupboard in the hall and opened the door. She listened and could hear no sound from the house. An idea had presented itself to Dorothy. She had noticed that Hubert had been wearing his heavy dark-blue overcoat during the last week or so. Hubert had three "out of doors" coats. His "Burberry", a light texture grey overcoat, and the very heavy dark-blue one. As the weather had been extremely cold round Christmas, he had been wearing the last-mentioned. On the sleeves of this coat, the heavy cuffs had been rolled back, as it were, thus giving Hubert a convenient receptacle in which to slip his various bus and train tickets. She had noticed him push them in there repeatedly when she had been travelling with him. Train tickets, of course, he had to surrender, but the habit meant that usually, during a week, several bus tickets remained tucked away within the roll of Hubert's left cuff. This was the state of affairs that Dorothy was about to investigate.

She found the coat, put her fingers into the cuff-roll in question, and extracted something like half a dozen used bus tickets. She examined them quickly. She was not in need of much time in order to carry out her purpose. A quick glance through them satisfied her as to what she desired to know. Three of the tickets were "returns" between Tudor and Cleves. On the direct route. She smiled as she turned away from the cupboard. Hubert must have spent quite an appreciable time in Cleves since Christmas! She wondered as to the manner of its spending. Had he been walking up and down, looking for her and Julian Kennerley? A tribute to his perseverance.

Dorothy went back to her chair and thought matters over carefully. At least one thing emerged clearly from this new combination of circumstances. Laurence and she must give Cleves a wide berth in the future. As far as she knew, she had never been seen with Laurence *anywhere* by anybody who mattered, and this condition she intended to preserve for as long as she possibly could. She would have to nominate a fresh rendezvous. The idea was aggravating, because Cleves suited both Laurence and her so admirably. In every way. For one thing, it was so easily accessible for them. She must discuss it with Laurence on the next occasion he telephoned to her. Cunning Hubert! And what amazing conceit and effrontery on his part to imagine that he could throw dust in *her* eyes.

As she thought in this way, another idea was born in her brain. She listened to see if the coast were still clear. It seemed to be. Dorothy went to the hall-cupboard again and carefully took from the sleeve of Hubert's coat one of the Tudor-Cleves bus tickets. She saw it was from the service which plied between Tudor and West

Parr. She carefully placed it on the mat outside the door of the dining-room. When Hubert came in again he would probably see it. It was a blue ticket which showed up prominently on the mat's surface. If Hubert didn't pick it up, she would pick it up and make play with it herself. She was interested to see how he would react to it.

When Hubert came in, he failed to see the ticket. But salvation was to hand. Alice came in shortly afterwards and stooped down to pick up the ticket. Dorothy wasted no time. She was in on the situation like a flash.

"What's that you've picked up, Alice?" Her voice was cold and eminently matter-of-fact.

"A ticket, ma'am. An old one. Somebody must have dropped it. I'll put it on the kitchen fire, ma'am."

"A ticket? What do you mean—a ticket? What kind is it? Do you mind showing me, Alice?"

Dorothy knew that Hubert was sitting up and taking notice. Alice took the ticket and handed it to Dorothy.

"Oh—a bus ticket. Yes—burn it, Alice. We don't want it littering up the place."

She affected complete indifference before suddenly changing her tone of voice. On the point of handing it back to Alice, she said, "Just a minute, though. Let me have another look at it."

Alice waited. For some days now Alice had realized that the atmosphere at "Red Roofs" was very far removed from the normal. She had not been able to understand why this should be. Dorothy, with much ostentation, carefully examined the bus ticket.

"Cleves," she exclaimed with dramatic emphasis. "A return ticket between Cleves and Tudor? This must be yours, Hubert! You must have dropped it when you came in. It certainly wasn't there before."

Hubert, surprised by the attack, reddened furiously and was incoherent. "Er . . . yes . . . I suppose . . . er . . . it is. I had to go into Cleves for Linklater this afternoon."

Dorothy assumed an expression of mock astonishment. "But nobody ever goes to Cleves. And fancy Linklater using you as a messenger. Is that where you've been going these last few afternoons? I wouldn't stand for it if I were you, Hubert. Why don't you tell Mr. Linklater to find somebody else to run his precious errands?"

By this time Hubert had partly recovered himself. "Don't be absurd. You don't understand—it's nothing of the kind. If you must know, I had to interview the accountant at Cleves. On important matters of finance. Affecting Tudor and Cleves. Questions of finance crop up from time to time between neighbouring authorities and when they do, they have to be attended to."

Alice stood by—scarlet and spellbound. This was an entirely novel experience for her. Dorothy suddenly seemed to become conscious of her presence. She handed back the bus ticket of contention.

"Take it away, Alice, and burn it. That will be all, thank you."

Hubert scowled as Dorothy dismissed the maid. In his heart he knew that Dorothy had turned the tables upon him most effectively, and he was feeling extremely annoyed in consequence. He was getting sick of the whole damned business! His world seemed to be falling about his ears. It all seemed so incredible to him. For two pins he'd like to take the entire matter into his own hands and let Dorothy see who was eventually going to be master. Perhaps that was what he should have done before. Before things had gone anything like as far as they had now! He cleared his throat in order that he might the more effectively deliver an ultimatum.

"Now look here," he said, pompously and belligerently, "let me tell you once and for all—"

Dorothy interrupted him incisively. "You didn't happen to meet Dr. Kennerley in Cleves, I suppose? If you had, you might have felt some sense of reward for having gone there. You know what I mean—that you hadn't altogether wasted your time."

Hubert, stung by the interruption, glared at her angrily. He knew that he was fast losing control of himself and his temper. "Look here," he almost shouted, "I've had enough of it. More than enough! Do you hear? I simply will not stand here to be insulted by you! Do you hear? And if I have any more of it—"

Dorothy, ignoring the tirade, went on with the utmost serenity. She had discovered that it was delightful fun to bait Hubert. The seeds fell on such fruitful ground. She continued, therefore, in the development of her previous remarks.

"And if you *had* managed to run across Dr. Kennerley—who knows but that you might have found me in the closest companionship? Hanging with loving abandon on his arm? Then, my dear Hubert, I'm perfectly certain that your afternoon would have been most completely rounded off. I can even see you dancing for sheer joy in the narrow streets of Cleves. And then, having so triumph-antly tracked down your guilty wife and her paramour (oh, Hubert, what a word), you could have—"

Her mocking eyes maddened him. Hubert saw red. Everything went from him excepting his raw rage. He took one step forward, raised his right hand and struck his wife hard across the face and mouth. Dorothy went as white as a sheet. Her eyes blazed blue fire at him. Hubert spoke no word. For some shattering seconds they stood and faced each other. Dorothy, white and trembling, Hubert, scarlet and enraged. Dorothy spoke.

"Thank you, Hubert. I shall remember that. I promise you that I shall remember that for a very long time."

Then she turned on her heel and walked from the room. Hubert Grant stood still and watched her.

CHAPTER XI

DURING the next few days, Dorothy completely ignored the pres-ence of her husband. She did not look at him. She did not speak to him. Hubert was sullen but defiant. Dorothy looked outraged but imperious. On the Friday morning, at the usual time, her expected telephone-call came through from Laurence Weston. After the normal preliminaries, Dorothy made her important announcement.

"Laurence darling, Cleves is no good for us this afternoon. Don't ask me why—it will take far too long to explain now—I'll tell you all about it when we meet. We must make up our minds about things quickly. Now listen to me carefully and please don't interrupt. Time's precious—as you know! Make it West Arragon—the station before Cleves. Make sure your train stops there. Some don't. I'll repeat it. West Arragon! There's a cinema there—I've seen it advertised in the local papers. Ask the way to it, and I'll meet you outside, same as we did in Cleves. Is that all clear to you? I'll get the time from the time-table. I'm *hoping* that your usual train will fit all right. *Toujours*, my angel—there's our time signal sounding for us."

No sooner had Laurence rung off than Dorothy flew to the time-table. She was delighted to find that the trains which usually brought Laurence to Cleves and afterwards took him back to town, both served the station at West Arragon. Good fortune indeed! So that one of her troubles, at least, was temporarily allayed. But she herself would be forced to travel to Cleves by her normal bus route and then, when there, to change into another midget bus which she knew ran out to the village of West Arragon. Annoying, certainly, but there it was—it couldn't be helped. The point about which she wasn't too clear was for how long would she be compelled to wait in Cleves. Another thing—Laurence would arrive at West Arragon sooner than he did at Cleves, whereas she, travelling in the other direction, and using two routes instead of one, would be later. This meant that she would probably keep Laurence waiting. Again—it couldn't be helped. She wished now that she could put her hand on a West Arragon bus service time-table. She knew that she hadn't one. She would have to chance it. Frances was all right. She had already arranged for Frances to have tea with Molly Neame. She had done this in advance to cover a possible assignation with Laurence.

She hurried through lunch, prepared herself carefully for Laurence and dashed out to catch her bus. The weather was utterly poisonous. Rain was falling in torrents. When the bus ran into Cleves, Dorothy put her head down and ran as hard as she knew how to the corner from where the West Arragon service started. Here she learned that she had a quarter of an hour to wait. All this was cutting to ribbons the time which she would be able to spend with Laurence and angered her intensely. The bus was waiting. She got in it and sat in it until it started. Only two other people entered, a boy and an old woman. It took another quarter of an hour to reach West Arragon. Half an hour had gone already—and in addition to all this she would have to start away earlier in order to get back home in time.

As she alighted, she inquired the time of the bus back to Cleves and noted it carefully. Luckily, she found the cinema she wanted without difficulty. It called itself the "New Regal". The title was a supreme example of the euphemism. But Laurence was waiting outside and for a time, at least, all the clouds on Dorothy's horizon were dissipated.

Laurence kissed her passionately, whirled her inside and instantly plied her with questions. The cinema was almost empty. Not a soul was near them. The audience, such as it was, was in the cheap seats. She had had time to notice that he appeared anxious.

"What's the matter, sweetheart?"

"I'll tell you. I've heaps to tell you. But before I start there's no need for you to worry. It all began with just a piece of rank bad luck. Now, listen."

Dorothy nestled down into her lover's arms. There was a film showing, but neither Laurence nor Dorothy had the faintest idea as to its title. Dorothy first of all told him about her encounter with Linklater and then went on to explain who Linklater was. Laurence listened with furrowed forehead. Several times he nodded and said "go on". Dorothy told him of what she had done. How she had waited to know for certain if Linklater had seen her and had afterwards informed Hubert. Laurence, when he heard this, nodded approvingly. Dorothy then went back with her story to the Christmas party at "Red Roofs". Laurence listened to her with the utmost attention. When she came to the story of Hubert's accusation against her fidelity, he intervened with an angry exclamation.

"Damned insolence. The idea of such a thing! Shows what his mind's like. Fancy thinking that you were that sort of girl."

Dorothy drew back her head and regarded him archly. "Well—I am—aren't I? I can't very well regard myself as an angel now, can I?"

"How do you mean?" he demanded.

"Well—us."

Laurence dismissed the idea imperiously. "That's very different," he said savagely. "But go on—tell me all there is to tell. It's pretty well making my blood boil."

Dorothy continued her story. She described her relations with Hubert since Christmas, how she had suspected his movements, how he had taxed her upon Linklater's mention of having seen her in Cleves, right up to the incident of finding out for certain that he had been snooping in Cleves. She could see that Laurence's jaw was set firm and his eyes dark and angry.

"Go on," he said yet again, in a hard, cold voice. "Tell me all."

She filled in all the blanks. Until she came to the time when Hubert had struck her across the mouth. She felt a sort of shuddering tremble run through Laurence Weston's frame.

"God," he said hoarsely, "if only I'd been there to see him do it!"

"Why—what would you have done?"

"Taken him by the throat and choked the life out of him. And have loved doing it! You'd have been the last person in this world that Mr. Hubert Grant would have damn' well struck."

His vehemence frightened her. Dorothy's femininity came to the surface. "Wouldn't you rather he hit me than . . . well . . . fondled me?"

"No! I hate and loathe the very thought of him doing either. The swine! I should like to think—"

Dorothy broke in. "I haven't slept with him for nights now. So that you needn't worry your head over anything like that."

"Suits me! And if I have my way you'll never sleep with the swine again."

Dorothy put her head on his shoulder as his arm went round her. There was silence for a time except for the low murmur of their kissing. Suddenly Laurence disengaged himself. When he spoke, he horrified her. Cold clutched at her heart. But the horror and the chill, strange to say, began to diminish as she listened to him.

"I've made up my mind," he said to her. "And after what you've told me, I've little or no compunction in the matter. I'll see that Hubert Grant doesn't bother you any more."

"Why . . . Laurence . . . what do you mean?"

She was frightened again. He laughed bitterly.

"What do I mean? One thing and one thing only—that's what I mean. I've made up my mind—once and for all. I'll get rid of the brute." She gasped, but Laurence was off again. "And it won't take me long either! I shall revel in the job."

"Laurence . . . you mustn't talk like that. It's wrong! Think what it will mean—if you're found out. There's a better way than that. I shall let him divorce me."

He shook his head roughly and fiercely and laughed again. With even more bitterness and harshness than on the previous occasions.

"Divorce you? With me as co-respondent? Have you thought what it means? The issues involved and the vital matters entailed?"

She shook her head. "I don't think I properly understand you, darling."

"I don't suppose you do. I don't suppose you've given it a moment's thought. Well—it doesn't matter. It's got to be faced. We'll face it now. It means two things. One—I lose my job and I should have hard work to land another anything like as good—and two—you lose Frances. The court in the circumstances would be bound to leave her in Hubert's custody. Now—do you see what I'm getting at?"

"But, Laurence . . . it's awful . . . it would be murder . . . it's like Mrs. Thompson . . . I mustn't listen . . . you mustn't dream—"

"Murder? Is that how you see it? Well—I don't! Justifiable homicide more like it! A man who strikes his wife in the mouth as he did you! Think what it means to us! A life together . . . all our days and nights spent with each other . . . comfort *and* Frances. I'll do the job 'pat' as Hamlet said. Nobody would be able to dream even of suspecting me. I'll see to that. Who in the world, save you, knows of any connection that I have with Hubert Grant? It's a cinch, my girl; don't you worry."

"They mightn't suspect you . . . but they'd soon suspect me. Everything I'd done would be combed out pretty thoroughly."

"So they might—*suspect* you . . . but if you had an unshakable alibi they couldn't touch you."

"If I had—no doubt! But I probably shouldn't have."

Dorothy said this deliberately. But she was already amazed at herself—talking so easily and so comfortably in terms of horror and murder. It all bordered on the incredible.

"But you *would* have, my dear! I should take damned good care to provide you with one. You aren't very complimentary to me. My plan will be perfect. Or as perfect as anything humanly conceived can be. I've never yet botched up anything in my life, and I certainly shan't botch this up. Too much at stake."

Dorothy almost held her breath. His coolness and complete confidence engulfed her. It seemed that there were deep waters stretched all round her. She attempted to remonstrate with him again. "But, my dear, it's dreadful! We *must* be able to find some other way of solving our problem."

"Look here, angel. You listen to me. As far as I'm concerned with your husband, the gloves are definitely off. For all time. When he hit you like you say he did, he signed his own death-warrant. Love and Passion and Murder are elemental. And so's Justice. You can't *play* at any one of 'em and you can't wear kid gloves for 'em either. You are over-civilized. That's all that's the matter with you. You put an entirely fictitious value on human life and recoil from stark realities. But your ancestors, faced with your problem, wouldn't have recoiled. They'd have done exactly what I'm going to do. Taken the law into their own hands! Hubert Grant's a dirty rat—and there's only one way of dealing with vermin. Get rid of it."

Laurence lit a cigarette, but his hands were shaking as he did so. The light of the match showed that clearly to Dorothy sitting next to him.

"Tell me," he said after a moment's silence, "are you sure that he has no suspicions of *any* person who might be me? You can see what I mean."

"None. He can't have. As far as you're concerned, I haven't made the vestige of a mistake. Ever since we've been going together."

"As far as you know."

"Yes, as far as I know."

"There's *one* slight risk, as I see it." Laurence spoke rather gloomily. His anger seemed to have departed from him.

"What's that?" Dorothy was anxious.

"That somebody *you* know, and who knows you, *may* have seen you with me. Without your knowing. Like this man Linklater seems to have done—only you spotted him."

Dorothy nodded. "Yes—it's possible—I see that—but I *don't* think so."

"Good. Then there's another slight risk that I've just thought of. It eluded me before."

Dorothy became more anxious. "What have you thought of now?"

"Tristram. Last June."

Dorothy, much relieved, shook her head at him. "Nothing much to worry about there. We didn't stop at the same hotel, for one thing."

"I know. That's lucky. The police will be bound to inquire. They'll look for the third side of the triangle. Always do. They'll try to link you up with a man somewhere. Unless I can throw 'em off the scent. Now let's have a look at Tristram again." He thought hard. "The inquiries they make will be at *your* hotel. Lucky I stopped at an inn where they didn't bother about visitors' books or receptionists. Now did any of *your* fellow guests see us together much? In any compromising circumstances?"

"I don't think so. I can't remember that they did. Besides—on a holiday like that—in the summer—"

"Exactly," said Laurence drily, "such an occurrence would make but the faintest impression. That's just how I feel about it."

It was at that precise moment that Dorothy thought of something. "By the way," she said impulsively, "there's just one other thing I ought to tell you about. With regard to him having suspicions of *you*. I meant to have told you about it before. But it slipped my mind. You know when you 'phoned me, just before Christmas."

Laurence nodded. "Yes."

"Well, Hubert tried to get through to me from the office at the moment you were on the line. It was just an unlucky coincidence. He asked me about it when he came home that night. Of course, I fobbed him off. Told him it was a wrong number call. That's positively the only occasion when the least thing has gone wrong with me—besides Linklater, of course."

Laurence frowned. "H'm. Makes you think. Has the skivvy ever *heard* you on the 'phone to me?"

Dorothy shook her head decisively. "Alice? Never. I take good care of that. Don't pay any attention to it. It was quite all right I tell you. Don't worry about it. I *know* it was all right."

"Good. I'll take your word for that. Trust your intelligence. But something else has occurred to me now. Something we can't afford to neglect to consider. We *must* look at everything. We've got to! To safeguard ourselves."

"Yes. Tell me."

"These cinema visits together. To Cleves on those few occasions, and now this one in West Arragon."

"You mean—"

"*You.* I'm thinking of *you.* You count. I don't. Unless I make a ghastly mistake, which I assure you I shan't do, there will be no avenue which the police can travel which will lead to me or even in my direction. But with you it's going to be different. This is the point that I'm trying to develop. With regard to these cinema stunts of ours. Let me put it to you like this. Supposing your photograph is published in any of the papers. That will include the local papers, naturally. What's the chance of it being linked up, say, by any of the Cleves picture people? I should doubt it, but there is a risk about it, or so it seems to me."

Dorothy was thoughtful as she considered the point which Laurence had made. "I should doubt it, too. Very much. The few times we've been. It's possible, I suppose, but . . ." she shook her head disarmingly.

"There's this about it. The times we come are not in our favour. They're definitely against us. We come when business is slack. No swarms of people coming out or going in with us. Another thing—" He paused and grinned.

"Still, another, Laurence?"

"Yes." He was still grinning. "If I may be forgiven for saying so, we are both *rather* distinguished."

She pulled his face down to her and kissed him just behind his ear. This was one of Dorothy's habits with Laurence. Then she ruffled his hair. "I don't know about myself, but you certainly *are.*" As she spoke she realized yet again where she was going. A revulsion of feeling came over her and shook her, "But, Laurence darling, this is madness. What are we dreaming of? This way disaster lies! Can't you see? You *must* see!"

But Laurence was adamant. He leant over and gripped her hands. "Neither madness nor disaster. Can't you—*won't* you see that I'm justified? I admit that I'm not squeamish—but when you doubt, remember your Bible! What about David, the great King David who desired Bathsheba, as I desire you? What did he do? Did he talk? He did not! He *acted.* He put Uriah the Hittite, and the husband of

Bathsheba, in the forefront of the battle. Gave definite orders that it should be done. That sounds all very picturesque when it's put in that way, but being interpreted, it means that David had Mr. Uriah killed. Murdered! In modern version—'bumped off'. And when he'd effected this, he proceeded to his affair with Bathsheba."

"Yes," agreed Dorothy, "but it was still wrong. It was still murder. David was guilty. Guilty in his heart. And both he and the woman were punished for it. And two wrongs will never make a right, argue as much as you like."

Laurence unloosed one of her hands so that he might caress it. "Yes—granted all that—but there's something you've forgotten—about David whom you're verbally castigating as a murderer. If you look in your Old Testament, you'll read there that David was 'a man after God's own heart'."

Dorothy looked puzzled. "Yes—I know—but—oh, I find it awfully difficult to find words—to say to you what I want to say. You see—it's like this. David might have been—"

Laurence threw her objections to one side and assumed supreme command of the situation. "Now listen. If you love me, as you swear you do, you'll fight for our future just as hard and just as fearlessly as I'm going to." He put his arms round her. "*Our* future, my darling! Don't you realize all that means? Like Villon, I can say, 'Methinks I see myself growing old sedately with Dorothy at my side. A little Laurence here, more virtuous than his father, a little Dorothy there, less comely than her mother . . .' but I won't go on and say 'run away, my little dream children', because in our case they're not going to be dream children, they're going to be real." He rained kisses on her eager mouth.

Dorothy thrilled at his touch. "You would fight," she said tremulously, "like Villon again, for love and life tonight. But if you fail, my dear . . . and . . . anything happens to you . . . anything unspeakably dreadful . . . I can't go on! You understand! I shall destroy myself." Her tears fell on his hands. "That would be the only thing left to me."

"Now listen to me carefully—you'll know nothing beyond what I'm going to tell you now. But I shall want you to do and arrange certain matters. We'll call them the preliminaries." He fished in his breast pocket. "You see these cards. You can see what they are. Look at them. They're eminently innocent and harmless."

There was enough light in the cinema for her to see what he held. Laurence went on talking. Clearly, concisely and earnestly. He obtained from her certain vital facts and noted them carefully. Facts concerning Hubert, Tudor and Bullen. Occasionally Dorothy shuddered—but curiously fascinated, she continued to listen.

CHAPTER XII

DOROTHY entertained Maureen Townsend, Ella Fanshawe and Ethel Thornhill. The proffered attractions were a "chin-wag" in the afternoon and a form of rather unambitious Bridge in the evening. After tea, and somewhere about seven o'clock, they would be joined by Chard, and the three husbands. During the evening they would all be regaled with light refreshments. Hubert and Dorothy ran little crushes of this kind fairly frequently and, as everybody knew everybody else, they usually turned out quite snappy and by no means boring. Certainly those who came were always quite prepared to come again. Hubert usually came home to tea and the other three men got a bite somewhere before they arrived, and thus were able to get right down to the game directly they did arrive. Dorothy had sent out the invitations about ten days prior to the event taking place, had told Hubert all about it, and had discovered, somewhat perhaps to her surprise, that Hubert was by no means ill-disposed towards the idea.

It must be remembered that Hubert had always liked these little social gatherings under his roof. But on the evening in question there were unpleasant disappointments. Maureen Townsend had been unusually late, and at 5.30 p.m. a message was received from Gervaise Chard apologizing for the fact that it was absolutely impossible for him to keep his appointment. This message was conveyed to Dorothy from Chard's office by one of Chard's typists. Gervaise had had to go somewhere on a most important mission at the eleventh hour and all that he could do to Mrs. Grant by proxy was to apologize humbly for his defection and profusely for his bad manners. The girl who spoke to Dorothy made it clear that Mr. Chard had no option in the matter. Dorothy put down the receiver after she had taken the message and returned to her three companions with a somewhat heightened colour.

Mrs. Fanshawe could see that her hostess was annoyed. She made a remark.

"Yes, I *am* annoyed," said Dorothy; "it's Gervaise. That call was from his office. He can't come this evening. Much too busy. I've never known Gervaise let us down before. It's positively sickening. Who would be a hostess and have to rely on men? When Hubert comes in I'll get him to 'phone to one or two other people. And I'll tick Master Gervaise off good and proper next time I see him."

"A lot he'll care about that," said Maureen with a thin smile.

"I know. Still—one must stick up for oneself these days. Master Gervaise isn't going to have it all his own way."

Everything had been ready for some time when Dorothy looked at the clock with a puzzled expression and then spoke to Ella Fanshawe.

"Ella," she said quietly, "do you see the time? I'm worried about it. Hubert should have been in over an hour ago. I can't think what can have become of him. The others will be here in less than half an hour."

Ella was unperturbed. "He'll probably come in with them. Got delayed at the Town Hall and then went along to the 'Ship' and had a snack with Dick. Plus other things," she added sapiently.

"Yes," added Ethel, who had been listening—"drinking probably and telling dirty stories. And I'll bet anything you like that my beauty's with them."

Dorothy shook her head doubtfully. "It's possible, I suppose, but it's unlike Hubert to do that. He likes to be home fairly early on these occasions. Likes to get things ready. You know how he fusses over people when they come in. He positively hates having to do things in a hurry. Says it disturbs his equilibrium. But why do I tell you? You know Hubert by this time almost as well as I do myself. Quite frankly, girls, I'm worried."

"You'll find he'll walk in with the others all right, you see."

Ella patted a cushion and made herself more comfortable as she spoke. The clock chimed a quarter to seven.

"'Phone the Town Hall, Dorothy, if you're worried," suggested Ethel. "May set your mind at rest."

"But, then, he may have left there with Dick, as Ella says. If Dick comes in without him, I shall certainly 'phone there. I know it's silly of me to get all worked up like this—but Hubert's so reliable on time." She smiled. "I must give the devil his due."

"We shall soon know," remarked Ella—"the others should be here in a few minutes."

Dorothy went into the kitchen to speak to Alice. Seven o'clock struck. Dorothy, having given Alice certain instructions, returned to the lounge. Maureen noticed how pale she looked. It was a dark night with a drizzle prevailing. But the lounge, with its warmth and its light and its comfort, soon made one forget the wretched conditions of the weather outside. Ethel noticed how repeatedly Dorothy glanced at the clock on the mantelpiece.

"Ella will be right," she said. "Hubert will arrive with the others."

But in this prognostication she was wrong. At ten minutes past seven Thornhill came in. He had seen neither Hubert nor Dick Fanshawe.

"No," he said cheerfully, "haven't heard from or seen either of 'em. I looked in at the 'Lion', too, on my way down."

"I'll say you did," returned his wife. "I should think the animal would die if it weren't for your constant attention. I wonder you didn't try the 'Ship' as well."

When Fanshawe arrived five minutes later, also minus Hubert or any knowledge of his whereabouts, Dorothy announced her immediate intention of ringing the Town Hall. The others at once approved the intention. Dorothy got through at once. When she returned to the lounge her face was even more white and strained.

"Hubert left the office at his usual time," she announced. "Now what am I to do?"

Fanshawe assumed control of the situation. "There may be a dozen explanations of Hubert's lateness—and all of them excessively simple when we come to hear them—I should wait till eight o'clock if I were you before taking any serious action. After all, if you look at it sensibly, nothing can have happened to him because if there had—you'd have heard by this time. That's a cast-iron certainty. Hubert's not a stranger in the district by a long chalk."

He looked towards Roy Thornhill for corroboration of his statement. Thornhill played up gallantly at once. "Yes. I think so. You'll find that Dick's about right. Perhaps Hubert's had a business call to make somewhere and has been unavoidably detained. He may not have told the office people he was going anywhere. You never know. It may have cropped up suddenly."

But Dorothy kept shaking her head at these well-meant efforts to allay her anxieties. "I hope you're right, all of you, but I think it's very strange. I know Hubert's habits so well. He's so very reliable."

After a time the two Thornhills and the two Fanshawes made an attempt to ease the situation and started to play. Maureen went over to a corner of the lounge and talked to Dorothy. But it soon became evident to her that Dorothy's mind was on Hubert and on what might have happened to him. Thus the evening dragged on—the atmosphere charged with drab anxiety. Eight o'clock, nine o'clock, ten o'clock were all sounded on the Grants' clock. No news came of Hubert Grant. At half past ten, in response to Dorothy's entreaties, Dick Fanshawe 'phoned to the police at Tudor police-station. He stated the bare facts. They were quietly noted by the station-sergeant who received them and Dick returned to Dorothy to report. By this time the anxiety at "Red Roofs" was general and the conversation forced and unnatural. Fanshawe himself was worried.

CHAPTER XIII

WHEN Hubert Grant came out of the railway-station at Bullen in the early part of the evening of the Bridge party at his house, he was annoyed to find that he was walking into conditions of darkness and drizzle. More than that, the raindrops clouded his glasses, interfered with his vision and added to his annoyance. He had taken but a few steps in the direction of his house, when he heard footsteps behind him and then, to his great surprise, felt a light touch on his arm. He turned quickly and saw a tallish woman, very smartly dressed, at his side. When she spoke, her voice was low and cultured.

"You will pardon me—but I believe I am addressing Mr. Hubert Grant. Am I right?"

Hubert blinked at her. "Good-looking woman," he thought, "but can't place her for the moment." He said "Yes—I'm Hubert Grant" and stopped. They faced each other. He felt that he had to say something. "But you have the advantage of me, I'm afraid. I'm sorry—but I can't recall—"

"You must forgive me for stopping you like this," said the woman, "but as far as I can see there's no other way. Do you mind if we walk on a little way and talk as we go?" She smiled at Hubert with expressive eyes and Hubert at once agreed to the suggestion. "My name," she said quietly, "is Ingram. I am Mrs. Ingram. Helen Ingram. My husband and I live at Cleves. I mention these matters because they're important. Mr. Grant," she concluded impulsively, "I want to speak to you about your wife—Mrs. Grant. Please will you give me—say—a quarter of an hour?"

Hubert tingled with jealous excitement. The flame was already there and this statement added fuel to it. "Well—Mrs. Ingram— this is rather—"

She took his arm. "Let us go where we can talk quietly. Down one of those side roads. It doesn't matter a lot, of course, seeing how far matters have gone now—but I suppose it would be better if we two weren't seen talking together."

Up to that moment no one had passed them, but Hubert nodded agreement. He suffered this exceedingly charming companion to pilot him down the first turning which conveniently presented itself, and his soul surged in righteous indignation at the disclosures he was fully anticipating to hear. The lady continued her story.

"I promise you that I can say all that I have to say to you in a matter of a quarter of an hour. What I am going to tell you, Mr. Grant, will, I fear, cause you a certain amount of pain. But I have suffered and you must suffer. It can't very well be avoided. You and I represent the unfortunate ends of two domestic triangles. Your wife and my husband, Mr. Grant, are lovers. They make assignations in Cleves. She goes to my husband's office. He's a house and estate agent. There is no doubt about it—believe me. I waited until I was absolutely certain before I decided to tell you. I have followed them and seen them. They have gone," she concluded in a low voice, "as far as they can."

As she spoke, Hubert found it impossible to analyse his feelings. He had no idea whatever which emotion was uppermost in his mind. Actually he grunted in indignation.

"Mr. Grant," went on Mrs. Ingram, "I love my husband—and I want him back. And I want your help to get him back." She stopped in her walk and gripped his arm. Her strength surprised Hubert. "Promise me that you'll give it."

"You may rely on me, Mrs. Ingram. To the fullest extent of my power. But you must realize that this news has come as a great shock to me." Hubert felt that his words were exceedingly well chosen.

Mrs. Ingram nodded. "I found a letter from your wife addressed to my husband—that's how I found out your name. He was careless enough to leave it in one of his pockets. The terms of the letter would have removed any doubts I otherwise might have had."

Hubert began to have certain troubled misgivings with regard to the time. "When can I see you again, Mrs. Ingram? This wants thinking about. And tonight I'm rather pressed for—"

"You're quite near your house," she said. "At the end of this road there's the footbridge over the Murmur. You know—where it rounds the bank at the back of the railway-station. If you cross that and turn to the right you come in the Wolsey Road. Ridgway Gardens is only a couple of hundred yards away from you, then."

Hubert looked and saw that Mrs. Ingram was right. He nodded and went along with her. He was actually on his way home.

"For one thing, Mr. Grant, I have no children. My husband is all I have and I do not intend to surrender him to another woman without putting up a fight. You have a little girl, Mr. Grant—that's right, isn't it?"

"How did you know?"

"I have made inquiries. When I knew it was your wife. I want your help. Badly."

"You shall have it. I'll promise that now. What's your full address, Mrs. Ingram?"

"44 Laud Road, Cleves. That's the private address. My husband's business is in the High Street. Number nineteen. You will write to me, then—and I shall know what you have done in the matter and also what you are going to do. Here's the footbridge, Mr. Grant. When you've crossed it, turn sharp to the right."

She stood very close to him and then held out her hand. "Good-bye and thank you. I am sorry if I have upset you. I must be getting back. Thank you for listening to me."

Hubert shook hands with her, turned and started to walk across the bridge over the Murmur. Then he heard the woman's voice calling him back. He turned and retraced his steps. The woman came to meet him. It was just about the time that Dorothy was presenting her anxiety to her guests at "Red Roofs" and it was perhaps somewhat extraordinary that Hubert and she at this precise moment were not much more than a quarter of a mile apart. Actually, some few minutes later he was even nearer to her than that. But by this time Hubert was dead. His body was travelling in the waters of the Murmur, and when Fanshawe rang up the police-station at Tudor, Hubert had been dead for over four hours.

CHAPTER XIV

HUBERT'S body was taken from the river in the early hours of the following morning. Dorothy was informed by telephone and she was asked to go down to the mortuary to identify him. The Fanshawes had stayed with her overnight so that Dick Fanshawe was able to accompany her on the journey. Later on she told the Inspector of Police all the things concerning which he questioned her.

"You say that as far as you know, Mrs. Grant, your husband never came home that way from the station?"

"As far as I knew—never."

She did not mention Hubert's recent visits to Cleves. She saw no reason why she should. She knew her lines perfectly and was going to play her part exactly as her producer had instructed her. Her exits and entrances had been carefully rehearsed.

"Your husband wore glasses, I believe? That was part of the description given here when you 'phoned us about him yesterday evening. A Mr. Fanshawe 'phoned on your behalf."

"Yes. Almost invariably when he was out-of-doors. Weren't his glasses on him when—"

"No, Mrs. Grant. The glasses have not been found. Was your husband extremely short-sighted?"

"His sight wasn't good. Obviously. He wore glasses."

"Er—yes. Of course."

"Do you think that he fell in the water, misjudged the bridge or something? Or the darkness caused the accident? I take it that he wasn't robbed?"

"He wasn't robbed." The Inspector shook his head.

"Was he hurt? Are there any signs of violence?"

"No. There don't appear to be any."

Dorothy shook her head in mystification. "Why he should have gone round that way—I haven't the slightest idea. I can't keep my mind from puzzling over it."

The Inspector turned away and conferred with a subordinate. "We have established these facts, Mrs. Grant. By inquiries this morning. Your husband left the Town Hall at Tudor at 5.5 p.m. We have three witnesses to that. He was at Tudor station at 5.17 and caught the 5.21 train for Bullen. Up to the moment, however, we have nobody who will testify that Mr. Grant left the train at Bullen station. Never mind that. We shall pick that fact up in time—never fear. Bound to! You were at home, I understand, all the afternoon and evening?"

"Yes. All the time. Why?"

"I was merely confirming my own remembrance of the facts as they have been placed before me." Inspector Sim again conferred with the other officer. "I fear, Mrs. Grant, that what I have to say to you now will come as a severe shock to you. You must prepare yourself to meet it. Do you mind, Owen, for a moment?"

He held out his hand towards Owen. Owen placed a piece of paper in it. Dorothy saw that the paper looked strangely crinkled.

"This, I regret to say, was found in your husband's overcoat pocket. Will you read it, please?"

Dorothy obeyed the request with flaming cheeks. This is what she read.

Wednesday morning. My darling Hubert, I simply must see you tonight. I will be waiting for you in the usual place and at the usual time. Yours always, V.

It was typewritten. Dorothy read it calmly and handed it back to the Inspector.

"You suggest," she said with equal calmness, "that my husband had an assignation with the writer of this letter?"

"It would seem so, Mrs. Grant. What else can I think? You have no idea, I suppose, who could have—" He tapped the dried piece of paper.

"None at all. I have never harboured the slightest suspicions of my husband. You suggest, I assume, that this letter was sent to my husband by a woman? If that is so, and I must admit that in the face of this you have grounds for thinking so, let me tell you at once that I have no knowledge of such a thing. It is a complete surprise to me."

"I see. Thank you. That doesn't get us very far, though, does it? I had hoped you might have been in a position to have helped us."

"I'm sorry I can't." Dorothy gestured with helpless hands.

"Well, then," said the Inspector, "I don't think I need detain you any longer. Bearing in mind what you have just said, we shall, of course, proceed with our inquiries. If we hear anything, we shall communicate with you at once. Goodbye, Mrs. Grant—and my sincere sympathy."

He rose and bowed gravely. Owen opened the door for her. Dorothy returned to her house and Frances. The child was quiet—almost silent. Dorothy observed that she shed no tears for her father. The days came and went. Hubert was put in his coffin and buried in the little cemetery at Bullen. The police followed up many avenues of inquiries. No women could be traced to whom the initial "V" could be reasonably attached. Statements were taken from various' people. By the exercise of extreme care, Dorothy saw that no photograph of herself appeared in any newspaper—local or otherwise. She was visited on several occasions by Police officials and answered all the questions put to her readily and satisfactorily. The Police were forced to the conclusion that any triangle entanglement was Hubert's and not Hubert's wife's. As the body showed no injuries or signs of violence, the jury, properly instructed by the Coroner, who exhibited considerably more intelligence than most, returned an open verdict. The insurance company with which Hubert had held a life policy paid his widow a thousand pounds. Hubert had been well insured and had left all his affairs in order. The Corporation of Tudor returned to Dorothy his superannuation contributions plus compound interest calculated at three per cent per annum.

Although she was in this manner made immune from immediate want, Dorothy decided to find employment. She knew that a considerable time must elapse before she and Laurence would see each other again. After a short interval, she obtained a post as cashier and book-keeper to a high-class printing and stationery shop in Tudor. The Fanshawes and the Thornhills fussed over and mothered her and were generally full of sympathy and kind in the extreme. After a few weeks, the sensation which Hubert's death had created both in Tudor and Bullen began to subside and gradually died down. Dorothy continued to live at "Red Roofs" with Frances, quietly and unostentatiously. She kept two lines of conversational conduct religiously in front of her and never swerved from their strict observance. Firstly, she did not discuss Hubert's death with anybody unless she were *asked* to do so, and secondly, she never refused to do so if she were invited. In other words, she neither laboured the matter nor fought shy of it. She was frank about its circumstances, but she always scrupulously avoided any semblance of volubility. Dorothy "boxed clever".

After three months' employment at her printers' and stationers', she went to a local house and estate agent and put "Red Roofs" in his hands with a view to sale. Two months after this action on her part, the agent reported that he had been successful. He had sold the house for her at a good price. The result was that Dorothy found herself in possession of nearly three thousand pounds. She decided to take a holiday at the seaside with Frances. When she suggested this as a possibility to the manager under whom she worked, he viewed the idea with strong disfavour. Dorothy outlined her position and pointed out calmly what she had been through in the early months of the year. Her arguments made but little impression. So Dorothy, courageous and independent, gave a week's notice, left the establishment with her chin in the air and promptly betook herself and Frances to Fowey, in Cornwall.

There they spent a wonderful month. She occasionally dreamt of Hubert—and it must be confessed that they were frightening, unpleasant dreams. But more often she dreamt of Laurence. When she did this, she was able to push Hubert to the back of her mind, but she was unable entirely to forget him. Before she came away from Fowey, she told Frances that they were going to move away from Bullen directly they got back. She explained her reasons. Although Frances was young, Dorothy wanted Frances to understand. "'Red Roofs' is sold," said Dorothy; "it held only sadness and memories for both of us, Frances darling, so I think it will do us both good to get away from the atmosphere at Bullen. The change will do us good. It must do. And after a time, I'm sure you will agree with me—even if you don't now, darling."

Frances nodded. They were sitting on a rock in the most glorious sunshine, looking at the blue sea.

"But where shall I go to school?" Frances puckered her face.

"I'll find a lovely school for you in the place we choose. I wouldn't go to live in a place where there wasn't a nice school for you. I'll promise you that, darling, now."

Frances listened to her mother and seemed eminently content with the prospect that had been opened up to her. "Have you any idea, Mother, where you would like to go? Surrey has been such a nice county to live in and I shall hate leaving it."

"I had thought of the other side of London. Say in Essex somewhere. I don't mean the East End—nothing slummy, my child. Just as though I would! There are some nice places, I've been told, between Blarum and Colneford. When we get back from this holiday we'll scout round and choose a nice place. You shall come with me and help me find it." She smiled encouragingly.

Dorothy kept her promise and early in the September, after saying farewell to the Fanshawes, the Thornhills and Hubert's parents, she and Frances chose a dear little bungalow at Simonstone—about twenty miles from London. Frances was able to attend the Secondary School for Girls at Brant—a matter of but two miles distant.

In the October, Dorothy showed Frances an advertisement in the local press which emanated from the honorary secretary to the Simonstone Amateur Dramatic Club. "I'm going to join," she said. "I'd love to act and it will give me something to do in the winter. I shan't start business again until after Christmas. The rest won't do me any harm. Later on, when you're a year or so older, you can join too, darling."

Frances was thrilled to the core at the delicious prospect. Dorothy applied for membership, attended an audition and was accepted. She was invited a week or so later to a reading of the club's next-intended production. The play which had been chosen was *The Barretts of Wimpole Street* and after the reading had finished Dorothy was introduced by the honorary secretary to a "Mr. Laurence Weston— one of our oldest members."

"Not in age, Miss Grant," laughingly returned Laurence Weston. "Miss Springthorpe is referring to my service when she makes that statement. I must defend myself."

Dorothy trembled as she took his hand. The moment for which she had waited so long was hers at last. But she quickly mastered herself and brought to her aid a measure of self-control.

"Not *Miss* Grant," she replied, "it should be *Mrs.* Grant. I must defend myself too."

"My sincere apologies," said Laurence Weston. "But may I sit down here and talk to you? You and I look as though we have something in common." She found herself trembling again.

His eyes devoured her. "At last," he whispered so that none could hear.

"At last," she whispered back. "At long last."

He took her to two chairs in a corner of the room. Home were the hunters—home from the kill!

Book Two
LAURENCE

CHAPTER I

ON CHRISTMAS Day Dorothy invited Evelyn Springthorpe, with whom she had quickly grown quite friendly, Evelyn's fiancé, Hedley Tucker, a school friend of Frances', Diana Bishop, and Laurence Weston.

"I want to be quiet," she said to Frances, before issuing the invitations, "but not too quiet. Six people should make things just about right for us. And you'll like the three people from the Dramatic Club, I'm certain."

Frances said she was sure she would. For some time, Dorothy dallied with the idea of inviting Gervaise Chard and Maureen, but finally decided against it. She felt that she definitely did not want any of the old Bullen atmosphere with her here at Simonstone yet awhile. Neither the Fanshawes nor the Thornhills could have come— it would have been an inconvenient journey for them—but Chard and Maureen, being more or less on their own as it were, might possibly have accepted her invitation if it had been forthcoming.

Everything went off splendidly. It was all very quiet and informal. Just as Dorothy said, a nice dinner with some bright talks and a little music afterwards. Frances and Diana enjoyed the gramophone records and the others just made themselves snug round the fire. Laurence looked particularly handsome and debonair, Dorothy thought, in a new, extremely well-cut dark lounge suit. She watched almost avidly his reactions to Frances and hers to him. For this was the first occasion of their meeting. What she saw pleased her on the whole. The guests went early and Dorothy went into Frances's bedroom to say "good night". She kissed her and then sat on the bed and began to talk.

"Had a nice day, darling?"

"Not bad, Mumsie. But not wizard—not like we used to have at Bullen. I missed all the old games."

Dorothy winced. "We couldn't have had those, darling. Not yet awhile. Things have changed. Still, it wasn't too bad considering everything, was it?"

"No-o," conceded Frances almost grudgingly. "I suppose it wasn't."

"Never mind—it'll all get better in time, sweetheart. How did you like the Dramatic Club set?"

"Pretty grim, I thought," replied Frances severely. "As far as I could see. Miss Springthorpe and her boy friend mooned in a corner by themselves best part of the time—holding hands. Feeble sort of business, I thought. Made me rather fed up. Diana thought the same as I did, too. Still—love's young dream, I suppose, makes people soppy." Frances wrinkled her pretty nose in sophisticated contempt.

"You must make allowances for them," explained Dorothy. "There may come a day, you know, when you'll be smitten with the same fever. Then, my dear, you'll think differently."

Frances tossed her head. "Somehow I don't think so—thank you very much."

Then Dorothy tried the thrust for which she had been preparing for some time. "I'm still young, you know, darling, and I look even younger than I am. And it's looks that matter with us women. I might marry again—if someone nice asked me. What would you say to that?"

"I should hate it," replied Frances uncompromisingly.

"All the same, not one of us should deliberately stand in the way of another's happiness. It would be wrong and selfish. I never should with regard to yours, my angel."

"Very likely—but it's not quite the same thing."

"Why not—what's different about it?"

Frances sat up in bed and assumed an air of judicial gravity. "It's difficult to explain. But you've already been married and I haven't."

"What does that matter?" Dorothy felt a twinge of anxiety.

"I don't know, Not well enough to explain to you. But I know what I mean myself—inside me."

Dorothy decided to go no further with the matter for the time being. So she kissed Frances and wished her good night. As she went to her own room and thought things over, she felt glad that she had not asked Frances a positive question about Laurence. Far better to prepare the ground gradually than by one fierce and sharp excavation. She was able to meet Laurence twice a week at Dramatic Club rehearsals. In this way, her meetings with him needed no special explanation to Frances. Laurence's plans, already made and perfected in every direction, were approaching maturity. In February, a little more than a year after the removal of Hubert Grant, he sounded Dorothy again as to the position with Frances. Since he had met Dorothy in the October, their relations had been eminently discreet. Dorothy realized that his self-control had been amazing. Laurence Weston was truly a man in a thousand and she counted herself thrice-blessed in his possession.

One evening, towards the end of February, Laurence walked home with Dorothy after a rehearsal. In the darkness of a side road he took her in his arms and kissed her passionately. She returned his kisses ardently.

"Sweetheart," he said, "I'm going to marry you at Easter. I have a week's leave due to me and I'm going to take it. We'll do it all quietly. It must be at Easter—I can't wait for you a day longer. As it is, I think I'm pretty marvellous." He grinned at her semi-ruefully. "Will the date suit you?"

"Yes. I'm ready, Laurence dear—I'm as starved for you as you are for me. Easter, then, it shall be. There are one or two problems, though. Shall we carry on for a time at the bungalow, or have you other plans?"

For a moment he hesitated before replying. "For the time being, I propose that we carry on at your place. It will save time and the worry of preparation for one thing. When we've been married a month or so, we'll have a look round. What's your other problem?"

"Frances."

Laurence frowned. "How do you mean, exactly?"

"Where shall we leave her—when we're on our honeymoon? I don't particularly want her to go to anybody at Bullen."

"No. I agree with you there. Isn't there anybody else?"

Dorothy thought. They had very nearly reached her bungalow. "I don't think I know of anybody suitable. I can't have the child unhappy."

"No. Of course not."

"I've thought of somebody," said Dorothy.

"Who?"

"Mrs. Bishop. Diana's mother. I don't imagine Frances would mind going there for a week. She and Diana are tremendous pals. Shall I see what I can do about it?"

"Yes. Do. Let me know on Tuesday evening. Now where shall we go for our perfect week?"

"Tristram," shyly suggested Dorothy.

"*Not* Tristram." His tone was decided. Dorothy realized that.

"I suppose not. And it will be Easter. There may be cold winds. We want somewhere warm. What about a little place in Devonshire somewhere?"

"Good idea. And I know the very place. Vinacombe. It's delightful. To my mind the pick of all Devon."

"Shall I like it?"

"You'll love it. I was there last summer. And thinking of you all the time. When you get there, carissima, you'll find fragrant pieces of 'you' peeping out at us from all sorts of unsuspected places. All because my thoughts were so concentrated. We'll be married at the Registry office on the Thursday before the Good Friday. It will give us a longer holiday."

"That will be Maundy Thursday. It's in Holy Week."

Laurence shook his head. "That doesn't matter. To us. We'll just walk in and when the job's done, walk out. That's all there is to it."

"I don't mind," returned Dorothy, "it just came into my mind, that was all—and here we are at the bungalow."

Laurence looked round before kissing her good night. "Good night, sweetheart."

Her lips were pressed hard against his and she clung to him passionately. When she went in, one thought was prominent in her mind. That she would be Laurence Weston's wife in less than six weeks' time.

CHAPTER II

FRANCES took the news of her mother's intended marriage rather hardly. For some days after the breaking of the news by Dorothy, Dorothy would find her in odd and unaccustomed parts of the bungalow crying bitterly. More than once, Dorothy tried to take the child into her arms to comfort her. But the old relationship was not there and Frances refused to be comforted.

"You mustn't be jealous, darling," said Dorothy, "and in the end it will be ever so much better for you to have somebody like a father living with you."

"I don't want a father—not another father," contested Frances, "I only want you. Just you and I together. Like we've always been. Why should we have a stranger to live with us? I wish you'd never joined that rotten old Dramatic Club, that's what I wish. Then you'd never have met other people and this awful thing wouldn't have happened."

"But Mr. Weston isn't a strange man. You know he isn't. He came here at Christmas. You know him and he knows you. He likes you, too."

"Well, so he may—but I don't like him. And I'm not *going* to like him, either. I *won't* like him. He's too cocky for one thing."

As Frances spoke, Dorothy felt a stab of resentment. But she deemed it wise to ignore the indictment and for some time after this left Frances alone. "Give her time," she thought, "and she'll soon forget her objections. Directly Laurence comes here to live permanently, and she gets to know him properly, Frances and he will get on like wildfire."

In the meantime, Dorothy went on quietly with the necessary preparations for her wedding, seeing Laurence twice a week at rehearsals and then once extra on the night of the show. A fortnight before Holy Week, she broached the subject to Frances about her going away. Frances, to her consternation, broke into a spasm of emotional weeping.

"Don't leave me. Don't leave me. I don't want you to go away. I can't bear it."

"I must," said her mother firmly; "you can't come with me, that's very certain."

"Why can't I? Please let me."

"You're going to stop with Mrs. Bishop while I'm away. You're going to sleep with Diana. You'll like that, won't you?"

Frances still sobbed. "And who will you sleep with? You'll sleep with a strange man—like you used to with Daddy."

To her own annoyance Dorothy reddened: "Now you must be a good girl and stop crying. I never heard of such goings on. Promise me now."

But Frances sobbed on and Dorothy, after a time, reluctantly abandoned what she considered was a most unequal struggle. When the morning of Maundy Thursday came, Dorothy kissed a sullen Frances and handed her over to the plump, eager to please, Mrs. Bishop. Frances suffered herself to be led away with head unbowed.

"I'll write to you directly I get to the seaside, darling," promised Dorothy, and a frozen-faced Frances heard the promise but made no response to it.

Dorothy met Laurence outside the Registrar's office in the early hours of the morning of that Maundy Thursday and within a surprisingly short space of time she found herself signing the register as "Dorothy Meredith Weston". A car was waiting for them when they got outside and they were quickly driven to Paddington. And Laurence's embraces, when it was seemly for her to receive them, were as deliriously delightful to Dorothy as ever. She did not think of Hubert once on the journey to Vinacombe.

CHAPTER III

LAURENCE and Dorothy were married at the Registrar's office in Brant on Thursday, the 5th of April. About fourteen months after the death of Hubert Grant. They arrived at the entirely charming little town of Vinacombe, in Devonshire, about five o'clock in the late afternoon of an almost perfect Spring day. Laurence had booked rooms at a small hotel, near the quaint harbour, known as the "Punch Bowl". Dinner was served to them at a private table in the dining-room, punctually at seven o'clock. There appeared to be but few other guests. Dorothy admitted, when challenged playfully by Laurence, that the dinner of his choice was excellent. Soup, sole, chicken and a sweet. They drank a delightfully dry sherry with the soup and after that a bottle of G.H. Mumm. Laurence toasted her over his glass of champagne. Her eyes sparkled as she listened.

"To you, my darling, and to our eternal happiness. Winter and Summer. Present and Absent. All through Life—and Beyond."

"To the happiness we snatched."

Laurence frowned, but otherwise completely disregarded Dorothy's remark. "You don't look shy enough for a bride," he said smilingly. "You don't really!"

She shook her head. "I hope that doesn't mean you're disappointed."

"I'm going to pretend," continued Laurence, "to myself, at least, that you are a virgin."

To his intense pleasure, she coloured. "Is it so frightfully important?"

He pursed his lips. "No. I suppose not. Not really."

"If giving myself to you means surrender of body *and* spirit, then I think, perhaps, I am. Does *that* sound terribly strange or absurd?"

"No. In that connection, I can always remember the words of Huguette the Wanton to Francois Villon. 'I have given many men my body, Francois, but to you alone did I ever give my soul.'"

"I love you more now that you have said that."

He leant across the table and caught her hands. They smoked cigarettes over the coffee and a Marc brandy.

"Shall we stroll along the cliffs before we turn in," asked Laurence, "or are you feeling too tired?"

"Let me see the time. It's only about a quarter past eight. No—I'm not so very tired. We'll go out for half an hour. The air will do us good."

"I'm with you," returned Laurence, "and it's quite warm, considering that we're only in early Spring. Still, put a coat on."

They walked along the red cliffs of Vinacombe for a mile out and a mile back. Few people passed them. Laurence put his arm round his wife's slim waist and Dorothy knew that she was content to be his possession until she died. His will was hers. Where he went, she would go also. He was her heart and her treasure. This would be her life. Frances was only partly hers, whereas Laurence was entirely hers. Every now and then Laurence stooped to kiss her. She was a girl again. She looked a girl. She felt a girl. She felt a bride in every sense, but when she had married Hubert . . . she skated quickly over the name in her mind as the thought registered itself, she had been incomplete, precocious and immature.

She went to their bedroom soon after they returned to the hotel and waited for Laurence to come to her with a fierce eagerness that she had never known before. Out of the anodyne which her passion had administered to her mind, she regretted nothing. The account was there somewhere. Tucked away at the back! But it had not been rendered. If it were ever rendered, she would pay it. There could be no evasion. But before that time came, there was Laurence. Laurence who had not shrunk from deadly sin for love of her. When, later, he gathered her into his arms, his passion frightened even her. For a time, he fought it courageously and held an even balance with it, but eventually there came his inevitable submerging. As she thrilled to him in rapid response, she saw his face and loved every line of it as he went under hopelessly and helplessly as sinks a drowning man, and then she began to understand for the first time that there are some forces, which, if they are once let loose, cannot be successfully opposed, and must be allowed to consume themselves in a wild and sweet despair.

When tiredness came and tranquillity, to take the place of fire and fever, Dorothy found herself in a state of profound humility. She felt that she wanted to pray. For herself, for Laurence, for Frances, and—strangely—for the soul of Hubert. She found this disquieting and tested herself so that she might assure herself of its truth. The testing effected no change in her. Her inclination was undisturbed. She leant over, kissed the sleeping Laurence, and then herself fell asleep.

As HER honeymoon proceeded, Dorothy knew yet more ecstasy. Laurence was ardent, devoted, splendidly virile, yet tenderness was never absent from him. Day succeeded day and night followed night and all the time Dorothy and Laurence revelled both mentally and physically in their new-found exhilaration. The conditions which they now knew, they had never known previously. They were now free to love. And not only to love. They were free to walk and talk with each other, without the fear of discovery. The furtiveness and the stealthiness were no more. Their chains and fetters had been knocked away. They walked for miles along the headlands. They drove in coaches to places of interest that were not too far away. They went to the cinema, to concerts on the little pier and generally filled the days with outpourings of delight. Until the afternoon of the Thursday of Easter week, or exactly a week after their marriage.

On this particular afternoon they had driven into the more popular resort of Mynton. As usual on these excursions, they at once made their way to the promenade and to the water's edge. It was on the promenade here at Mynton that Dorothy's mood of sheer, unadulterated happiness was broken. She saw a man and a woman approaching her and Laurence, and her first impressions as she watched them come nearer were that the man's figure and general appearance seemed vaguely familiar to her. A split second later she knew that the man was Linklater . . . the Borough Treasurer of Tudor. She tried to control herself as he passed, or more properly her appearance, but she knew at once that she had been far from succeeding. Linklater raised his hat punctiliously. There was no real greeting on his face. Mrs. Linklater looked hard and frigid. To her own extreme annoyance Dorothy knew that she herself was blushing furiously. The thought shocked and sobered her. The Linklaters were already past when Laurence spoke his thoughts to her.

"Two questions, my angel. One—who was it? And two, what's the matter?"

Dorothy clung tightly to his arm. "I was taken unawares. Off my guard. I can't understand myself—behaving like a silly school-girl. I blushed."

"Like hell you did. And why—pray? Haven't you ever been out with a man before?"

"We're unlucky—that's all. Oh—how I wish we hadn't come here today! The news of our wedding will soon be all over Tudor and Bullen."

Laurence frowned. This was certainly not to his liking. "Why—who were they? The town crier and his assistant?"

"Almost! Or as good as. They were Mr. and Mrs. Linklater."

"Linklater?" Laurence furrowed his brow. "Linklater? Why, isn't that the chap you thought spotted you in Cleves one afternoon?"

"That's right. And look at my hands even now—they're trembling."

"Good Lord—why? What's it got to do with him that you and I are spending a few Easter days in Devon? Let the self-satisfied beggar mind his own business. Who *is* he—anyway?"

Without thinking, and the explanation is that the entirely unexpected encounter had shaken her, Dorothy replied. "He was Hubert's chief at Tudor."

The lines showed suddenly on Laurence Weston's face. "Hubert? Who's Hubert? Never heard of him."

Dorothy realized with something like a stab at her heart that she had broken one of the pacts she had made with Laurence within the first week of her life with him. "I'm sorry, Laurence," she said, humbling, "I'm frightfully sorry. I said that because I was upset. Forgive me, please."

"Skip it," returned Laurence Weston, "and pull yourself together, or you'll never find yourself cast as a good conspirator. Linklater's nothing to you and less than nothing to me. Understand, my sweet?"

"Yes . . . I know. But I'm afraid that he'll—"

"Talk? Let him. Who cares? 'They say—what do they say—let them say!'"

"I've just thought of something else, Laurence. Something that's dreadfully worrying. Supposing that afternoon in Cleves, when he saw me—"

She paused.

Laurence turned to her, impatient and expectant. "Well? Go on. Suppose what?"

Her lips trembled as she framed the words. "Supposing he had seen you as well, say a minute or two beforehand. *With* me—or even without me? If that were the case, he *might* be able to piece things up, put two and two together . . . and—" Again she paused.

"And what?" His tone was curt and his eyes dominated her.

"Well . . . connect you with me. And Linklater's a nasty piece of work. I've always understood from those who knew him in Tudor, that he'd stoop to any dirty trick if he thought he would. Or to gain his own ends. No scruples at all over anything."

"He's welcome to try," said Laurence, "and if he does I'll deal with him. So once and for all—forget him! I refuse to let a man like Linklater spoil my honeymoon."

He pulled her into the lee of the harbour wall. "Is this where I kiss you?" he asked.

"No," she said with tears in her eyes.

"That's where you're wrong," said Laurence.

CHAPTER V

BUT Dorothy's misgivings with regard to Linklater were far from over. She and Laurence were due to return from Mynton to Vinacombe by a return coach which they picked up by the pier at half past four. As she and Laurence entered the coach, she saw to her dismay that Mr. and Mrs. Linklater were standing on the kerb at the other side of the road. Dorothy made no remark or sign to Laurence as they entered the coach and took their seats. Or, did she give any sign to the Linklaters that she had noticed them. Five minutes' drive away from Mynton she spoke casually to her husband.

"The Linklaters saw us as we got into this coach. Was it a coincidence—or were they trying to find anything out? What do you think, Laurence?"

Laurence's lips curled. "Snooping us—eh? Damned cheek! But do as I'm going to do. Forget 'em. A thousand to one that's the last we shall ever see of them. Over which fact, I shall lose no sleepless nights—believe me." He lit a cigarette.

Dorothy shook her head at his confidence—a confidence which she felt by no means sharing. "I'm not so sure. That last piece looked too deliberate for me. Looked to me as though they had been waiting for us. They may attempt to follow it up in Vinacombe."

"They'll have to move then. From now onwards. Seeing that we return to Simonstone on Saturday. Oh—blast them! Forget it."

But Dorothy was unable to. Try as she might. Even that night when Laurence's passion for her was at its height, the Linklaters were with her in her thoughts. She was unable to banish them. If she "shoo'd" them away, they were not away long. They came back. When she awoke on the Friday morning, her waking thoughts were of the Linklaters.

She turned in bed and looked at the figure of Laurence recumbent at her side. The light through the window was making a faint shadow across his neck. She shuddered. Laurence half-turned in his sleep and threw an arm across his pillow. His dark hair was tumbled on his forehead. His cheeks were a little flushed. She contrasted him with Hubert, and his physical beauty took Dorothy by storm. She bent over him and kissed him. For a second or so she had forgotten the Linklaters. Laurence awoke at her kiss and pulled her head down by his.

"This is the last time," he said playfully, "that you and I will sleep in this bed. But there are other beds. So don't let the thought distress you. Kiss me!"

Dorothy obeyed. When she sat down to breakfast at the "Punch Bowl" she felt more cheerful. A morning in Vinacombe with Laurence, their last morning before they returned home and with a glorious Spring sun shining, added to that cheerfulness. Before very long there would be, thank God, many miles between her and the Linklaters.

After lunch, she and Laurence decided to do some shopping. Amongst other things, she wanted a present for Frances. "Buy her a book," said Laurence; "you can never go wrong with a book when you're dealing with a kid like Frances."

Dorothy was secretly amused. "How do you know that, my lord?"

"Because I've seen her. Don't I know that she's intelligent? Why—when I was a small boy, I simply loathed any present that wasn't a book."

"What's that got to do with it?" asked Dorothy with a touch of mischief. "To hear you talk, anybody would think you were the child's father."

"I should have been," said Laurence with superb egotism, "but for your flagrant infidelity. You should have waited for me. Been faithful to me before you knew me." He grinned. "Any decent girl would have."

"You said decent. It's a euphemism surely! A few weeks with you and it seems to me I shall be the epitome of indecency."

"Which will only make me love you even more." He squeezed her arm. She returned the affection and wished that it was dark so that he might kiss her.

Laurence went into the shop with her to assist in the choice of Frances's book.

"Don't forget," advised Dorothy, "she's old for her age. And, I fear, more sophisticated than she should be. It's probably my fault. I expect I've more or less encouraged it."

"Probably. Like you have with me."

"I like your style. Well—any suggestions before we arrive at the book counter?"

"Yes. Definitely. Give her a copy of the finest romance in the English language. In my humble opinion."

"Since when has any opinion of yours been humble?"

He smiled good humouredly at the sally.

"What's the book?" asked Dorothy.

"Esmond," replied Laurence—"give her that and she'll love every word of it. If she doesn't, I'll eat my hat."

"There's one thing I like about you, Laurence, you do know your own mind."

He grinned again. "Only one thing?"

"Yes. Only one thing. If I admit any more I shall make you more conceited than you are. Then you *will* be a horrid little fellow."

The girl behind the bookseller's counter was able to produce a copy of *Esmond* with little difficulty. "Get her a better edition than that," prompted Laurence, "and I'll go 'fifty-fifty' with you. When I'm with you only the best is good enough for me."

Dorothy flashed him a smile of gratitude. She looked a picture. Her honeymoon had painted her with radiant colours. "Have you a better copy than this?" she inquired.

The girl appeared doubtful. "I'll see," she said with a certain amount of hesitation. She vanished and was absent for some little time. Eventually she came back with a much superior edition of Thackeray's masterpiece. "I'm afraid this edition is rather expensive," she announced with diffidence.

Laurence pounced on the book immediately. "This'll do. It's wizard. How much is it?"

The girl told him. He accepted the price at once. "That's all right. We can afford it, Dorothy. Good Lord, we shan't have a honeymoon every week. Worse luck!" He turned to the shop-assistant. "Wrap it up nicely, will you, please?"

The book was done up in the neatest of parcels. Dorothy knew delight in Laurence's action. Always he pleased her. She caught him impulsively by the arm as they left the shop.

"That was very sweet of you, Laurence. I know that Frances will be thrilled."

He laughed away her thanks. "Gertcher! You'll make me blush. I wilt under the heavy fire of gratitude."

They crossed the road on the way back to the "Punch Bowl". When they reached the corner where the hotel stood, Dorothy's blood turned to ice. For there, standing outside, were two figures which she had hoped she would never see again. Mr. and Mrs. Linklater were standing there looking up at the hotel. They had not seen her and Laurence. Without saying a word, Dorothy swung her husband in the opposite direction. Surprised at her sudden action, he let himself be swept on.

"The Linklaters again," she said in a low tone, "looking up at our hotel. I spotted them just in time. What are they nosing round for?"

"Stark bloody curiosity, my girl—and nothing more. For two pins I'd—" Laurence Weston paused abruptly.

"What? What would you do? You can't prevent them standing in the street."

"Go up and ask them what the merry hell they wanted," replied Laurence with rising anger.

"I'm frightened," said Dorothy simply.

"What of? Them? Don't be absurd."

"I'm frightened he knows something."

"Well—he doesn't. He can't. Take that from me. I know what I'm talking about."

He stopped suddenly and pulled Dorothy back to his side. "Look here—it's no use us going on like this. We're inclined to panic. We *mustn't*—understand? It's daft—and it's dangerous! Our way is as clear as crystal. Can't you see it?"

"What is it, then? What is our way?"

"Take no notice of them. Or of anybody else either. Face everything with courage and sangfroid. Why not? That's always the best policy. Face the music. See things through. And to hell with the blasted Linklaters. What is he? Borough Treasurer of Tudor? Let him go back there and wallow in his blinking old Sinking Funds. May they choke him! And I'll thank him to leave you and me and our business alone. Come, my girl. Right about turn. If they're still there, garping at the 'Punch Bowl', see me look at them as though they're two lumps of bad liver."

Laurence turned her head in the direction of the "Punch Bowl". In a small degree, his avowed determination to face whatever came had given Dorothy courage and some comfort. When they reached the hotel again, the Linklaters had gone. Dorothy wasn't sure whether she was pleased or sorry. In a way, she would have liked Laurence to have seen them and annihilated them with his battery of scornful looks. On the whole, though, perhaps it was as well that they had gone. The less they saw of her and Laurence, the better.

Dorothy enjoyed her dinner and when she went into the lounge to listen to the radio she felt much more serene and tranquil than she had done for some hours. When she went to bed she felt much the same. Tomorrow she would be back at Simonstone. To live with Laurence and Frances. The second half of her life had begun. The past was over . . . buried for ever in the grave of Time.

CHAPTER VI

FRANCES was overjoyed when Dorothy returned. She delighted in the nearness of her mother, she was thrilled by her present, and she accepted Laurence with a friendliness and a humour that boded well for the immediate future. Life at the bungalow proceeded more or less uneventfully. After more dramatic performances, Spring passed and Summer weather came. The garden became more delightful day by day, because the year was a good year. Sunshine and silver rain came alternately. There were no terrific downpours. There was no drought. Dorothy wrote and told her intimate friends at Bullen that she had married again and received in return their various congratulations. In none of these letters was there any mention of the Linklaters or of any reaction that might have come from them. Towards the end of May, Dorothy told Laurence that she was pregnant. He was intensely pleased when he heard the news and a smile rippled over his face.

"My dear," he said, "that's the best news I've had for a long time. It will do us all good. You yourself, and me and Frances. Frances will be bucked no end to have a little sister."

"I should prefer a boy," remarked Dorothy thoughtfully, "then there'll be a pigeon pair."

"I think I should, too," said Laurence, knitting his brows, "but we can't arrange to have what we want in this world. We have to put up with what we get. You should know that by this time, Mrs. Weston." As he spoke, another smile transformed his face.

"I'm glad you're pleased," said Dorothy, "but I'm a little worried about Frances and how she'll take it."

"You worry too much about Frances," he replied, "and when our affair comes along I'm afraid that Miss Frances will have to leave centre stage a bit and take a back seat. It won't do her any harm, so don't look so disturbed about it."

"I didn't know that I was. But I wouldn't have Frances hurt for anything."

"Frances must take her share of the tribulations as well as of the good things in life. You mustn't expect her to be singled out for

special treatment. As I told you before, it's not good for the kid."
Laurence spoke with decision.

Dorothy nodded. She knew that in the main Laurence was right.
Early on the morning of Whit Monday, which was the twenty-eighth
of May and a day of glorious sunshine, Dorothy was mowing the
lawn in the front of the bungalow. Frances had gone to a school
camp for the whole of the week. Dorothy saw a car slow down and
stop in front of her. When the people got out, she was amazed to
see that they were Dick and Ella Fanshawe. Dick grinned at her
affably as he came in the gate.

"How now," he said, "surprised to see us? We've taken pot luck—
hoping to catch you in. Seems we've succeeded. Well, my dear, and
how are things with you and yours?"

He shook hands effusively, while Dorothy murmured how glad
she was to see them. Actually, she was not too sure on the point.
Ella followed her husband up and kissed her warmly.

"Darling, I'm so pleased to see you! We do hope you aren't going
out anywhere and that we haven't put you out."

"Not a bit, Ella. I'm ever so pleased to see you. You and Dick
come in and I'll introduce you to Laurence."

She took them through from the front garden. Laurence was at
the back of the bungalow. He came forward, wiping his hands on
a piece of rag he had been using. "Laurence," said Dorothy, "this
is Dick and Ella Fanshawe. You've heard me speak of them several times."

Laurence at once made the best of himself. "Oh . . . good! Jolly
sporting of you to come over. Afraid you've caught us bending, as
it were, but do make yourselves comfortable. What will you drink?"

Laurence dashed away for the drinks. He returned with a couple
of tankards for himself and Dick Fanshawe, and glasses of sherry for
the two women. The Fanshawes soon made themselves at home. In
due season Dorothy produced cold lamb and salad for lunch. After
lunch, Fanshawe suggested a run in the car.

"You'd better take the back ways," said Laurence, "the main road
to Sudmore will be merry hell on a Bank Holiday."

After an hour's cruise round the country lanes they returned
for an early tea, as the Fanshawes had to cross London in order to

get back to Bullen. During tea, Dorothy began to talk more freely. "Laurence and I met through an Amateur Dramatic Society. Quite romantic, wasn't it? I came over here, as you know, to help forget and then—after a time I began to find myself more or less at a loose end. You know how it is after you come to a new place?"

Ella Fanshawe nodded brightly. She was listening to Dorothy's recital with considerable interest. This was the particular information which she had really come to glean. "Yes. Of course. How interesting."

"Well, one day in one of the local papers I saw an advertisement of the local Amateur Dramatic Club. They wanted new members. It gave me an idea. I had always had the feeling I could act, so I applied for membership."

Ella purred more and more. "Yes, dear . . . and what happened after that?"

Dorothy knew that both Laurence and Dick Fanshawe were listening to her intently. The realization of this made her feel a trifle uncomfortable. But on the surface she kept entirely calm and collected.

"Well—I was invited to an audition. Perhaps it would be as well if Laurence carried on the story from that point."

Laurence assumed his best debonair manner. "You want me to carry on? Well, I don't mind. As a matter of fact, there isn't a great deal more to tell. Dorothy turned up for the audition, won golden opinions from everybody whose opinion counted and was offered club membership. The next invitation she had was to a reading. The committee allotted her a part in a show in which I was also playing . . . and the inevitable happened." He beamed gallantly towards his wife. "I began to meet her at rehearsals . . . two evenings a week . . . and she bowled me over. When I asked her to marry me, to my utter astonishment she said 'yes'. There you are, ladies and gentlemen, there you have the full story of our love-lit career. And finally, let me say this. You don't know what a lucky chap I am." He looked across at Dorothy and raised his cup. "To you—my dear."

The others took this cue and joined in boisterously. Ella was round-eyed in excited admiration. "How perfectly charming! Just like out of a book. I've wondered—in fact Dick and I have both wondered—how you and Mr. Weston did meet. Not idle curiosity, you understand, but a genuine interest in you and affection for you, my dear Dorothy. We were simply thrilled when we got your letter with its shattering news."

She leant forward over the cake-stand and patted Dorothy on her arm. Dorothy smiled back.

"Of course, my dear. I thoroughly understand."

Dorothy saw her chance. She determined to take it. The trend of the conversation had presented her with the opportunity. "But tell me, Ella dear, how is everybody at Bullen?"

"All right, I think. Everybody you knew. The Thornhills are flourishing."

"Yes. I had a card from them at Christmas. I thought things were well with them. Now tell me about some other people." Dorothy went on to mention several families by name. Ella Fanshawe was able to supply the requisite information. "How are they with Dick? At the . . . er . . . Town Hall?"

Dorothy contributed to her query an artistic hesitation. Ella recognized it and inwardly paid homage to it.

"Oh—very well—most of them. Dick's had a promotion." She turned to her husband. "Not out of its turn, was it, darling? Not a lot. From the money angle. Another £100 a year—that's all. Of which most will go in income tax. Still—it helps. And it will help towards his superannuation allowance. When it comes! I often long for the day when Dick will retire—but then I say to myself—Ella, you mustn't wish your time away. It's wrong, and you may be punished for it." She laughed on a high note.

Dorothy steeled herself for the question which for some time now had been her goal. "Do you ever see anything of the Linklaters?"

"Yes. But not a lot. Just occasionally. At the Mayor's reception, of course. Oh—and at the officers' dinner. It was at the 'Troc' last year. I remember that—because Mrs. L. looked awful. She wore an orange something and with her sallow complexion and muddy eyes it made her look more hideous than ever." Ella Fanshawe smiled sweetly.

"I asked you," said Dorothy, rather too demurely, "because what do you think happened? Talk about coincidences. You can't beat this one. Laurence and I actually bumped into them when we were on our honeymoon."

"You don't say! Well, that *was* a coincidence! If you'd tried to do it, you might have picked a hundred places and not brought it off. Well, I never! Did you hear that, Dick?"

"Yes. Darned funny." Fanshawe puffed at his briar.

"I wonder Linklater himself didn't tell all of you at the Town Hall. I made quite sure that he would. Told Laurence so. He was always a sensation-monger of the first water if he had a reasonable chance."

"Still," replied Fanshawe, "this was hardly an occasion for that sort of thing, was it? They may not even have seen you."

Dorothy laughed scornfully. "They saw us all right, don't you worry, Dick. They took good care to—didn't they, Laurence?"

Laurence grinned at the reminiscence. "I'll say they did. They actually went to some lengths to track us down at our hotel. Wherever we went—we fell over Linklaters."

Ella came forward again, her eyes gleaming with excitement and curiosity. "They did that? How do you mean, Mr. Weston—exactly?"

Laurence took the trouble to explain matters. "We were at Vinacombe. Staying—I mean. They were, I should imagine, at Mynton. Mynton's eight miles from Vinacombe." He went on to tell the Fanshawes what had happened.

"They were certainly uncommonly interested," commented Fanshawe. "Can't understand what they were after. They seem to have exceeded the canons of good taste."

Dorothy spoke bitterly. "Those considerations don't weigh with the Linklaters. They're laws unto themselves. So you needn't feel surprised about anything."

"I'm sorry we haven't seen Frances," said Ella Fanshawe. "I should have loved to have seen her again. I said so to Dick, coming along. I expect she's grown a fine big girl by now and that I should hardly recognize her. Where did you say she was, Dorothy?"

"At a camp—it's a school affair—near a place called Rettenford, about twenty miles from here. She went last Saturday and returns next Wednesday. She was mad to go. I hadn't the heart to stop her. Laurence was the same." She smiled in the direction of Weston.

"You may not believe me, but he spoils her almost as much as I do. He'll deny it, of course, but it's true all the same."

"It's nice to hear you say that," returned Ella; "shows that you've struck an excellent working arrangement. That's how it should be. When I marry a second time, I'll endeavour to work to the same end." As she concluded her sentence, Ella leant over to Dorothy and dropped her voice almost to a whisper. "I suppose you never heard any more, did you?"

"What about, Ella?"

"Poor Hubert."

Dorothy realized that the red colour was mantling her cheeks. "No . . . of course not. How could I? Please don't talk about it . . . especially as Laurence is here with us. Since I told him all about it, he's never once mentioned it. He does his best to help me to forget. I think it's very sweet of him, and I appreciate him all the more for it. Some men—similarly placed—would have been more like detectives than husbands. And that would have been too awful for words. I simply could not have stood it. So you see, Ella dear, that's how it is. Don't you think I've been very lucky?"

Ella Fanshawe nodded her understanding. "I'm sorry, dear, frightfully sorry. I shouldn't have breathed a word. Forgive me."

Dorothy squeezed her hand impulsively. "That's all right, Ella. Don't worry about it one little bit. Forget it."

As she spoke, Dick Fanshawe rose from his chair and stretched his legs. "Well, my dear, we must be rushing off, I'm afraid. Don't want to be too late. The main roads'll be pretty lousy this evening, and if there's one thing I loathe it's motoring in a procession. Well, Dorothy, many thanks for your hospitality and you too, Weston. Pleased to have met you and I'm sure that that goes for my wife as well. You've made us feel glad that we came."

The two men shook hands warmly. "You must come again," said Laurence. "It's been charming having you. Done Dorothy good."

"And you must come and see us." Fanshawe was hearty and sincere in the invitation. The women kissed their farewells.

Laurence and Dorothy accompanied the Fanshawes to the front door of the bungalow. The Fanshawes got into their car and drove off. Ella leant out of the car and waved her hand from the window.

As Laurence and Dorothy stood there by the gate watching and waving back, Laurence noticed that their immediate neighbour had left his porch and was coming towards them. He was carrying something and was striving to catch their attention. He came up to them, red-faced and apologetic.

"Awfully sorry, Mrs. Weston, but the postman delivered this at my place this morning when we were out. We went out extra early, I'm afraid, and the maid unfortunately didn't notice it was addressed to you. Many apologies and all that."

Dorothy smiled graciously and took the package. "Thank you, Mr. Pemberton."

"We've only just come in—the wife and I," said the penitent—"otherwise I'd have run it round before."

It was a squarish parcel tied with thick string. It was addressed to "Mrs. Dorothy Weston, 'Brockhurst', Rossall Avenue, Simonstone, Essex". The address had been typewritten. The postmark was London.

"A present for you," said Laurence jovially, "a present for Whitsuntide. Some people have all the luck. It's arrived a little late—that's all. Blame the post."

Dorothy untied the string. Inside the parcel was a book. Dorothy took it out wonderingly and looked at it. *Famous Trials Series. The Trial of Frederick Bywaters and Edith Thompson.* Once again cold fear clutched at and held her heart. Laurence Weston was quick to observe the ashen pallor of her face.

"What's the matter?" he cried sharply. The deathly look on her face frightened him.

She nodded to him weakly and vaguely. The book slipped from her grasp and fell on the grass of the lawn. Dorothy herself swayed and then suddenly crumpled into a dead faint.

CHAPTER VII

LAURENCE was quickly at his wife's side. He carried her indoors, laid her on the settee, opened the windows of the room and brought cold water. It had occurred to him that her faintness was probably due to her physical condition and on that account he did not feel unduly alarmed at Dorothy's entirely unexpected collapse. Dorothy soon showed signs of coming to. The water revived her. She opened her eyes to find Laurence bending over her as she lay on the settee. She shook her head vaguely.

"Come, come," Laurence was saying, "this sort of thing won't do, you know. This isn't the way to build bonny babies. Chucking dummies on the grass, like this."

Dorothy realized that Laurence had not yet understood. "The book," she said, "the book. Where is it? Oh—get it, please."

Laurence stared at her in something like astonishment. "Why— what about it? I didn't trouble to—"

He dashed back to the front garden to retrieve the book from the grass where it had fallen. The title at once hit him hard. He brought the book into the house with a look of grave anxiety on his face. His thoughts were a medley of anxiety and astonishment.

"I didn't realize," he said to his wife simply.

Dorothy got up from the settee. "I feel better now. Let me look at it again, please, Laurence."

They sat, at the table and examined the book. For a time neither of them spoke. Occasionally they looked at each other.

"What are we going to do?" at length asked Dorothy.

Laurence was already beginning to recover himself. He held his wife's hands. "Do you remember the counsel I gave you at Vinacombe at Easter? On our honeymoon? When the Linklaters were standing outside our hotel and you were trying to take me in the opposite direction so that we might miss them? I said then that we mustn't panic. And I say the same thing now. We simply must *not* panic! That must always be our first line of action. After all—what have we to fear? Nothing at all. In a Court of Law. At the worst—mere suspicion. Ten to one, this is somebody doing a spot of pin-pricking. Somebody who has heard that you've married again, is probably damned jealous about it and is absolutely letting off a gun in the dark."

Dorothy shook her head. "I'm not sure that I agree with you, Laurence. Much as I should like to. That title frightens me. It's so awful."

Laurence took the book into his two hands and opened it. At the title page there had been inserted a slip of paper. On this was something like a message. This was typewritten like the address had been on the outside of the packet. The words of the message ran as follows:

My dear Mrs. Weston. Whitsun! Herewith the first of my Greetings. More will follow at strictly regular intervals. At the moment you have nothing to fear—from me. I shall let you know in good time when I intend to move. And, of course, you don't need me to tell you what the end will be. On the particular morning, you are allowed, I believe, to choose your breakfast. Till next time, therefore, believe me to be, "Harry the Hangman".

Laurence Weston read this and went white with anger.

"What is it, Laurence?" cried Dorothy. "Tell me quickly—please." Her fingers clutched at his arm.

Without a word Laurence passed over the slip of paper. Dorothy read it with frightened eyes. When she handed the slip back to Laurence, he saw that her fingers were trembling. "What does it all mean?" she asked him.

Laurence was remaining reasonably calm. His second shock had tried him more than his first, but again his natural resilience was helping him and recovery was not a great distance away. "I don't quite know," he answered thoughtfully. "It looks to me that there is somebody who's got it in for us. Not by taking any drastic action, but simply through a sort of war of nerves. It's somebody with a grudge. A grievance either real or imaginary, as I said before. I should say against you. Rather than directed against me. Although the postmark here is London, I should say it's someone in the Bullen vicinity. He doesn't really *know* anything—but just chancing his aim. Trying to put us on the spot, as it were. Well—as far as I'm concerned—he's not going to. I flatter myself I can hold my own against that sort of stabbing in the back. And my wife must make up her beautiful mind to do the same."

Dorothy's face was still blanched with fear. "If you're right in your surmise—we haven't very far to look. In Bullen—I mean. I should say that the Linklaters filled the bill remarkably well. Don't you agree?"

Laurence nodded.

"It's probable, I think. But not necessarily a foregone conclusion. You know the wretched people, I don't. But from what you've told me of them, and from what I saw of them in the West country, I don't know that the style of this message patterns up any too well. In other words, they didn't look too subtle to me, whereas I think the phrasing of this message here suggests a more than average amount of subtlety. I may be wrong, of course, but that's how matters look to me at the moment."

Dorothy repeated aloud certain parts of the letter which she had remembered. "'More will follow at strictly regular intervals.' That's what I can't understand. What do you think that means, Laurence?"

"Don't know, What *can* one think? It's no more than a leap in the dark. Give me that book."

"What are you going to do with it—tell me, please."

"Destroy it," returned Laurence curtly. "Even though it may be the trial of two guilty lovers, they paid the penalty of their wrong-doing. Let them rest, therefore. Why should their memories be continually raked over to provide amusement and entertainment for the masses? That sort of muck-raking absolutely disgusts me."

Dorothy gave him the book. "I don't want to see it any more. Take it away and burn it, Laurence."

Dorothy went to bed early that evening. She was both tired and worried. At midnight she awoke in a fright. She had the fancy that Hubert was standing at the end of the bed. As she stared, horrified, she saw water dripping from his hair.

CHAPTER VIII

INASMUCH as Laurence had been given an early leave in April, he was compelled to take the balance of his summer holiday in September. Mainly to please Frances, Dorothy had suggested that they should all go to Fowey for a fortnight. Laurence had instantly fallen in with Dorothy's suggestion. For one thing, Dorothy was not at her health's best. Her doctor was far from being pleased with her. He had had a private word with Laurence on the subject and had told him with an unusually plain directness that Dorothy was going to need a considerable amount of care and attention during her trying period. Laurence, therefore, had been kindness itself to her. He relieved her of most tasks in the house when he happened to be at home and generally waited upon her hand and foot. But Dorothy's real trouble was one of which he was unaware. Since the night of Whit Monday, she had seen Hubert twice more. And more plainly on each succeeding occasion. He was always in the same place. At the foot of her bed. Staring straight at her. Water always dripped from his hair and it seemed to her, too, that there was a pool of water on the floor round his feet. His staring eyes held an agonized appeal. He never spoke to her, but she was haunted by the fear that one day he would. That particular day she dreaded with an ever-increasing horror.

No further communication had been received from "Harry the Hangman", but any parcel that came addressed either to her or to Laurence gave her a thousand choking apprehensions, before she was able to open it. Laurence, on the other hand, remained calm and unruffled. His superb self-confidence had always stood him in good stead and never had it proved of greater worth than during these days. He watched Dorothy ceaselessly as the doctor had advised him and clung to the hope that after her time had come she would return without difficulty to her usual health and spirits. Frances was due back at school on the 14th of September and the stay at Fowey had been arranged to end on the 11th of September. This meant that Frances would be at home in Simonstone from the 22nd of July, when the school went into vacation, until the 28th of August, the day when Laurence started his holidays.

The hot, dry, Summer days dragged by for Dorothy until the August Bank Holiday Monday. Soon after breakfast that morning, there came a loud knock on the front door of "Brockhurst". Laurence was nearest to the door at the moment so that he answered the knock. The postman handed him two letters and a brown paper packet. Directly he handled it, Laurence knew that it was a book. Before he had time to decide what action he should take with it,

Dorothy was at his side in the hall. She was pale and trembling. He was unable to hide the parcel from her.

"I knew it was," she exclaimed in strangely gasping tones, "and it's addressed to me again."

Laurence nodded. She was right. The address was exactly the same as it had been on the previous occasion. Laurence looked at her. She knew what his question was going to be.

"Where's Frances?"

"Still in her bedroom—but she may be getting up any minute. Why do you ask?"

"What do we do with this?"

"What can we do with it? We must look at it in the first place. It may tell us something more than we know. With regard to the sender. There may be a clue. It would be sheer negligence on our own part not to look for one. Don't you see what I mean?"

"The postmark's London again."

He turned the packet over as though he were assessing the value of what Dorothy had just said. "All right. Let's take it into the lounge and open it in there." He strode away.

Dorothy followed Laurence into the lounge. She watched him cut the rather thick string of the parcel. He took out a book. The title of it was plainly to be read. *The Trial of Mrs. Maybrick*. Laurence nodded almost to himself. It seemed that the book was in accordance with the terms of an expectation.

"Yes . . ." he heard Dorothy whisper . . . "it's just the same as the other one was. Look inside the cover, Laurence. See if there's any message like there was before."

"Bound to be, I'm afraid." His eyes were hard and unyielding.

He opened the book. There, tucked away between the leaves, was the typewritten slip of paper which they were seeking. They read it together.

My dear Mrs. Weston. August Bank Holiday! Herewith the second of my Greetings. You see that I have not forgotten you. How could such a calamity be possible? And I'll wager that you have not forgotten me. Permit me to remind you, however, that you are now two months nearer what we will term "the inevitable hour". *In other words "all heedful of their doom, the little victims play". The next time, therefore, believe me to be as before, "Harry the Hangman".*

"Cold-blooded swine!" muttered Laurence, with singularly short memory. "Same technique as before. Exactly. Continuing the war of nerves—that's the idea."

Dorothy stared straight in front of her. "If it's a war of nerves, Laurence," she said, "it's succeeding with me. I'm ready to admit it. I don't think that I can stand much more of it. I'm sorry, dear, if I disappoint you."

Laurence turned on her. There was more than a hint of asperity in his voice. "You've got to pull yourself together. You've got to. For my sake! For both our sakes! Good God, Dorothy, you must see the truth of that! This is all a try on, I tell you! Nothing more! I'm absolutely certain of it. Where's your pride? Your courage? Your gentility? What's gentility worth if it can't stand fire?"

She shook her head at him weakly. Laurence continued in the same strain, his voice rising.

"Do you mean to tell me that you're prepared to give in, to surrender, to lower all your defences at the first few shots that are fired in your direction? Because I tell you, you're not—for the single reason that I'm not going to let you."

"It's the Linklaters," said Dorothy in a kind of numbed voice, "it must be. They're responsible for all this. There's nobody else. I feel sure of it."

"I don't. I told you before that I didn't. And I shall refuse to regard the threat as serious. It's just somebody who thinks there's a—"

He broke off suddenly as he could hear Frances coming out of her room. "Mind—there's Frances. Leave this to me. I'll take charge of it for the time being."

Dorothy nodded acquiescence. She was only too glad to accept. There was breakfast to see to. There was the holiday to prepare for at the end of the month. Clothes. Hers and Frances's. She felt that she had lost interest in nearly everything. More than that even— she felt that she had lost interest in Life itself. It was useless, too, for Laurence to be annoyed with her. It wouldn't do the slightest good. He didn't know about what was happening with regard to Hubert. If he did know, he might be able to understand her feelings better. She wished she could tell him. Tell him about the water which dripped out of Hubert's hair. Tell him of the mute appeal in Hubert's eyes. But she couldn't tell him. Without breaking her pact with him. She dreaded that look of intense annoyance that crossed Laurence's face. Perhaps because it came so much more often now than it used to. She went wearily to see to the breakfast. Frances was already sitting down waiting to be attended to. Dorothy forced a smile on to her face, for Frances's sake. Perhaps she would feel better when she got to Cornwall. She would do her best. As she entered the breakfast-room, she saw that Laurence's eyes were fixed on her. That look was on his face again.

"Come on, Dorothy," he said rather aggressively, "we haven't all day for breakfast."

As she took her seat and began to pour out the coffee, she remembered that she had not yet told Frances of the child that was coming.

CHAPTER IX

THE holiday at Fowey came and went. It brought Dorothy but little real enjoyment. Partly because of her sudden and increasing weariness—of both body and spirit—and partly for the reason that Hubert went to Cornwall with her. She saw him on several occasions. On the last occasion, he acted differently from the normal. He laughed and then pointed at her. It was a soundless laugh, but she knew that he was laughing because she could see the contortions of his face. She knew, too, that she herself was becoming less of a companion for Laurence day by day. Often she stayed in the hotel whilst he went out with Frances. She hoped that he would explain these matters to himself, if he needed explanations, on the score of her physical condition. Gradually the idea came to her and began to develop, that he was worried about her. She found this belief disturbing and disconcerting.

On the Sunday evening immediately following their return to Simonstone and after Frances had gone to bed, Laurence told Dorothy that he wanted to discuss something of importance with her. She nodded and listened to him. He sat in an armchair in the lounge and spoke very quietly. He had evidently given a deal of thought to what he was about to say.

"My dear," he said, "sit down here with me. I want to talk to you. I'm sorry if it's a bit painful—I can't very well avoid that. I've been thinking things over. I had a good deal of time at Fowey during which I could think—and for a good portion of that time I was turning over in my mind what I'll call for want of a better description at the moment, 'the Linklater matter'."

He saw Dorothy turn pale and almost wince at the words.

Laurence continued. "I'm sorry—but I had to call it that, so that you'll be able to understand properly what I'm about to suggest." He paused to put a cigarette stub in the ash-tray.

"Yes, Laurence," said Dorothy. "What is it you want to say to me?"

"I'm sorry to spring it on you, as it were, but I think it would be excellent policy on our part to move. To move, say, at the end of this quarter. That is, in about a fortnight's time."

"Why, Laurence? What's the point about moving?"

"I want to find out if the 'Linklaters', as we are calling them, will trace us. I shall not inform the postal authorities as to where we go. I shall leave no loose ends here so there should be no need for that to be done." He paused again. "Get the idea?"

She nodded at him. "I think so. Partly. Though I don't know that it will have much effect."

"That remains to be proved. To an extent, it will have the effect of forcing our unknown correspondent into the open. If he doesn't reach us in our new home, we shall know that our move has eluded him. If he *does* reach us at our new address, wherever it may be, he will only do so by actively finding out where we have gone. That is to say, he will have to make inquiries. Be forced to show himself a bit. Show his hand. And in doing these things, it's on the cards that he may give himself away. See where I'm getting to now?"

"Yes—but you're more hopeful of good results from it than I am."

"You agree to the idea of the move, though?"

"Yes. I don't *want* to move. Indeed, I shall hate leaving here. Because I had come to love the place. But I can see that it may turn out for the best. But there's Frances—though."

"How do you mean? How does it concern her?"

"Her school. She's been moved once already. It's hardly fair to the poor kid to send her from pillar to post. These particular years of her life are so important from the point of view of her education. Constant chopping and changing must be prejudicial."

Laurence frowned. What did Dorothy want to drag this up for? It wasn't as though it were of real importance to the point at issue. "Oh—she'll be all right. We'll find a place for her. Don't let that worry you. In the end a change may turn out to be all to her advantage. She's the right age for transplanting. Very often children of her age get into a groove which is fatal. A thing like this would get her out of it."

Dorothy thought over his reply. "All right, then. Where are you thinking of going? Far?"

"No. Not over far. We'll stay this side. To the coast. Sudmore. That's the place I've been considering. It's about eighteen miles farther from town, but there's a much better train service altogether. The sea-air will do you a world of good and should benefit Frances as well."

Dorothy brightened perceptibly as she heard Laurence's proposal. "I think I rather like the prospect. It does one good to move from time to time. It makes a change and it's in a good cause."

Laurence leant towards her—his face stern and unyielding. "Now don't breathe a word to anybody where we're going. I'm deadly serious about that. Don't even tell Frances—yet awhile. She can be told all in good time. Plenty of time for that when we're there. Let it be a kind of pleasant surprise for her. You know what I mean—living at the seaside all the year round and all that sort of thing—when she hears the news she'll be no end bucked about it. Don't breathe a word about it to the Bishops or to Evelyn Springthorpe. Or to any others of the Dramatic Club crowd. Keep it all under your hat. All the bills will be paid up before we go so that there'll be no hounds on our track in that direction and we'll have a clean sheet everywhere. In other words, when we walk out of here, let nobody know where we're going except our two selves. I'm not running away because I'm afraid of anything—I'm just endeavouring to seal up an end like we used to in the old days." He stuck out his chin determinedly.

"All right, Laurence. I see what you mean and I'll do my best. But there are the removal people to consider—you mustn't forget them. They'll know where we're going because they'll take the things from here. Anybody could put an inquiry through to them."

"I've thought of them. There *may* be a way of circumventing that particular difficulty. I'm not so sure there isn't. As a matter of fact, I'm already toying with one or two fairly bright schemes. Leave all that to me. I think I can make it all right. Now for more immediate plans. I propose that next Saturday we'll fix Frances up somewhere and you and I will run down to Sudmore. To have a scout round. We may pick up a nice little place. There are plenty going. Either in Sudmore or just outside. What do you say?"

Dorothy puckered her brows. "What do we do with 'Brockhurst'?"

"I've considered that, too. My proposal is that we put it up for sale. Put it in an agent's hands. Through my office address. So that all communications with regard to it can be sent to me there. It ought to go pretty quickly. It's an attractive little place in a rather charming district and we ought to get a good price for it. Actually we should be prepared to drop a few pounds over it. But that can wait."

"I agree. We wouldn't put up a haggle over the price. After all, I've lived in it for a year."

"That's settled then. And next Saturday we'll run down to Sudmore house-hunting. Good! We shall see then what cards our friend Harry *does* hold up his sleeve. And when we do that, I may be able to find a trump for most of them. I shall certainly be disappointed if I can't."

Dorothy shuddered at the words.

CHAPTER X

THE journey to Sudmore on the Saturday following was not unproductive. Laurence naturally took charge of the expedition and soon had Dorothy interested in some new bungalows out in the direction of a suburb of Sudmore called Westwood. In shape, style and general design they were not at all unlike their own "Brockhurst" at Simonstone. This fact Laurence was not slow to point out. He found Dorothy in ready agreement. Instructions in one of the front windows enabled them to find the builder and after a short interview, Laurence expressed himself as willing to enter into a quarterly tenancy. Various forms were signed, wallpapers chosen and all arrangements were completed for the Westons to enter into occupation of the bungalow they had chosen commencing from the Michaelmas quarter.

Coming back in the train that evening, Laurence felt that he had accomplished an extremely satisfactory afternoon's work. Dorothy felt the same without confessing an equal measure of enthusiasm. For the next few weeks she and Laurence kept their own counsel. "Brockhurst" was placed in an agent's hands, in accordance with Laurence's original suggestion, and any business that might result therefrom was arranged to be transacted through his business address. The furniture from "Brockhurst" was removed to a furniture repository in Brant, where it remained for two days only. From here it was conveyed to Sudmore by a different firm from that which had carried out the first job. Laurence's idea was that the men who took the furniture out of "Brockhurst" should have no knowledge as to where it was ultimately going. The two days' interval which were thus brought about were spent by Laurence, Dorothy and Frances at the Palace Hotel, Sudmore. Laurence was always thorough in the things which he undertook.

As the time for the migration had come nearer, Dorothy had felt a strong sense of relief that she was getting away from Simonstone. The place had seemed changed to her since the—she had to face the truth—since the Whit Monday. Frances was a little bewildered at the (to her) surprising turn which things had suddenly taken. But her first feelings of annoyance at leaving her school at Brant, and all the rather delightful friendships which she had made there, quickly gave way to the spirit of adventure. For Adventure will always find an entrance to the hearts of the young. The problem of her new school at Sudmore had not yet been considered, let alone been found a solution. Laurence promised Dorothy that he would deal with it directly they were anything like settled in Sudmore. Dorothy accepted the promise without demur.

Frances adored the two days which she spent in the hotel with her mother, as they afforded her a glimpse of something she had never seen before and, of course, had not seriously considered. Laurence went to the office each morning and on the last day of the month the furniture came down from Brant in a noble-looking pantechnicon and the Westons moved into their new bungalow on the Westwood road. Laurence had chosen the name of "The Wave" for the new abode, and when Dorothy had questioned him with regard to the choice had replied laughingly with the line from Shelley, "Swiftly walk o'er the western wave, Spirit of Night". Frances listened eagerly for this reply, as, like it had her mother, the choice had puzzled her. When she heard it, she was observed to make a grimace. She had her own ideas had Frances!

The three months to December and Christmas passed quickly. For one thing there was so much to do in the new surroundings. And Dorothy was becoming heavy and tired with the child she was carrying. In the middle of October, Frances started at her third secondary school—the Westwood High School for Girls. Dorothy had one great objection to it. To get there from the bungalow entailed the crossing of a nasty four-road junction where, as she put it to Laurence, when first describing it to him, a child wanted eyes in the back of her head to be absolutely safe. Frances, however, appeared to negotiate the difficulties satisfactorily and adroitly avoided trouble and after a time Dorothy became more reconciled to the thoughts of the child's daily journey to and from school.

Ever since the removal from Simonstone had taken place, Laurence had uncompromisingly maintained his stand with regard to Dorothy passing on any news concerning the change of address. To this end, he had rigorously forbidden her to send any Christmas cards or presents. In reply to her somewhat half-hearted protests against this rather drastic course of action, he had said to her "never mind about seeming discourtesies *this* Christmas—we shall be able to make it up to the various people later on. Not that there's anybody of much account as far as I can see."

After a time, Dorothy accepted the position as Laurence had outlined it. "Very well—I'll do as you say. And I'll hate myself inwardly for seeming to be so mean."

Laurence laughed it off. He had certain ideas with regard to Boxing Day, that is to say, *the next Bank Holiday*. Get that over and he might be able to see things a little more clearly. He didn't wish to discuss this particular point with Dorothy. He knew that it would upset her. So he kept his own counsel about it. The new doctor in Sudmore to whom she had gone shortly after her arrival was, like his predecessor at Brant, not too pleased with her. Dorothy herself had told Laurence this. Laurence felt strongly that he would be relieved when February came. Almost as relieved as Dorothy herself. He consoled himself with the thought that the worst of the waiting was over and that the last two months would quickly pass.

Dorothy did not see Hubert in the new bungalow until the week before Christmas. The shock of the encounter almost shattered her. He came to her in the same manner as he had always come. At night. When she was lying in bed, trying to get to sleep. He suddenly appeared and stood at the foot of the bed. The water dripped from his hair on to the floor. Again, she could see the pool forming round his feet. Again, his lips seemed to part as though he were endeavouring to say something to her. Again, no sounds came. But that laugh was on his face. She started up in bed, her elbow supporting her on the pillow. She dared not speak for fear of waking or disturbing Laurence. She wondered if Laurence *were* awake, whether *he* would see what she saw! She felt that if Hubert persisted in visiting her in this fashion, the night would come when she would be compelled to wake Laurence so that he could take his share and burden of the visitation. It wasn't fair that Laurence should sleep like he did, while she bore the brunt of what came out of hell to visit them. And yet—at that moment, Hubert, or the shape of Hubert, went away. Back to the bourne from which it seemed he had returned. Dorothy fell back on to her bed, gasping. Her forehead and cheeks were wet with laboured sweat. Hubert had found his way to her again. In her new abode. Where he had come once, he could come twice . . . he could come as often as he liked. He would get to come regularly . . . gradually Dorothy found sleep, to awake in the morning looking like the soul of Tomlinson—"white as a rain-washed bone".

A quiet Christmas Day came and dragged by. The Westons went to bed early. On the Boxing Day morning, each knew very well what the other was thinking. No post came at the usual time. But Laurence and Dorothy well knew that Christmas posts, especially those *after* Christmas Day itself, were irregular and entirely unreliable. At eleven o'clock a parcel post came. Laurence went to the door to take it in. Beyond a parcel for Frances from a school friend at Westwood, there was nothing. Laurence went and spoke to Dorothy. On his face was an expression of quiet triumph.

"Nothing for us," he announced laconically. "I've called his bluff. Let me see a smile in your eyes, wife of mine, and quickly at that."

"The smiles will come back one day," replied Dorothy. "You must be patient with me and wait for them."

Laurence went to the sideboard and poured himself out a drink. "Confusion to friend Harry," he called; "may his ears drop off and the dogs of the city devour them!"

Dorothy looked up to see Laurence grinning at her over the rim of his glass. She raised her glass and smiled back at him.

CHAPTER XI

IT HAD been for many years the custom of the firm for which Laurence worked to give their more or less senior officers the day's holiday immediately following Boxing Day. Laurence regarded it as a valuable concession. He rose on the morning which came after the Boxing Day so recently described, full of good spirits and brimming over with any amount of *joie de vivre*. For one thing, he had a free day in front of him, for another, he felt fit and well, and for a third he had for the time being eluded the disconcerting correspondence of "Harry the Hangman". He whistled to himself as he went round the various rooms and pulled back the curtains to let in the daylight. Get January and February over and things generally would begin to look even better. He made tea in the kitchen and took cups to both Dorothy and Frances. In the saucers of the cups he put sweet biscuits. Frances complained if he didn't. He began to get the breakfast. Christmas Day and Boxing Day breakfasts had both been away from the normal routine. Today, they'd go back to the best breakfast of all—bacon and eggs. That knocked all the tongue and pork pie. Laurence proceeded cheerily with his preparations. So much so that he scarcely heard the knock on the door which came not long after nine o'clock. Frances called out to him from her bedroom.

"Laurence—there's a knock at the door."

The child had called him Laurence from the start of his life with them and Dorothy had encouraged rather than disapproved the arrangement. Laurence, in his comfortable morning shoes, padded his way up the passage to the front door. He opened the door and a man in a familiar uniform put a brown paper parcel into his hands. Laurence received it almost mechanically.

"Name o' Weston, sir? Thank you very much. Compliments of the season, sir."

The postman touched his cap and walked away from the door. Laurence stood just inside the hall with the parcel in his hands. The typewritten address caught his eye. "Mrs. Dorothy Weston, 'The Wave,' Westwood Road, Sudmore, Essex." It was similar in style to those addresses he had seen before. And the postmark was London. As he turned the parcel over, Laurence cursed softly under his breath. In spite of his confidence, all his carefully laid plans had gone for nothing. As this thought took hold in his brain, he heard his wife's voice from the bedroom.

"What is it, Laurence?"

From the peculiar timbre in her voice he knew exactly what she meant. "It's all right," he answered as casually as he could; "a letter for you. Don't worry. I'll bring it in to you in half a sec'." He slipped into the bedroom where Dorothy was. He gestured towards the room where Frances slept as an indication of certain precautions. Then he pointed gravely to the parcel he carried. "It's come," he said in a low voice. He was irritated beyond expression to see that Dorothy was trembling. He felt as a man feels who has been cheated.

"You see," she said, and her voice shook, "I was right after all. He must know all about us, too. How else could he have found us out here?"

"He?" he questioned rather savagely. "Why not 'they'—if we stick to the Linklater tradition?"

"What are you going to do about it?"

"See what he says this time," he declared with a show of anger.

He cut the string with savage strokes of his pocket-knife and pulled off the brown paper covering. The book's title was *Mrs. Major and Mrs. Bryant*. Two modern Borgias. He looked inside. It was entirely according to precedent. There was inserted the usual note. Laurence read it—his eyes alive with resentment.

My dear Mrs. Weston. Boxing Day. Herewith the third of my greetings and I hope that the post will deliver it at the appropriate time. So you have run! But only a little distance. Further away we may say, as regards actual distance, but another spell of Time nearer the knell of doom. What a glorious phrase for guilty hearts! This time I have news for you. News that should intrigue you greatly. The Police are on your track. Early in the New Year, they will visit you. Be sure that you make them very welcome. The inquiry will be, on the surface, of a most innocent nature . . . but . . . well, you know Police methods, don't you? Better probably than I do. This will be their first move. The first move in along game. Many others will follow. Until the final scene comes. Till next time, therefore. Believe me to be, "Harry the Hangman".

He passed the book to Dorothy without comment. She read the message as he had. When she looked up at him again, there was a hopeless and helpless look in her eyes.

"It's no good, Laurence," she said, "you see—"

"I see what?" he countered.

"That it's useless for us to try to get away from them. They must be very close to us. That's obvious from this, isn't it? Closer than we imagined. Much closer!"

Laurence thrust his hands into his pockets and stared moodily at the floor. Dorothy's words evidently made him think of something. "That's an idea," he muttered. "Closer than we imagined. I wonder if there's anything in that point. It might bear looking into." There were ugly lines round his mouth.

"How do you mean?" she asked.

"Why this! That if we looked round a bit we might be able to identify our Bank Holiday correspondent. The people who know our new address, outside my own office, are extremely few and far between. See what I mean?"

"It's amazing!" Dorothy half whispered the words to herself. "Yesterday I thought we had steered clear of it. I should have known better, I suppose. Now that this has come this morning, I feel that we shall never escape these horrible parcels and messages. If we went to the ends of the earth, I feel that they would still follow us and find us there. It's dreadful!"

"Don't be ridiculous. Keep your sense of proportion. Look at it like this. If these people really *knew* anything about us, they wouldn't content themselves with vague and nebulous allusions. Oh no! They'd act. They wouldn't remain on the edge of things and just yap about them. I tell you straight, Dorothy, I'm not going to let them frighten me. Not on your life! I don't see myself taking this lying down."

"I don't see what you can do," she responded; "you're in the position of a man hitting out in the dark. You don't know who your opponent is. Let alone hit him. As I see things, your hands are as good as tied behind your back."

"We'll see about that," hinted Laurence darkly. "Light and dark are relative terms. For all you can say to the contrary, I might take a smack in the dark and hit the right person. You never know . . ." he chuckled, "attack is often the best weapon of defence, despite the reluctance of so many white-livered scoundrels to try it for once."

Dorothy listened to him without hearing properly what he was saying. Her mind was the prey of so many disturbing thoughts. She wished that she could see the end of it all.

CHAPTER XII

WHEN Dorothy looked out of the window on the morning of the last day of January, she had little idea of the tragedy which the day was destined to bring. Because the sun shone brilliantly, the air was like fine champagne, and the whole atmosphere of the day's morning was full of the promise of the Spring and Summer which were to come. Dorothy was near her time. Her health had fluctuated considerably since the week of Christmas. No more correspondence had been received of the kind she dreaded, although she wrote early in January to Mr. and Mrs. Grant, Hubert's parents, telling them of her second marriage and of the move to Sudmore. She had deliberately procrastinated over this, but when she had written, she immediately felt a strong sense of relief.

But although she had been free from another dreaded postal communication, she saw Hubert at least once a week now. And he came to other places than the end of the bed. One dark afternoon, she had been looking out of the window and had seen him cross the bottom of the garden. He walked stealthily—with stooping shoulders and furtive footsteps. His clothes were wet—she could see that—and as he disappeared under the hedge he turned to her and waved triumphantly. Then there had come another evening when she had gone into the lounge in the dark. Before she could find the switch for the electric light, she knew with a dreadful certainty that Hubert was in the room. Sitting in the room in the dark. In one of the big armchairs. Waiting for her to come in. She heard him chuckle to himself at the catch in her breath which he couldn't help hearing. She had a feeling that if she stayed in the room without putting on any light, Hubert would take advantage of the darkness and come across and strangle her. So she snapped on the light at once, fearful and trembling. When she looked again, Hubert had gone, but Dorothy could see the wet patch on the carpet directly underneath where he had been sitting. As she looked at it with a horror that had by now become all too familiar to her, the patch began to dry up, as though a magical means were being used on it, and Dorothy saw it gradually fade away before her eyes.

Laurence had made arrangements for her to enter the maternity ward of the hospital at Westwood for her confinement. She had agreed with him directly he had put forward the suggestion, that she would rather go away to have her baby than stay at home. She was due to enter the hospital on the third of February and as she looked out of the window on this last day of January, she realized that little time was now left to her before her ordeal. When Frances had been born, Dorothy had stayed at home in Bullen, but things were different now and she knew that it would be far better, in every way, for her to go away. Besides being better for her it would be better for both Laurence and Frances. The hospital to which she was going was not much more than a quarter of an hour's walk from the bungalow, so that there arose no questions of inconvenience from any point of view. She knew that a tremendous relief would come to her after she had given birth to Laurence's child. That besides ridding herself of a physical burden, she was hoping against hope to shed a mental burden at the same time. She even clung almost pathetically to the idea that perhaps Hubert would cease to trouble her when he saw her with a child in her arms! Surely that would be the time when he would extend her mercy!

On the afternoon of this last day of January, Dorothy had a light lunch and then read on the settee in front of the fire. She intended to stay where she was until Frances came home from school. After that, she and Frances would have tea and muffins also, in front of the fire, before it was time to see to Laurence's dinner. Laurence left the office at five o'clock, caught the 5.22 train from town and usually arrived at the bungalow in the region of ten minutes to seven. If he were kept at the office late, for any reason for which he had been unprepared, and of which, therefore, he had failed to advise Dorothy when he had left home in the morning, he invariably telephoned her. His old quality of supreme reliability had not diminished one iota.

Dorothy looked up from her book and at the clock. It was most unlikely that Laurence would be late that evening as things at his office, at this particular time of the year, were distinctly on the slack side. As she looked at the clock, Dorothy saw that Frances was late. She hadn't realized this before as her thoughts had been mainly on the Westwood Maternity Hospital. Twenty more minutes passed with no appearance of Frances and then, to Dorothy's chill uneasiness, the telephone-bell rang in the hall. Dorothy left her comfortable position on the settee and walked to answer it. An unknown voice greeted her ear.

"Who is that speaking, please?"

"Mrs. Weston."

"This is Inspector Farquhar, speaking from Westwood police-station. Please don't be alarmed, but I had to make sure that there was somebody at home. But I'm sorry to say that your little girl has had a bit of an accident. Crossing the road. Don't worry for the time being. She's in Westwood Hospital. In good hands. I'll be along to your place in a quarter of an hour or so in a car. Then we can have a little chat about it. Now don't forget what I said—you're not to worry. Everything that can be done for her is being done. Expect me along in a few moments."

Before Dorothy could frame words for reply, he had rung off. The pain in her heart almost paralysed her. Her hands shook as she replaced the receiver. Frances! Hurt! Lying in hospital. Perhaps maimed for life. Perhaps even . . . worse than that. Perhaps dead! Dorothy felt that she must cry for mercy to the supreme Arbiter of Life and Death. That she must fall on her knees to pray . . . just where she was. For she had loved and still did love Frances. It was really for Frances's sake that Laurence had . . . that Laurence had . . . done what he had done.

She stumbled back to the room of the settee and the fire. Her feet and legs were wavering and unsteady, her body almost disobedient to the impulses of her brain. She lay on the settee. She could not cry. She was gripped tight by an inexorable fear. She just stared in front of her. What had they done to Frances? What had she done to Frances? She castigated herself mentally with supreme mercilessness. Whatever it was, whatever had happened to Frances, she would make it up to her directly she was able, a thousandfold!

Even though there would be another child in her arms and on her lap, Frances shouldn't suffer in the tiniest particular. She would devote her life to Laurence and her dual motherhood.

Dorothy stared into the red heart of the fire. That Police Inspector who had telephoned would be at the door before very long. Within the next few minutes probably. She would know then the extent of Frances's injuries. There was one comfort, if such a matter as a comfort could be extracted from so tragic an entanglement—she would be near to Frances when the time came for her to go away.

They would both be in the Westwood Hospital. Fate certainly did play strange tricks. She and Laurence would go to see Frances that evening. Directly he came in. She had already made up her mind on that point. Perhaps this Inspector Farquhar would be able to drive them over after Laurence had had his dinner. She heard the wheels of a car stop outside the bungalow. A footstep sounded on the step outside and the bell rang. Dorothy went slowly to the door. A man in a Police Inspector's uniform stood in the porch. Even before he spoke to her, she thought that he looked unusually grave and serious. She began to tremble.

"Good evening, Mrs. Weston. You were expecting me . . . Inspector Farquhar? Is Mr. Weston in?"

"No. Only me. Mr. Weston doesn't get in till later. Please come in and tell me how Frances is."

"Thank you." He slipped into the hall. "Nasty night," he said quietly.

"Come in here, Inspector. It's warm in here."

"Thank you, Mrs. Weston."

Farquhar took a seat by the fire.

"Now tell me, please. I must know. What has happened to my little girl?"

As Inspector Farquhar looked up at her to answer her question, he saw with a certain sense of shock how close she was to her time. He wished himself a thousand miles away. Dorothy sensed his hesitation.

"Tell me—please," she said with a fierce insistence, "is Frances badly hurt?"

"Yes, Mrs. Weston. I'm afraid she is." His eyes seemed afraid to meet hers.

"Very badly?"

He nodded. "Yes."

She rose from the settee and held the end to support herself. "Do you mean that she's—she's dead?"

Her voice held the unmistakable note of hysteria and Farquhar saw to his dismay that she was swaying as she spoke. Why the hell wasn't the woman's husband with her at a time like this? He bowed his head in answer to her last question. He spoke no word. As she took in the dread importance, her eyes opened wide and her lips parted. Her breasts rose and fell. A sharp, cutting, blinding pain seemed to twist itself into her being . . . was it Death? Dorothy prayed that it was. But sharply sudden judgments are rarely the instruments of Nature for either the just or the unjust. Dorothy swayed like a bush harried by the wind and fell to the floor fainting at Farquhar's feet.

CHAPTER XIII

WHEN Laurence arrived home that evening, he was surprised when an Inspector of Police opened the door to him. For a moment it must be confessed that he was badly shaken by the unexpected incident. But he put a bold front on the matter and jocularly inquired when he entered as to why he had been thus honoured. The Inspector's manner, however, was both courteous and cordial. Laurence Weston's usual poise soon returned to him. He was annoyed that it had ever deserted him.

"I'm sorry, sir, to have planted myself on you in this fashion—when I explain how things are, you'll understand that I had no option. But come in here and sit down, will you, Mr. Weston?"

Inspector Farquhar ushered Laurence into his own lounge. Farquhar wasted no time in coming to the point. "I'm afraid, sir, that I've got bad news for you."

Laurence went white as he sat himself in one of the arm-chairs. "My wife?" he asked, his voice a little out of control.

"Partly, sir—although she's all right now, I'm pleased to say. There's a nurse and doctor with her. I had to telephone from here for immediate medical assistance. Mrs. Weston collapsed."

"But why? Why isn't she in the hospital? I've made all the arrangements—"

"I'm aware of that, Mr. Weston, and you have my sincere sympathy. But the truth is, Mrs. Weston's had a bad shock this evening . . . prepare yourself, sir . . . the little girl was run over late this afternoon by a motor-coach. She died in Westwood Hospital soon after being admitted. The skull was fractured."

Laurence Weston sat in his chair as though he had received a heavy blow which had stunned him. Nearly a minute went by before he spoke. "What time was Frances killed?" he asked at length.

"About half past four, Mr. Weston. As I said, she died a few moments after being taken to the hospital. There was little hope of her recovery right from the first."

"What time did my wife collapse?"

Inspector Farquhar consulted his watch. "A little over an hour ago, sir. I broke the news to her as gently as I could. I even prepared her first by getting through on the telephone."

"I see. Where is she now?"

Farquhar gestured with his thumb. "In the bedroom, sir. With a trained nurse and Dr. Appleyard in attendance. As I told you just now, Mr. Weston, I 'phoned for them when I saw how things were with your good lady. I did my best for her in every possible way."

Laurence nodded. "Thank you. I'm sure that I appreciate all you've done. How is my wife now?"

"From what I can hear, Mr. Weston, she's pretty bad. If I were you, I should screw myself up to the idea that it'll be touch and go with her. Prepare yourself for the worst. I know that's Dr. Appleyard's opinion."

Laurence Weston did his best to collect his scattered thoughts. This was all very terrible. Frances . . . and Dorothy herself! One blow would have been bad enough, let alone two coming in such quick succession. And he was certainly helpless. He could do nothing at all to help. He realized that Farquhar was watching him closely.

"I think," said Laurence, rising, "I'll go and snatch a mouthful of something to eat. There'll be some for me in the dining-room. I'm pretty well all in. If I don't take some nourishment, I won't answer for the consequences."

"Do, sir. You couldn't do anything better—seeing how you're placed."

The Inspector encouraged him. Laurence walked almost blindly into the dining-room. He made tea and found food for himself. He supposed that in time either the doctor or the nurse would come out and speak to him. He drank a cup of tea. The warmth of the liquid helped him to pull himself together. Every now and then, he listened to certain sounds which were coming from the bedroom. The room where a doctor and a nurse, neither of whom he knew, neither of whom he had ever seen before, were fighting for the life of his wife. He heard low murmuring sounds and the noise, from time to time, of quick footsteps across the room. A knock at the dining-room door startled him. It was Inspector Farquhar wanting him.

"Yes," said Laurence wearily—"what is it?"

"I think, if you don't mind, sir, I'll go. There isn't much more that I can do now." He paused as though reluctant to go on. "I'll see you again, sir, in a day or two's time about the inquest on the little girl. Good night, Mr. Weston."

Laurence answered him mechanically. "Good night, Inspector." He drank more tea and cut himself some slices of cold beef. He wondered if the people in the bedroom knew that he had come home. Perhaps he ought to tell them. He disliked, however, making the necessary interruption. Suddenly this problem that faced him was solved. The nurse came into the room, carrying a kettle. Laurence rose.

"I'm Mrs. Weston's husband," he said simply.

The nurse smiled at him. "She's a little better. But we're having a rather sticky time with her. It was the shock she had, poor girl. It couldn't have come at a worse time. I'm so sorry."

She disappeared into the scullery and Laurence heard the sound of water running. When she came back, she smiled at him again and said "I'll tell Dr. Appleyard you're here. Perhaps he'll come and have a word with you later on."

Laurence nodded. "I shall be in here. Let me know if I can do anything—or if you should want anything."

She shook her head. "There's nothing you can do. Sit here and rest yourself—and be as quiet as you can. I'll tell the doctor that you're here."

She went out of the room. Laurence sat by the dining-room fire. He became the victim of his thoughts. Dorothy . . . Frances . . . Frances . . . Dorothy . . . and then . . . Hubert! An unreasonable anger seized him for a short spell. By an effort he shook it off. The warmth of the fire began to get hold of him. He was dog-tired now. He felt that he was going to fall asleep. He fought against this insistent inclination. For some time he maintained what rapidly became an unequal struggle. Eventually he gave in and he slept in his chair in front of the fire. He did not know how long he slept. He was awakened by a man clutching at his shoulder. He heard what this man was saying to him.

"Weston! Wake up, man. I want to talk to you."

Laurence opened his eyes and blinked at this stranger.

"I'm Appleyard," said the man. "I'm the doctor who's been looking after your missus. We've had a rare scrap, I can tell you, to keep her the right side of the river. But I think she's turned the corner now. Sleeping nicely. It's a girl. I think the missus'll do now, but of course you mustn't bank on it. I've just come out for a breather. Nurse Eadie is carrying on for me."

"A girl?" muttered Laurence Weston.

"Ay—a girl."

"Is the child all right?"

"Well"—Laurence thought that Appleyard found the question a trifle unwelcome—"I think she'll do all right. We're hoping so. It's early days yet, remember." The doctor changed the subject. "I hear you've had a stroke of bad luck this evening. My sympathy. Damned shame. Rough on your missus to run up against it when she was like that. Pity they broke it to her when they did. Might have waited."

Appleyard rattled on. It was patent that he was doing his best to be sympathetic. The clock struck on the mantelpiece. Laurence was surprised at the chimes. There were two of them. Appleyard noticed the expression on Weston's face.

"Yes, sir—it's tomorrow. I don't suppose you realized that, did you?"

"No. Had I been asked, I should have said it was about ten o'clock. I must have slept longer than I thought I had. How long is it since the child was born?"

The doctor glanced at his watch. "About three-quarters of an hour. Almost exactly. We were in the thick of it for a hell of a time. You can put down her birthday as February the 1st. A daughter of Aquarius. The Water."

His words hit Laurence. "February. Water." Two years ago the month had been February when the waters of the Murmur had closed over Hubert Grant. Laurence shivered at the reminiscence. It was the small hours of the morning and his body was low . . . but it was an unusual occurrence for Laurence Weston to shiver. Appleyard didn't miss this shiver. He looked shrewdly at his companion.

"Why not turn in, man? You can do with it as you are. You can't do anything. And I can't allow you to see your missus. Even were she a darned sight brighter than she is, I'm dead set against that sort of thing. Always have been. Ever since I started as a G.P. My motto has always been 'when a person's ill, keep the chowers away'. Not that you'd do a lot of chin-wagging."

Laurence nodded. "What are you going to do yourself, Doctor?"

Appleyard consulted his watch again. "I'll give the patient another 'look-see' and then if everything's O.K, I think I'll clear off. The nurse is here—and you'll find that she's quite capable of looking after both the cases. I'll pop in there again now. Hang on for another five minutes or so."

Appleyard departed with an incredible quietness for so heavily built a man. Laurence waited in patience for him to return. He hadn't to wait very long. Within about ten minutes Appleyard came into the dining-room on tiptoe and with his finger to his lips. "Thumbs up," he said. "The kiddie's not too bad and the missus is still sleeping nicely. She'll do very comfortably if she stays like that for another two or three hours. Sleep's a grand thing for a tired and shocked body." He held out his hand. "Good-bye, Weston. Good luck over this job—and all my sympathies with regard to the other. I'm a family man myself and I can guess how you feel."

Appleyard shook Laurence by the hand and patted him on the shoulder. Then he went out and closed the door.

"Decent chap," thought Laurence as he watched him go out. "Pity there aren't more like him about. World would be a better place. Told me to go to bed. Point is where? I can't face Frances's bed—poor little kid. Think I'll stay in here. Use these two chairs. What was that noise? Like somebody crying. The new little girl, of course. Mustn't wake Dorothy up. Fancy the Police greeting me when I came in. The Police! Fancy that—considering what had been promised by Harry the Hangman . . . curse him!"

CHAPTER XIV

A WEEK after Frances was buried, they broke the news to Dorothy Weston that the baby had been born blind. Laurence had known of this before. Appleyard, fearing the worst, and in deference to Laurence's desires, had called in a specialist. This gentleman, a Dr. Langsdon, had looked grave from the beginning of his examination. He very soon gave Appleyard his opinion. "Ophthalmia neonatorum" was his pronunciation. "And I don't like the look of it at all, Dr. Appleyard. There has been infection, with discharges from the maternal passages which has caused a most severe corneal ulceration. To all intents and purposes the eyesight of this child has been destroyed. There is absolutely no hope that she will ever see. The damage that has already been done is much too far advanced."

Laurence was badly hit by the blow. Dorothy, for a time at least, comprehended it but dully. Her grief for Frances held the field against every invader. Her one wish was that she might be permitted to die. That she had nothing to live for, she felt convinced. She felt it impossible to analyse her feelings towards Laurence. It wasn't exactly that she didn't love him. It was that she felt that she *should* not love him . . . that she was doing wrong to love him. Laurence was quick to notice the change, but he decided to say nothing about it, for a time at least. The house became like a garden full of weeds where no blossom grows. Dorothy grew more and more silent. She withdrew into herself. Laurence, eminently patient, bided his time. He had such an implicit belief in the healing power of Time. He knew that his future happiness now hung on the most precarious of threads. He moved and trod softly, lest this gossamer thread snapped and scattered his happiness beyond salvation and recall. He never discussed with Dorothy the blindness of the little girl.

On the 1st of March, St. David's Day, and exactly a month after the birth of the little Faith Weston, a visitor in the person of Police-Constable Young called at the bungalow. He asked for Laurence. Dorothy told him that if he wanted Laurence, he must come in the evening. He accepted the position and called again about half past seven. Laurence invited him in. Young seemed uneasy. Laurence waited for him to open up. Young's first question shocked him and amazed him.

"I believe you were in Cleves the other afternoon, sir? In the Tudor district. Yes?"

Laurence caught sight of Dorothy's white face on the other side of the table. What was behind this question? He remembered vividly the threat contained in "Harry the Hangman's" most recent effusion. What on earth was this copper driving at? Young noticed Laurence's hesitation. And Laurence *knew* that he had noticed it. His mouth felt dry and horrible. He told the truth.

"Sorry, Constable—but you're wrong. You've got the wrong man."

Young looked surprised. "To be exact, sir, on the twenty-second of last month."

Laurence shook his head. "Sorry—nothing doing, as I said."

"Are you sure, sir?"

"Positive. I suppose I should know, shouldn't I? What makes you think I was? In Cleves? It's nowhere near here, for instance."

Young took out a pencil and note-book before replying. He sucked the top of the pencil. Then he carefully read from his book. He looked up. "My information is that you were in Cleves. I can't quite understand this. When were you last in Cleves? Would you mind telling me that?"

Laurence gave a quick glance at Dorothy. He saw plainly the ordeal through which she was passing. He determined to be bold and resolute. He crossed the Rubicon.

"To the best of my memory I have never been in the place you mention in my life."

Well, there it was—there was no going back now—he was committed now. He'd soon see whether he had played the right card.

"Never, sir?" came the Constable's query.

"That's what I said."

"Well, sir, it's all very strange, I don't know what to think about it."

Laurence flung out his challenge. "This is all very well, Constable, but you don't tell me anything. You leave me floundering in the dark. What's it all about? Why not tell me, man, and clear the air?"

"No, sir. I don't think I'd better—if you don't mind. You deny having been there—that's as far as I'd better go for the time being.

We shall have to get matters sifted out. If you've never been in Cleves—and I take your word for it, sir—it's certain the cinema people have slipped up somewhere. Leave it at that, sir."

Constable Young rose to take his departure. He replaced his note-book and pencil. Laurence's face showed signs of temper.

"I think I'm entitled to a fuller explanation, Constable, than you've so far given me. It's all very well, you know, but there's a good deal here that's distinctly puzzling."

Constable Young steadfastly refused the challenge that had been trailed in front of him. He remained what he had been all through the interview. Jovial, rather unintelligent and entirely good-tempered.

"That's all right, sir. You mustn't take offence where there's none intended. We do get instances of mistaken identities. Perhaps that's what's happened in this case. Anyhow, I'll report what you say, sir. If you don't hear any more from us, don't let it worry you."

"It may not be your fault, Constable—but I tell you frankly I don't think it's good enough."

Young smiled again. He was chock full of brotherly love and totally unperturbed. "Good night, sir."

"Good night, Constable, and make my representations to your superiors—will you? I shall be obliged." The tone was hostile.

Laurence closed the door behind the representative of the law rather forcibly. Dorothy's lips were set tight when he returned to the room and her face looked drawn of all its blood.

"Well," said Laurence, with exasperation in his voice, "and what do you make of that?"

"I remember," she replied evasively, "and I know that you remember too."

He laughed with cold scorn. "'Harry the Hangman', you mean, I suppose?"

"I do. It's just what he said would happen. What he threatened. You can't argue about it, Laurence, and you know you can't."

"Well, there's one thing," retorted Laurence in anger, "he's out in his time. He said 'Early in the New Year'. You can't call March the 1st that by any stretch of imagination. I'm delighted to find that our mysterious correspondent is not infallible. It's a relief."

"There's no comfort will come to us from thinking like that, Laurence. Unless it's cold comfort." She put down her knitting. As she did so she burst into tears. Laurence was cross. She saw it. "Don't be hard on me. Bear with me, if you can. God knows I need all the sympathy I can get. But all this insidious attack to which we're being subjected by this man or these people, is slowly killing me, Laurence! It's all so secret, so clandestine, so stealthy, so furtive. It isn't as though he came out into the open and attacked us direct. We should know what to do. We could face it. To face it and lose . . . I sometimes think . . . would be preferable to this appalling suspense."

Laurence made no immediate reply. On the whole, he was in agreement with her expressed opinion. He thought, however, rightly or wrongly, that if he did acquiesce in her statement, he would weaken her already fast-diminishing powers of resistance and sap her resources of courage still more. Eventually he spoke sharply to her. In the now all too familiar strain.

"Listen to me. It's not the slightest use your giving way. It won't get us anywhere. You've got to face up to things. You simply *must*! I know—none better—that you've had hard knocks. Cruel knocks. Too cruel for most women to bear. But if you're the woman I think you are, the woman I loved, the woman I married, you'll rise above them and prove your true worth."

He bent over her and kissed her. Dorothy wiped her eyes and at once harked back to the recent interview with Constable Young.

"That policeman, Laurence—what was the meaning of all that? The real meaning? Those cryptic references to Cleves and the cinema people and possible mistaken identity?"

She noticed as she glanced up at him that Laurence was looking tired and fine drawn.

"Candidly," he replied, "it's got me guessing. I don't mind admitting it. I can't fathom it at all."

"But there must be *some* meaning in it. Some *reason* for the visit and the mentioning of those things."

"I suppose there must. All the same, I don't get it. I should say, if I had to answer, that they don't know anything and that those remarks are no more than chance shots in the dark. Damn it all—how *can* they know anything?"

"That's what we don't know, Laurence. Where *we*, you and I—are in the dark. That's our weakness. Our heel of Achilles. That's what worries and frightens me."

"I suppose you're right," he assented gloomily. "But I'm afraid there's nothing we can do about it."

"That's very true, Laurence." For once Dorothy was quite calm. Resigned, perhaps, would be the better word. Laurence wasn't sure whether this new condition of hers gratified him or not. Dorothy continued. "It's because we don't know anything, and in consequence can do nothing, that I'm so scared with everything. When I had Frances here with me things weren't so bad. I could stand up to things better because I felt that in a way I was fighting for her. Now I feel just helpless and so horribly alone."

"That's not very complimentary to me," he returned shortly. "I'm here with you. Unless your intended meaning is that I don't count with you any more. If you do feel like that, please say so. Then we shall know exactly where we stand. Which, from my point of view, will be all to the good."

When he had finished saying this, he saw that Dorothy was crying quietly—almost to herself.

"It's not that at all," she said between her tears; "you're different. You aren't a child."

"You have *our* child. Surely that means something to you. Or doesn't it?" He regretted this speech almost immediately he had spoken.

"Yes. As you say, I have our child. But you don't expect me to be ecstatically happy because of her, do you, Laurence?"

"Because of her blindness? Is that what you're hinting at? Some mothers would love her all the more because of her affliction. I think that my own mother would have."

"I don't love her less. Because that would mean that I was denying my motherhood. But to see her suffering and helpless, and to be helpless myself in regard to it, doesn't make for happiness. Does it make you happy?"

"I at least attempt to be brave about it and to understand it."

Dorothy shrugged her shoulders. "All right, Laurence, we'll say no more about it."

Laurence, looking sulky, changed the subject. "Tell me," he said, "I have a reason for asking. Have you written to anybody at Bullen with regard to Frances?"

"Yes."

"To whom have you written?"

"To Ella Fanshawe, Ethel Thornhill and to the child's grandparents. I felt that I had to. That they had a right to know. Do you mind?"

"No. I wanted to know—for another reason, that was all."

Laurence Weston took a cigarette and began to smoke it quickly and nervously. He paced the room. For the first time in his life his nerves were beginning to master him.

CHAPTER XV

IT WAS shortly after this incident that Hubert began to visit Dorothy with a much greater degree of regularity. But when he came now, there was a different look in his eyes and a changed expression on his face. He came to her at new times and appeared in places which, previously, he had not favoured. The climax, as far as she herself was concerned, occurred one evening during the second week in March. She was returning home in the dusk of the evening with the baby Faith in the perambulator. As she turned into the Westwood Road, she heard footsteps a short distance behind her and, looking up, saw that Hubert was walking with her at her side. Her hands trembled as they gripped the front of the perambulator. In the hope of shaking Hubert off, she quickened her pace, but the effort was ineffective. Hubert kept pace with her. Suddenly, to her indescribable horror, he began to laugh. The laugh chilled her blood. He pointed towards the sleeping child and laughed again. All she could do was to avert her face from her companion and pray hard that he might vanish from her presence. When she reached the gate of the bungalow, her prayers were answered.

She opened the door, badly shaken, laid the baby down in her cradle and sat down herself so that she might recover from this new menacing experience which had just come to her. After a time, she felt a little better. It would have afforded her some measure of comfort if she had been able to confide in Laurence. But she knew, irrevocably, that she daren't whisper a hint of this present trouble to him. It was part of the original promise that she had made to him when they had married and, up till now, she had faithfully kept that promise. She was afraid that if things got worse with her she would be forced to break it.

When Laurence came in that evening he was unusually silent and it was some time before he spoke. When he did, it was to say "I ran into Dr. Appleyard on the way home. He's coming in to see you. I didn't know you'd been 'phoning him."

"I didn't want to worry you over it. I try not to worry you over ordinary domestic matters. I know that you're tired when you get home. When's he coming—did he say?"

"No. In a day or so, I believe. What's the real trouble?"

"I want to ask him about Baby. Nothing much—so don't you start fretting about it."

Laurence shrugged his shoulders. "Don't start building on false hopes. I'm afraid that even modern medical skill can do nothing for her."

"I shan't fail from want of trying, Laurence."

Laurence nodded. "You have observed, I take it, that there has been no further development over that Police inquiry affair. It's ten days now since that constable was here. And why? Because it was all a try on—that's why! I can visualize the time when the famous 'Harry the Hangman' will send his Bank Holiday parcels and we shall laugh like fun when we open them. 'Harry the Hangman'! Hangman, my foot!"

"Well, then—why has it been done? If that's the case? What's their point in sending to me? What sense is there in it?"

"No sense at all. It's all nothing more than what is popularly known as a practical joke—and there's no sense in any of them. They're never funny—and they're usually painful to the victims."

"But who would want to play a practical joke on us—and such a practical joke?"

"You don't know. You can't tell. That's part of the so-called fun of a practical joke. But anyhow, I'm going to leave it at that. Dismiss it from my mind—and I want you to do the same."

"I don't think I can—but I'll try to."

Thus Dorothy closed the conversation. Laurence went to bed that night with a lighter heart and in better spirits than for a long time, but Dorothy saw Hubert again. This time he came to her in the still watches of the night. Instead of staying at the foot of the bed, as he always had done previously, he came right up to her and stood right by the pillow. And, to her unutterable horror, Hubert went down and spoke to her. His lips came close to her ear. His face and hair were wet. She trembled violently as she heard what he said to her. Twice she endeavoured to remonstrate with him. To tell him that his tongue spoke false things—but his voice was always stronger then hers. Relentlessly it beat her down. It dominated her. She gave up the unequal struggle. Hubert stayed with her for quite a long time, and after he had gone Dorothy lay awake and heard the Sudmore parish church clock strike three, four, five, six and seven. Sleep would not come to her, woo it though she might. At a quarter past seven she got up to attend to the baby. Faith was crying. Laurence was sleeping his usual untroubled sleep. Dorothy suddenly gave way to an unreasoning anger. Why didn't Hubert worry Laurence?

CHAPTER XVI

EASTER came that year at the end of March or about three weeks after Laurence had made his announcement with regard to the practical joking propensities of "Harry the Hangman". "This Bank Holiday," he declared to Dorothy, "I'll wait on the mat for the literary offering to be handed on to me. To show how much I care about it. No ring at the bell is going to make me 'jumpy'."

Dorothy made no reply. All the sunshine, all the poetry, all the colour had gone out of her life. She feared they had gone for ever. All attempts that she had made to recapture them had so far ended in failure. True to his expressed resolution, Laurence prowled round the front door on the morning of Easter Monday waiting for the post to arrive. He was not destined for disappointment. But no parcel came. Just an ordinary letter arrived with the same London postmark and the address typed similarly to before. When he saw the letter, Laurence felt quite "bucked". He thought that he detected here a diminution of effort on the part of their unknown correspondent. Something akin to a slackening in attack. As he was thus sizing matters up, Dorothy joined him.

"See this?" he said with a tinge of triumph in his tone. "Just an envelope this time. No book. Variation of technique. I wonder why. Anyhow, it won't take us long to find out. Come into the dining-room and we'll open this."

She went with him. Her heart began to beat furiously. Although the letter was addressed to her as usual, Laurence opened the envelope to read the following.

My dear Mrs. Weston. Easter Monday. Herewith the fourth of my Greetings and the completion of what may be termed the annual cycle. You will have observed by now that on this occasion you are minus the customary literary contribution. No paper parcel—just an ordinary letter. But don't get too optimistic on that account. You would be making a grave mistake if you did. There are two reasons for the absence of the book. I will detail them to you. The first is that Mesdames Major and Bryant have had no recent successors dans cette galère. I mean by that phrase "murderesses who have been discovered and who have subsequently paid the penalty of their crimes". You will readily see the point, I am certain. And the second reason is this. If I had been able to buy a book for you, which could be justifiably described as being in the true tradition, I very much doubt whether you would have found time to read it.

You are wondering as to what I mean by this last statement? Yes? Well then, I shall be delighted to make myself clear and precise on the matter. In a very short time from now the Police will swoop on you! Remember the visit you had from them the other day, concerning a little trouble to do with Cleves? Remember how I predicted that visit in my previous bulletin? You must be convinced by now that I know what I'm talking about. The usual programme with regard to the Police will then take place. Arrest, trial, sentence, execution. Knowing you as I do, I feel that you will be bound to appeal. After all, it does delay matters for a few weeks, doesn't it? And so we have come, you and I, in imagination at least, to that last morning (probably somewhere round about next October) when they take you out and hang you. There are, of course, a number of gruesome preliminaries and unpleasant formalities which I wouldn't dream of going into here. The official in charge, a colleague of mine, most obviously, will rarely have attended to anybody quite so charming as Mrs. Dorothy Weston!

Still—that's neither here nor there. The one fact that does emerge clearly from this rather lengthy effusion, is that I shall be unable to write to you any more. Because I shan't be sure of your new address. When the feast of Pentecost is fully come, you will be either in prison (I shan't know which particular one) or in a certain corridor of Hell. Again—I shall be unaware of the exact locality. Hence my difficulty! I therefore bid you farewell. Not au revoir, you observe, but a direct adieu. Our acquaintance has been all too short, I fear, but it has, nevertheless, been singularly delightful. Wishing you a happy landing on the other side of the Styx, where doubtless Hubert will arrange to meet you, I remain, sincerely yours, "Harry the Hangman".

There was a curl on Dorothy's lips when she and Laurence had finished reading the letter. Laurence saw it and was uncertain as to why it was there. Also he wasn't sure as to whether he liked seeing it there.

"There's one thing," Laurence said critically, "he comes out of his shell more this time. Shows quite a lot of his hand. In this respect. His main attack, if not his entire attack, is directed against *you*. I'm ignored. Notice that? Not in the picture at all. I rather fancy that we shall be repaid by a closer study of this communication. I won't destroy it. Yet awhile. All I wish is that I knew *his* address or *their* address so that I might take the war into the opposite camp. It's the only way to put a stop to it. That'd suit me down to the ground."

Dorothy smiled at his enthusiasm. The smile developed into a laugh. Evidently, Laurence considered, she was at last coming round more to his point of view.

"What are you laughing at?" he asked.

"The fool that writes and sends these ridiculous letters," she replied with a new strength and resolution in her voice. "The fool who misses the entire point," she continued; "that's what made me laugh like I did."

"Which one? Which point?" queried Laurence.

"*The* one! He writes as though a crime had been committed. Whereas I know better."

Laurence stared at her. Dorothy rattled on. "This fool who writes on Bank Holidays doesn't know what I know. He thinks Hubert's dead! But he's wrong! For I know that Hubert's not dead. He's alive!"

The room rang again with her laughter.

CHAPTER XVII

FOR some days after this, Laurence watched Dorothy closely. She slept badly and dreamed heavily. As she lay at his side, she muttered strange sentences. But, to his relief, she made no attempt to enlarge on the alarming statement which she had made with regard to Hubert. Nor did she refer to it in any way. She knew that something which she couldn't explain had caused her to break the pact she had made with Laurence, and she was annoyed to think that she had been found wanting in this respect. Moreover she wasn't able to mention Hubert now, on any account. To Laurence of all people! She knew what Laurence had said to her and she knew what she had learned from Hubert and there was a vast difference between the two. A vital difference which could not be altogether ignored. She knew that if she wanted to be happy ever again, she had to establish a basis of understanding with both the men to whom she had been wife. Her problem was how could this be most effectively settled. To solve it became the major interest of her existence. She wrestled with the problem for some days before she was able to discern even a glimmer of light. When the light did come to her, she felt greatly relieved. She even smiled on Laurence when he came home that evening. Laurence caught her mood and the meal that followed was the brightest that the Westons had enjoyed for some appreciable time. Laurence asked her about the baby and she talked with animation about the blind child.

"I think I'll pop up to town tomorrow," she said after a time; "the jaunt will do me a world of good. I feel that I simply must have a change of some kind. I'll get Mrs. O'Gorman to look after the baby for me: She's much better than she has been. Dr. Appleyard gave me a mild sedative for her when I took her to him on Monday. I shan't be away from here too long, naturally—although I *may* do a 'flick'."

Laurence approved. "By all means go, my dear. For myself I'm only too delighted at your suggestion. Go early and get back here in the late afternoon."

Dorothy nodded and said she would. That evening, whilst she was ironing in the little kitchen, he heard her talking to the baby. Her voice was light and eager. He was pleased at this fight she was putting up. He went and listened to her. A mother talking to a child! Amazing! Laurence realized that this new phase through which Dorothy was passing was going to mean a lot to him. When they went to bed he was tenderness and kindness personified. Dorothy turned to him and snuggled into his arms. He used lovers' words to her again.

"Protect me, Laurence," she said almost imploringly, "don't let them come and take me away from you."

"Or even me from you," he added, "because that would be just as bad."

Laurence Weston meant what he said.

After a time Dorothy went to sleep. Laurence gently removed his arm and laid her head softly on the pillow. Then he listened to see if she dreamt and talked in her sleep again.

"I'll tell you what," he said at breakfast the following morning, "meet me somewhere for lunch. It'll seem like old times to meet you somewhere. Do say 'yes', darling."

"All right," she said—"I don't mind. Where shall it be? 'Simpson's'?"

"That will suit me nicely," replied Laurence. "Twelve-forty-five at 'Simpson's', then—and mind you aren't late."

"Was I ever?"

"No. You weren't so bad. I've met worse."

"Then you had no business to," replied Dorothy with a flash of her old spirit.

When he had left, Dorothy waited for Mrs. O'Gorman and gave her certain necessary instructions. She caught a train to town before ten o'clock. Punctually at a quarter to one, she met Laurence and they lunched together at 'Simpson's'. He asked her where she had been and all that she had done. She made her way to the Haymarket and saw *Empty Vessels*. Garbo, she thought, was at her incomparable best.

Dorothy caught the 4.22 train out of Liverpool Street. The baby was well and happy when she arrived back and Mrs. O'Gorman declared that little Faith was and had been a perfect darling.

"She's been ever so good, Mrs. Weston—she has, really! I have had no trouble with her at all."

Dorothy thanked her for her kindness and shortly afterwards Mrs. O'Gorman left to return to her own home. Laurence came in that evening a little earlier than usual. He explained that he had been lucky enough to catch an early train. He showed great interest in Dorothy's day in town. Discussed the merits and demerits of the film she had seen and questioned her with a rather charming, if possessive, insistence as to her other calls.

"You don't know," he said, "how pleased I am to see you taking hold again. To tell the truth, I was getting distinctly worried about you."

"You needn't worry about me any longer, Laurence," she said in a strangely subdued voice; "for one thing, it doesn't do any good, and for another, it isn't worth it."

"I'm the best judge of that," replied Laurence with a smile, "so once again we'll agree to differ."

After dinner, Laurence found an excellent musical programme on the radio, to which both he and Dorothy listened with unusual interest. When Dorothy went to bed that evening she felt that she knew exactly what to say to Hubert, when next he came and visited her. When Laurence came to bed, half an hour or so later, he was whistling the catch of a song. Dorothy, knowing him as she did, wasn't certain whether this indicated that he was really light-hearted.

"There's something wrong," he said as he got into bed, "with our radio. I can't make it out. It will have to be seen to. It persists in 'fading-out'."

Dorothy nodded to him sleepily. Of what importance was the radiogram? Hubert would come again before the morning!

CHAPTER XVIII

ON THE following morning, Laurence Weston waited for the postman to come. He was anxious to receive, if possible, before he went out, an important letter. When the postman came, about twenty-two minutes past eight, he found Laurence waiting at the front door. He handed the letter to Laurence, who thanked him smilingly.

"What I've been waiting for," Laurence explained. "Didn't want to come home and find it here this evening. Would mean the waste of a day."

The postman grinned at him understandingly. Laurence called out "Good-bye" to Dorothy, waited for the reply and accompanied the postman down the garden path as far as the front gate. He waved a good morning to the postman who was evidently going in the opposite direction to himself, changed his attaché-case from one hand to the other, and made good pace to Westwood station for the 8.37 train. Sometimes, if he were extra busy, he caught the train before this, but more often than not this was his morning train. His attaché-case was a light burden on this particular morning, containing no more than a few books connected with his business and his morning paper.

On the whole, he found himself looking forward to a pleasant day. The most pleasant day perhaps for some time past. The only cloud on his horizon at the moment was the thought of his blind child. He had by this time convinced himself that his mysterious correspondent, "Harry the Hangman", knew nothing tangible and that his bark was considerably worse than ever his bite could be.

Dorothy, he was certain, had turned the corner and would give him no more trouble. When he got to the office, he took things quietly and strolled through the morning's tasks with even more than his usual smooth efficiency. When he went out he purchased a midday paper and took an early lunch.

He went to the restaurant that he favoured when he felt on good terms with himself. At the table he chose—in the corner by the window—he was joined by a tall, good-looking man whom he fancied he had seen in the restaurant before. Laurence ordered his usual good and satisfying lunch. Soup, fish, joint and a sweet. For the first time, however, his tall, good-looking companion entered into conversation with him. Laurence found him entertaining and did not resent, therefore, what might have been an intrusion. Amongst other things, he was able to discuss, with both knowledge and discernment, music, literature and the stage. Laurence found that he was enjoying his lunch rather more than was his usual custom. His companion ordered a light sherry and asked Laurence to join him. Laurence, who invariably drank water with his meal, was willing, and after a suitable interval, returned the compliment. The meal ran to its conclusion. Laurence sat back comfortably in his chair and asked for his bill. The waitress brought it. The tall man then asked for his bill and paid it at once.

"By Jove," he said with an exclamation of dismay, "I had no idea it was so late. Sitting here talking to you has caused me to lose all sense of time. That's by way of being a compliment, isn't it? I shall have to be off—I've an appointment at half past one. Good afternoon to you, sir."

"Good afternoon," returned Laurence.

After the man had gone, Laurence took his time. He was in no hurry to leave. He sat and smoked a cigarette at his leisure. At twenty minutes past one he looked at his watch. He could still stay for another five minutes and be back at the office at half past one. He looked through the midday again. No news of any kind worthy of recording. Really, this edition wasn't worth buying. After a slight argument with the waitress as to the amount of the bill, he found his gloves and prepared to take his departure. He looked round.

He mustn't forget anything. Laurence Weston prided himself upon his general efficiency.

He rose and walked towards the door. On the way there, he felt strange. His head was funny and he had come over giddy. Also he realized that something had gone wrong with his eyes. He wasn't able to see clearly. His lunch must have upset him in some way. He was worried. Then he became desperately afraid. The symptoms weren't passing from him. On the other hand, they were becoming much more acute. He felt stupefied. The next thing he knew was putting his fingers on the handle of the restaurant door. As he did so, he felt himself sinking into a deepening insensibility. Laurence Weston sank to the floor as several people rushed to his assistance. As he showed no signs of rallying, a doctor was at once sent for. He arrived in the space of ten minutes and, after a swift examination, immediately commenced artificial respiration.

"Bring me a hot sponge," he ordered. "Let the water be as hot as possible."

When the sponge was forthcoming, the doctor applied it to Laurence Weston's heart. To no avail.

"It's no good," said the doctor eventually. "I'm too late, I'm afraid. The man's dead. And unless I'm very badly mistaken, he's been poisoned." He turned to the manager. "You'd better get into touch with the Police. We may be dealing with a case of murder."

CHAPTER XIX

AFTER Dorothy had said "good-bye" to Laurence on that same morning, she was pleased to see that the baby was sleeping so nicely. The medicine which Dr. Appleyard had prescribed for her had certainly been beneficial. She decided that after she had seen to the breakfast things, she would "do out" the dining-room. It wasn't one of the days that her woman came to help her, but Dorothy's frame of mind this morning was such that she felt like working extra hard all day. It would take her mind off things. She thereupon entered the dining-room and started her self-appointed task. The time was early and she had all the morning in front of her. Like Laurence, she felt easier in her mind this morning than she had for a long time past. She felt that at last she had been able to throw off the despondencies and inhibitions which had possessed her for so long.

She looked at the clock. Laurence would be in his train by now and on his way to business. She thought of the things that made up his morning's work at the office, the duties which he had more than once discussed with her, way back in the old days. She went on working. She began to sing to herself as she worked. Yes . . . her mind was easier. Much seemed to have been taken off the burden of her soul. She smiled to herself. Suddenly her attention was aroused by a strange noise in the bungalow—a noise that sounded to be not very far away from her. Then, to her apprehension, she heard the noise of a footstep that sounded right behind her. She half turned, with the duster she had been using still in her right hand. The figure that closed in upon her seemed to her fear-haunted eyes to be vaguely familiar . . . she had seen the face before somewhere. Her head was jerked up cruelly and something fierce and frightful tightened round her throat. Everything went black . . . she fought for a few seconds with convulsive futility . . . until there came the inevitable end. Dorothy Weston sank to the floor in her own room but nobody rushed to her assistance as they did to Laurence Weston's some short time later, when the full debt to Hubert Grant had been paid.

Mrs. O'Gorman, a neighbour of the Westons, was disturbed about midday by the persistent crying of the Weston baby. The little girl cried so loudly and evidently so despairingly after a time, that Mrs. O'Gorman came to the rather unwilling conclusion that this crying was something she wasn't able to explain or understand. The child invariably ceased crying when Mrs. Weston picked her up. It then occurred to Mrs. O'Gorman that she hadn't seen or heard Mrs. Weston since breakfast time that morning. She listened to the baby crying. It had been going on now for nearly half an hour. After a time she began to feel somewhat anxious. Later, she decided to investigate. There was something here which she couldn't understand. She was able to use the side-entrance to enter the Weston bungalow. She had used this means once or twice before. The kitchenette was empty. The noise of the baby crying came from the room which Mrs. O'Gorman knew to be the Westons' bedroom. She went in here to find little Faith Weston crying in her cradle. There was no sign of Mrs. Weston, and Mrs. O'Gorman's anxiety increased. She picked up the child and endeavoured to comfort her. In this, being no stranger to the baby, Mrs. O'Gorman was partly successful. She laid the child back in the cradle in the hope of obtaining a few minutes' respite, which she would be able to devote to further exploration.

A few short steps took her into the dining-room and directly she arrived here her heart turned cold with horror. She saw the body of Dorothy Weston, her neighbour, lying on the hearthrug in front of her. She knew that this was death at which she looked. She had no doubt of it. Then her sharp eyes caught sight of a white slip of paper which had been pinned to the front of Dorothy Weston's dress. Fearful of touching or disturbing anything, Mrs. O'Gorman summoned all her courage to go down on one knee to see what this piece of paper was. She saw that there were words typed on this white paper slip. She read these words with an emotion of increasing horror.

Wishing you a happy landing on the other side of the Styx, where doubtless Hubert will arrange to meet you, I remain, sincerely yours, "Harry the Hangman".

Mrs. O'Gorman rose to her feet again, gasping. What on earth should she do? What could she do? And there was that poor darling baby all alone in the house—with this cold, dead mother. Mrs. O'Gorman shivered. She thought of Dr. Appleyard. She knew that he was the Westons' doctor. Forgetting entirely that there was a telephone in the hall, she remembered there was a telephone kiosk not very far away. She could run to it quite easily. Wouldn't take her much more than a minute. She hesitated. Was this the right procedure for her to pursue? Ought she to go to the Police first—before she called in any doctor? Mrs. O'Gorman's fright and fear increased. To think that she should be faced with a situation of this kind. Then she cast her cares aside. She would call the friendly doctor rather than fly to the evils which she knew not of. She 'phoned in the kiosk to Dr. Appleyard. Fortunately for her peace of mind, he happened to be in. He listened to Mrs. O'Gorman's agonized story, realized the probability of the tragedy behind it and told her to get back to the address concerned to which he would come at once. Mrs. O'Gorman was much relieved to obey. When she returned she waited in the hall of the abode of death for Dr. Appleyard to arrive. She hardly realized that the baby Faith had started to cry again and was still crying.

The doctor was as good as his word. He was at "The Wave" in less than five minutes. As he entered he strode past Mrs. O'Gorman and said curtly "Where is she? Take me to her immediately."

Mrs. O'Gorman obeyed. Dr. Appleyard at once went down to the body of Dorothy Weston.

"Dear, dear," Mrs. O'Gorman heard him say, "this is too bad. Nothing I can do. Nothing at all. Been dead three hours or so. Yes—quite that. Her watch has stopped at ten minutes past ten."

Mrs. O'Gorman asked a question.

"What was it, Doctor, that killed her? Her heart?"

She saw that Dr. Appleyard was staring at the dead woman's neck and at the message pinned on her clothing. At some peculiar marks on her neck to say nothing of the other matter. The doctor muttered something to himself which Mrs. O'Gorman was unable to catch. Suddenly he stood up and looked at *her*, gravely.

"Mrs. O'Gorman," he said, "this is a nasty job. A much worse job than I anticipated when you 'phoned me."

He looked round the room, as though he were in search of something.

"Is there anything I can do, Doctor?" inquired Mrs. O'Gorman fearfully. "Because if there is—please tell me."

"Yes," he said slowly. "While I stay here. Go to the telephone in the hall and ring up the Police. Ask for Inspector Chetwode—say I told you to 'phone. Tell him to come here at once. That I'm waiting for him. Say nothing beyond that. Not half a word! This is a case of 'Wilful Murder'."

Mrs. O'Gorman's eyes and mouth opened in amazement.

BOOK THREE

INVESTIGATION OF THE WESTON MURDERS BY ANTHONY LOTHERINGTON BATHURST

CHAPTER I

IT IS conceivable that the murder of Laurence Weston in the "Greatorex" Restaurant would never have been brought to the notice of Sir Austin Kemble, Commissioner of Police, New Scotland Yard, had it not been for the more sensational murder of Dorothy Weston at some time during the morning of the same day. Chief Inspector MacMorran sat in his room with the Commissioner.

"The Sudmore people have been on the 'phone, Sir Austin, and asked us to take over. In view of the Weston murder up here that we already have on our hands. It's a case of husband and wife."

"Tell me, MacMorran." Sir Austin endeavoured, unsuccessfully, to look important.

The Inspector recounted the details. Sir Austin's brows corrugated. "Amazing," he said, "really amazing," as MacMorran concluded his story.

"There must be some connection between the two crimes, sir, and I've no doubt that the same man killed both Mr. and Mrs. Weston. Our job will be to find him and prove it."

"'Harry the Hangman'," quoted the Commissioner reflectively. "Does that name suggest anything to you, Inspector?"

"No, sir. Not a thing. It's a blind, no doubt. As I see things, this fellow strangled Mrs. Weston soon after the husband had gone to business and then popped up to town in order to get him. He hung about until Weston went to lunch, followed him into the 'Greatorex' and then slipped him the poison in some way."

"Why?" demanded Sir Austin blandly.

MacMorran shrugged his shoulders. "Who can say at this stage of the case, sir? Revenge, I should say, if I were forced to make a choice. The triangle again—verra likely. Disappointed lover lurking in the background. I'd like to bet on it."

Sir Austin Kemble turned over the first report of the restaurant murder.

Statement by Dr. Inescort, called to the "Greatorex" Restaurant about 1.35 p.m. "Death in my opinion from poisoning. Probably cyanide of potassium."

Statement by Divisional Surgeon, Dr. Sugden. Agreement with Dr. Inescort's opinion. Deceased died of poisoning by cyanide of potassium—impossible to say how administered. Autopsy 10 a.m. tomorrow.

"H'm," grunted Sir Austin, "highly eloquent, I must say. Clear as mud," he added almost venomously. Suddenly he wheeled round on the Inspector. "I've made up my mind, MacMorran. I trust you won't be displeased. If you are, say so at once. Don't bottle it up."

"I'll endeavour not to be, sir—whatever it is that you've decided."

"I'm going to call in Bathurst. Before any time's wasted. Don't think I can do better. Now what do you say to that?"

The Inspector coughed behind a large hand. A hand which, in the earlier days of his career, had darkened the sky on traffic control. "It's all the same to me, Sir Austin. Whatever you wish, although I don't fancy there'll be much in this case—or rather these cases—when we get right down to them. I'm convinced the solution will be a simple one when we find it."

"Yes. When you find it," growled the Commissioner, "that's just the point."

The telephone-bell rang on his desk. "See what that is, Inspector, will you? If it's Capper, tell him I'm engaged. Man's becoming a damned nuisance. Never lets me alone. If I've told him once, I've told him a— "

"It's not Major Capper, Sir Austin, it's the Sudmore Police with regard to the Weston murders. Shall I take it, sir?"

"Yes—certainly. But don't tell them anything, Unless you have to. Don't believe in it. Never did. Let the other fellow talk."

Having delivered himself of this eminently sound piece of advice, Sir Austin proceeded to chuckle. He was still chuckling when he heard MacMorran say "certainly and thank you very much" and replace the receiver. When MacMorran turned to him he saw that the Inspector was looking grave and certainly rather worried.

"What is it, Inspector?" demanded the Commissioner. "What's the trouble?"

"There's a new development down there, Sir Austin," returned MacMorran. "The Sudmore authorities report that the murdered woman, Mrs. Weston, was formerly, that is to say before her second marriage to Laurence Weston, the wife of a man named Hubert Grant. This Hubert Grant met his death in most mysterious circumstances almost two years ago. At Bullen—in Surrey. His body was taken out of the river there and it was never discovered how he got into the water. The Coroner returned an open verdict. Funny," added MacMorran contemplatively.

The Commissioner stared at him across the room. "Funny?" he echoed questioningly.

"Yes—funny—three of 'em dying violent deaths in the space of two years! Don't you agree with me, sir?"

Sir Austin tapped his front teeth with his thumbnail. "I do, Inspector—most certainly—I do. And I'm damned glad I've decided to send for Anthony Bathurst."

Chief Inspector Andrew MacMorran grinned. "I won't say that I'm sorry myself, Sir Austin."

CHAPTER II

WHEN Anthony Bathurst was shown into the Commissioner's room at New Scotland Yard, he was delighted to find MacMorran already in there. He shook hands with Sir Austin and then with Andrew MacMorran in such a manner that it left no doubts as to his pleasure in answering the invitation which had been sent him. The Commissioner ran his eye over the tall, lithe figure, clothed in a light-grey suit of superb quality and cut. He noticed how well Anthony Bathurst looked.

"You look very fit, Bathurst. What's the secret?"

"Moderation in all things, Sir Austin. Even to the degree of my admiration for the 'Yard'." Anthony's eyes twinkled.

"Sit down," said the Commissioner. "I told MacMorran to send for you. We're up against a case that's absolutely after your own heart."

"I'm delighted to hear you say that," returned Anthony. "I should hate to run to rust. But what's the trouble? All I hope is that it's fresh."

"Dates back as far as yesterday. Not a minute farther. Tell Bathurst, Inspector; give him the facts."

"I presume," said Anthony, "that you're alluding to the Weston murders? Am I right in my presumption?" He smiled.

"You are," MacMorran answered him. "First time. How did you guess?"

"My dear Andrew! Don't forget my most admirable morning paper. My *Morning Message*. Could I fail to be struck by the extraordinary coincidence? A husband and wife murdered on the same day! And forty miles apart at that! As far as I am able to remember, the affair is unique in the annals of crime. A most attractive crime, Andrew, without a doubt. The facts, please. Start at this end, will you? With the murder of the husband at the 'Greatorex' Restaurant."

MacMorran nodded, used his file of notes and recounted the details of the murder of Laurence Weston. His recital included the result of Dr. Sugden's autopsy of that morning.

"May I see Sugden's notes?" asked Anthony.

MacMorran pushed them over to him. Anthony read them carefully. "Poison—eh? Cyanide of potassium. Introduced into the body but a few moments before the man died. And Weston had just dined at the restaurant! Extraordinary! What did his meal consist of, Andrew?"

Anthony handed back the Divisional Surgeon's report. MacMorran answered his question. He detailed the various courses.

"Tomato soup."

"I might have known," murmured Anthony.

"A small piece of halibut. Roast beef, potatoes and cabbage."

"Exactly," said Anthony.

"And finished up with apple pie and custard."

"Of course—inevitable! Did he dine alone?"

"No—there was a man at the table with him. A man whom so far we haven't been able to trace. Although they spoke during the meal, the waitress who served them is of the opinion that they were strangers to each other."

"Who went out first?"

"The other man. He left the restaurant a few minutes before Weston got up to go out."

"I see. What did Weston drink?"

MacMorran consulted his paper again. "To begin with—water. After that he had two glasses of a light sherry. This, by the way, I am told, was unusual for him. He usually drank nothing but water with his lunch. Apparently, from what the waitress tells me, each bought the other a glass of sherry. There was no trace of poison in Weston's last-used glass. I suggest that the other man asked Weston to join him in the first glass, and that afterwards Weston returned the compliment?"

"Very likely. I take it then, Andrew, from what you have just told me, that Weston usually lunched at the 'Greatorex'?"

"That is so, Mr. Bathurst. He lunched there fairly regularly. Nearly always alone."

"What was he by profession?"

"In an accountant's and auditor's firm. Their place isn't more than five minutes from the 'Greatorex'."

"Tell me this, Andrew. If you hadn't heard of the wife's death at Sudmore, would you have thought of Weston's death in terms of murder—or of suicide?"

"Exactly," cut in Sir Austin Kemble, "that's the very question I was about to ask. Answer that, Inspector."

MacMorran pursed his lips before replying. "Murder, Mr. Bathurst," he eventually answered.

"Tell me why, Andrew."

"Because he got up from his seat and walked to the door. Had he intended to die and had administered the poison to himself, he'd have stayed still in his seat—and died there. Why give himself an entirely unnecessary effort?"

Mr. Bathurst rubbed, his hands again. "Excellent. I agree with you, Andrew. I agree with you *in toto*."

Sir Austin also entered the lists. "And I too, Bathurst. Strikes me as a piece of eminently sound reasoning."

"Anything found on the body, Andrew?"

"Nothing at all out of the way, Mr. Bathurst. Cash and a few private papers. Nothing to cause the slightest comment. I've been through them all myself."

"Good. Nothing, then, to be picked up in that direction?"

"Afraid not, Mr. Bathurst." The Inspector shook his head.

"I'll accept that position then. Now let me take you to the other end of our story. To the Sudmore end. Where Mrs. Weston died. Let me have the facts there, please."

MacMorran consulted more notes and recounted more details. Anthony listened attentively. Right from the statement taken from Mrs. Lucy O'Gorman through the medical opinion of Dr. Appleyard to the bizarre message from "Harry the Hangman".

"That last part," asserted Mr. Bathurst eventually, "seems 'phoney' to me. What do you think yourself, Andrew?"

"I'm inclined to agree, Mr. Bathurst. But it's difficult to say without having seen the actual outfit."

"Death by strangulation—eh? Murderer crept up behind her and took her unawares, I suppose. We've had instances of that before. I should like to have seen that body. Too late now. Shall have to go down there, though. Sooner the better."

"And what about visiting the 'Greatorex', Mr. Bathurst? Is that on the bill, too?"

Anthony deliberated for a few moments. "Yes, Andrew. I had better do both. I'll come along to the 'Greatorex' now with you. It will be as well. Before the waitress's memory wilts and dies. Though Pelmanism should flourish indeed midst pies and puddings and pastry." Anthony rose. "Goodbye, Sir Austin. And thanks for the retainer. I'll be seeing you."

The Commissioner shook hands with him heartily. "Let me know when you go to Sudmore. I'll run down with you. If I can manage it. It'll be like old times again."

"Sudmore this afternoon, sir. Not a minute later. Where shall I pick you up?"

"Going by road, Bathurst?"

"Yes, sir. I thought so. If that's O.K. with you."

"Suits me," returned Sir Austin. "Two-forty-five here this afternoon."

"Andrew," said Anthony Bathurst, "come along."

Inspector MacMorran turned and grabbed his hat.

CHAPTER III

ANTHONY and MacMorran went into the "Greatorex" together. The Inspector had arranged for them to close for half an hour while he and Anthony had their walk round. It was comparatively early and considerably before the busy period started so the proprietors raised no objection to MacMorran's suggestion.

"By the way, Bathurst," he said as they stood on the threshold of the restaurant, "something I forgot to tell you. About the Sudmore end of the case. Mrs. Weston's first husband—a man by the name of Hubert Grant—was drowned about two years ago, in rather remarkable circumstances."

Anthony stopped short of the door of the restaurant. "Where?" he inquired.

"He was drowned in the River Murmur, near the little town of Bullen, in Surrey. The Coroner's was an open verdict. There was scarcely any evidence to show how the body got into the water."

Anthony turned the knob on the door. "Interesting," he said. "I'll come back to that later on. Here's the manager, I fancy."

The manager came forward. MacMorran explained matters to him. He nodded. "What would you like us to do, Inspector?"

"Take us to the table where Weston sat for his lunch. And have the waitress who served him standing by. We may want some questions answered."

"Very good, Inspector."

The manager went away for a moment to give certain orders to members of the staff. He came back. "This way, gentlemen, if you please."

MacMorran and Anthony followed him. "This is the table where Mr. Weston lunched. He was almost a 'regular' here. The table was as good as reserved for him. He liked to sit in this corner."

"By the window," commented Anthony.

"Yes—overlooking the street. Or rather looking into the street." The manager smiled at the correction of his own mistake.

"H'm," said Anthony. "Bring the girl who attended to him, will you, please?"

The manager raised his eyebrows. "Miss Gibson, please?" A dark, pale-faced girl stepped forward. Anthony smiled at her.

"Please show me the seat in which Mr. Weston sat."

The girl gave the indication.

"So that the left-hand side of his face was towards the door?"

"Yes, sir." The girl nodded.

"Now show me, please, where Mr. Weston's companion sat."

"Exactly opposite to Mr. Weston, sir," replied Miss Gibson.

"So that Mr. Weston's glass was on his right and the other man's glass on his left? That right?"

Again the girl nodded. "Yes, sir. That's right."

"Did you know this other man?"

"No, sir."

"Seen him before?"

"Yes, sir. In here. Two or three times before, I should say from memory. But he didn't always sit at this table."

"Were he and Weston all right together? Did they seem on good terms?"

"Yes, sir. Very friendly indeed, sir. They bought drinks for each other. There was no quarrelling or anything."

"And this man went out of the restaurant and left Weston here?"

"Yes, sir. There was about five minutes between them, I should think." She stopped.

"Well?" prompted Anthony.

"More than five minutes, sir. Because I made a little mistake on Mr. Weston's bill and he pointed it out to me. I've just remembered. I added the bill up wrong. Say that the interval between them going out was about eight minutes. You'll be nearer."

Anthony thought for a moment or so. "How much was this mistake that you mention? What did it amount to?"

Miss Gibson furrowed her brows in thought. "Fourpence."

"Which way?"

"Which way? How do you mean, sir?"

"Was it against Mr. Weston or in his favour?"

"Oh—I see what you mean. It was against him. I had charged him fourpence too much."

"And he complained about it?"

"Not exactly 'complained'. He just pointed it out. He wasn't in a temper about it—or even hot and bothered. He simply called my attention to the mistake."

"What did he say? Can you remember his exact words or near enough?"

Miss Gibson produced a little "moue". She conveyed the impression to the others that Mr. Bathurst was asking rather a lot. She nevertheless "played up" as well as she could. "Mr. Weston called me and said, 'My dear young lady, you must stop regarding me as a millionaire because I assure, you I am not one'. As far as I can remember, they're pretty well the exact words he used."

"Thank you, Miss Gibson—I'm certainly in your debt." Anthony turned to the Inspector. "I shall have to see Sugden. There are one or two questions I must ask him."

MacMorran nodded. "Right you are. Leave that to me. I'll see to that for you."

Anthony went back to Miss Gibson. "Forgive me if I ask you one more question."

The girl nodded.

"When Mr. Weston was alone at the table and discussed the amount of his bill with you, did you notice what drink he had in his glass?"

"No, sir."

"You didn't notice, for instance, whether he had drunk the whole of his second glass of sherry?"

Miss Gibson shook her head. "No, sir. I didn't notice anything like that. But when he got up to go, he had drunk it all."

Anthony nodded and walked from the place where Weston had sat to the restaurant door. MacMorran watched him. Anthony came back to the Inspector.

"I believe, Andrew," he said, "that all my experience tells me that there is little delay in the action of cyanide of potassium. In fact, I believe that its effect is very nearly instantaneous. What do you say?"

"I agree, Mr. Bathurst."

"Well, in that case, the poison must have been given to Weston just before he got up to leave the restaurant. Seems pretty conclusive to me—that."

"It certainly does, Mr. Bathurst. Whichever way you look at it. I came to the same conclusion. myself."

Anthony swung round to the manager. "Well—good morning, sir! And to you, Miss Gibson. Many thanks for the assistance."

He and Andrew took their departure. "Two-forty-five at the 'Yard', Andrew. I'll pick up both you and Sir Austin Kemble."

The doors of the "Greatorex" restaurant closed behind them.

Miss Gibson tossed her head and flung cutlery on tables.

CHAPTER IV

"I KNOW the Westwood Road," said Anthony as the powerful car neared the seaside town of Sudmore. "I used to travel in this direction quite a lot a few years ago."

"A woman?" queried Sir Austin with a hint of censure in his voice.

"No, sir. Sport."

The Commissioner looked a trifle taken aback.

"I arranged for the Sudmore Police to be at the bungalow." This from MacMorran.

"Good," exclaimed Mr. Bathurst. "I was beginning to be afraid we might have to wait for them.".

MacMorran leant forward and touched him on the shoulder. "Here we are, Mr. Bathurst. Next turning on the right. Westwood Road. The name of the house is 'The Wave'."

"'Wave'—or 'Waves'?" queried Anthony.

"'Wave', sir. Singular."

"Very," remarked Mr. Bathurst. He then threw a remark to Mac-Morran over his shoulder. "The owner must have been poetic—with a penchant for Shelley, Andrew. Percy Bysshe! Wonderful bloke, too!"

"Who? The owner?"

"No—the aforesaid P.B.S."

MacMorran changed the subject. "Here we are," he exclaimed. "Second on the left from here. 'The Wave'."

Anthony stopped the car and they descended. Directly MacMorran led the way in, two men in plain clothes came to meet them. MacMorran shook hands and made the necessary introductions.

"Inspector Chetwode and Sergeant Gerrard, sir."

The five men went into the bungalow. The Commissioner led the way. Anthony looked round. Inspector Chetwode pointed out where Mrs. Weston's body had been found.

Anthony went over and looked at the side-entrance down which entrance and exit were so simple. He came back and listened to what the Police were saying. Suddenly he heard Chetwode say something to Sir Austin Kemble which arrested his attention.

"What was that, Inspector?" he asked. "Would you mind repeating that for me?"

"Why, yes, sir. What I said was this. 'That the noise of the wireless set probably prevented Mrs. Weston from hearing her murderer approaching.'"

Anthony looked puzzled. "What makes you say that, Inspector Chetwode?"

"The wireless set was switched on when the Police were called to the body. One of the men noticed the light on the indicator."

Anthony was more puzzled than ever. He shook his head. "I'm afraid I still don't understand. Correct me if I'm wrong: The facts, as I understand them, were these. Mrs. O'Gorman, a neighbour of Mrs. Weston's, came in. After a time she called up Dr. Appleyard on the telephone and he came along. Those facts all right?"

"Yes, Mr. Bathurst. Quite right."

"Well—what strikes me is this. Why didn't either of them notice that the wireless was on? Surely it would have struck a discordant note—to say the least of it? Don't you see my point?"

Chetwode nodded, but embarked on an effort of explanation. "Yes. I see what you mean. But perhaps I can help you. In a way you're inclined to jump at conclusions. This wireless business, as I've put it to you, isn't all plain sailing. It's a radiogram. And although it was switched on, when my chaps arrived, no sounds were coming through of any programme. Which means that there's a fault in the set somewhere that had caused it to 'fade out'. Does that help you at all, Mr. Bathurst?"

Anthony rubbed his chin with his fingers. "H'm! Interesting. I hope you aren't forgetting its significance, Inspector."

MacMorran was looking puzzled—uneasy. Inspector Chetwode handed to Sir Austin the slip of typescript which had been signed by "Harry the Hangman".

"Come over here, Bathurst, will you? You'd better have a look at this."

Anthony read the typed words.

Wishing you a happy landing on the other side of the Styx where doubtless Hubert will arrange to meet you. I remain, sincerely yours, "Harry the Hangman".

He looked towards Chetwode and Sergeant Gerrard.

"Hubert, I take it, gentlemen, was the name of Mrs. Weston's first husband?"

"Yes, Mr. Bathurst. His name was Hubert Grant."

"Drowned, wasn't he?"

"Yes, Funny business—so the Bullen Police tell me. Never satisfactorily cleared up."

"Did you make any contacts with it, Inspector?"

"No, sir. No inquiries in connection with it came this way."

"I was wondering if the Police on the case ran against Weston at all during the inquiry?"

"Don't think so, sir. From what I've been able to gather. But you will be able to refer to their file, sir, if you should want it."

"Afraid I shall. Thanks very much." Mr. Bathurst took the slip of paper over to the light. After a few moments spent in examination, he beckoned to the others to go over to him. "This paper's been cut from somewhere. See the indication on the edge? Point is, was the paper cut prior to the typing being done or was more typing done and this piece specially cut off from it?"

Chetwode took it and looked. "The latter, I think, sir. It would be a very small piece to be cut off first and then used."

"I'm inclined to agree with you, Inspector Chetwode."

"Well, Bathurst," cut in the Commissioner with a certain irritability, "what do you make of it?"

"Oh—it's murder, all right. Both Mr. and Mrs. Weston have been murdered. And in each instance considerable cunning has been used. It's our job to find the murderer. And it's going to be difficult."

"I have a theory," interpolated Sir Austin; "it's been insistent now for a long time. Weston murdered his wife and then committed suicide! How's that? Does it appeal to you?"

Chetwode broke in. "When Weston left the house his wife was alive. That's been proved. By independent testimony. Weston went straight to the railway-station about half past eight and from there to his office. In all probability, from the evidence of her watch, Mrs. Weston died at ten minutes past ten. All Weston's movements have been verified."

Anthony listened to him carefully. Sir Austin looked a little annoyed at this summary disposal of his theories. When Inspector Chetwode had finished, Anthony came in.

"Now it's my turn, sir. With regard to Weston himself. I can assure you that Laurence Weston did not commit suicide. Two pieces of evidence in connection with his death cannot possibly be overlooked." He smiled at the Commissioner. "So that between us, Inspector Chetwode and I have been rather merciless to your theory, I'm afraid."

Sir Austin had the grace to smile back. He said no more, however.

"Any finger-prints?" inquired MacMorran of Sergeant Gerrard.

"No. The doors of the room seem to have been open—the murderer came in, did the job, and walked out again. No doubt used the side-entrance."

"Anything missing?"

"Nothing at all. That's as far as I can tell. Certainly nothing of value. Mrs. Weston's money was untouched. That's a pretty good guide in itself."

Anthony heard these remarks and carefully noted them. He went over and spoke to MacMorran. The latter nodded. "I'll speak to the Guv'nor," he said—"that'll be all right."

"Also," said Anthony, "there's the matter of that wireless. I should like an expert's report on it. On its condition. Just as it is. Just as it was at the time of the murder. I should also like to have a few minutes' conversation with Mrs. O'Gorman and also the doctor, Dr. Appleyard."

"That can be arranged at once," replied Chetwode. "Before you return to town this afternoon."

Anthony and MacMorran, accompanied by the Commissioner, made a tour of the bungalow and its garden. In the bedroom, obviously used by the two Westons, Anthony came across a wooden box. In this box was a collection of cards, banded together with an india-rubber ring. He took them out, as their appearance struck him as curious—unusual. He soon saw what they were. They were trade postcards, issued by various firms of coal merchants with the respective price lists printed on the back of each card. The price lists covered the various grades of coal and coke. Anthony saw that they were all addressed to "Mrs. D. Grant, 'Red Roofs', Ridgway Gardens, Bullen, Surrey". Somewhat to his surprise, he saw that they had been sent by various firms of coal merchants whose addresses were all over the London area. None of them was local. "The Tees Main Colliery Co., Paddington", "Rothwell and Stuart, Kings Cross", "Messrs. Harrington and Lovelock, Westbourne Grove", "Adam Arnold & Sons, St. Pancras", "Errington, Lockett and Co., Chalk Farm", "Davey Jones, Lockyer & Co., Willesden". The foregoing names were typical examples. Anthony went through the cards one by one. Yes . . . all London addresses without an exception. What had been Mrs. Grant's interest in coal and coke? In all, there were twenty-two. In each instance, the addresses had been type-written, with two exceptions. These exceptions were cards from "Beckett and Somerville, Canning Town E." and from "Hoare, Hatch and Sons, London Wall". In these two cases the address had been written and the handwriting, strangely enough, was the same in each instance.

Anthony found this fact difficult to understand—unless the two firms concerned employed the same agent. Yet Canning Town and

London Wall were a reasonable distance apart. He made a note of the two names. He had a friend who had been appointed as Local Fuel Overseer to a London Borough during the second German War. He would make inquiries as to whether there were any connection between these two firms. On the whole, Anthony found these coal "trade-cards" both interesting and intriguing. Again—why had they been retained? Brought from the house in Bullen to this residence in Sudmore. Wherein could they be in any way worthy of retention? The argument was there at once that they represented something more than their ordinary significance. Anthony Bathurst felt more interested in the case than ever. He showed them to MacMorran.

"What do you make of these, Andrew?"

MacMorran, looking puzzled, glanced through them. "Had a relation in the coal trade, I should think. There are no marks on any of them."

He handed them back to Anthony Bathurst. Anthony slipped the pack into his pocket. After having learned nothing from either Dr. Appleyard or Mrs. O'Gorman, on the way home he turned to the Commissioner.

"Well, sir, did you pick up anything in the Weston bungalow?"

"Can't say that I did, Bathurst. As far as I could see, there wasn't a lot to be picked up. What did you think yourself?"

"As I see things, there are two highly important clues, Sir Austin— the incident of the radiogram—and these coal trade cards." Anthony fished in his pocket. "Have a look at 'em, sir."

He handed the pack over to the Commissioner. Sir Austin played with them for over ten minutes.

CHAPTER V

ANTHONY Lotherington Bathurst studied the report of Victor Gosling, "Radio Engineer" to the firm of "Oliver Saxon and Co., High Street, Sudmore". This report ran as follows:

I have examined the Radiogram at "The Wave", Westwood Road, Sudmore, and beg to report as under.

"The fault in the set is due entirely to the switch. The switch is worn and a condition of looseness has resulted which causes an intermittent 'fade-out'. Reception will be good for a time and then suddenly 'fade-out'. If the set be then switched off and switched on again almost immediately, reception will be re-established. This will happen with disturbing regularity."

Anthony considered the report for some time. He began to realize the implications which the report established. There was much food for thought here. On the other hand, a further examination of the coal price lists had failed to reveal anything more. There was nothing whatever on them beyond the address and the prices of the different grades of fuel. With regard to the agency question, his friend who had been Local Fuel Overseer had been unable to help him. He looked at the clock. The time was a quarter to eleven. MacMorran was due that morning in a quarter of an hour's time. Anthony hoped that the Inspector would bring with him both Dr. Sugden and certain vital information. Anthony wasn't disappointed. Punctually at eleven o'clock, MacMorran arrived accompanied by the Divisional Surgeon. The Inspector had always been reliable on time.

"Before we start, Andrew," said Mr. Bathurst, "I want to have a few words with our good friend the doctor here. In this particular respect, he's the man in the case who can help me."

Sugden smiled. He knew Bathurst of old. "Shoot, Bathurst," he invited. "As far as I'm concerned, this case is pretty well plain sailing."

"Right, Doctor. I will. Now tell me this. Weston died of poisoning. Cyanide of potassium. Right?"

"Absolutely. No doubt of any kind about that."

"Good, then. Am I right in thinking that the action of this particular poison is extremely quick?"

"You are. Extremely so. It loses no time in doing its dirty and deadly work."

"So that Weston must have had that poison given to him just a few minutes before he died. Yes?"

Sugden nodded. "In my opinion, just before he got up to walk out of the restaurant."

"Good again. That's what I was hoping you would say."

"Glad to have you satisfied. Know what a beggar you are." Sugden smiled again.

Anthony came at him with more questions. "What were the contents of the stomach, Doctor?"

Sugden referred to certain notes that he took from his breast pocket. "He had breakfasted, probably about six hours before, on porridge, bread, bacon and egg. At his last meal—there were indications that he had eaten heartily, by the way—he had partaken of beef, vegetables and an apple dish. Probably apple pie. Oh—and fish. I found halibut and halibut oil. The latter in small quantities."

"And of drink, Doctor?"

"Sherry—and water, I should say. Now what else do you want to ask me?"

It was obvious that the Divisional Surgeon enjoyed his encounter with Anthony Bathurst. *"Bon chat, bon rat"*, he used to say.

"Was Weston a healthy man?"

"Absolutely. Both healthy and well-nourished. And in top-hole condition. Barring accidents he should have lived to a ripe old age. In build and general stature he wasn't unlike yourself, Bathurst. In other words—a fine specimen physically."

Sugden's eyes twinkled. Anthony drummed on the table with his fingers. "Forgive the next question, Sugden. How do you think the poison was administered?"

"Weston took it through his mouth just before he rose from the table. Beyond that, I can say nothing. It would be absurd and extremely unprofessional to guess. There you are, my dear Bathurst. In the words of my newspaper-seller, 'you can pick the bones out of that'."

"Thank you, Doctor. Then I won't trouble you any more."

"In that case I'll be off. I've a couple of P.M.'s to get through before lunch. Good-bye. If there's anything more you should want to ask me, don't hesitate to give me a tinkle."

Sugden dashed out. Anthony turned to Andrew MacMorran.

"What have you got for me, Andrew?"

MacMorran handed over several green dockets. "What you asked for. *(a)* Dossier of Hubert Grant. *(b)* Complete accounts of the inquiries into Grant's death at Bullen. With statements of all witnesses interviewed by the Police. *(c)* Full report of proceedings at the Coroner's inquest. That lot satisfy you?"

"Don't know yet, Andrew. Shall have to wait and see. Depends on what I pick up. You can never tell what the Police have missed, Andrew!" The grey eyes gleamed with the Bathurst banter.

"Well," returned MacMorran, "you always did have a liking for ancient history—you can have your fill there. Fair revel in it."

"Had you been through it?"

"More or less. Don't *think* you'll find anything. And if you're looking for Weston in that woodpile—you won't find him. I'll present you with that from the kick-off. It was Grant himself who was playing the game, not his missus. Not she with him. That came out in the evidence. Still—you have a rout round yourself—there's nothing like it for your own peace of mind. When shall I come and see you again?"

"Tomorrow," returned Anthony—"same time."

"By the way," added MacMorran, "I may be able to save you some more trouble. The note from 'Harry the Hangman' was *not* typed on the same machine as the one found in Grant's pocket. In case you think so. I've checked up on 'em."

CHAPTER VI

THE following is the Tudor Police file report on Hubert Grant. It had been compiled by Inspector Sim.

Body of man identified as "Hubert Grant", address "Red Roofs", Ridgway Gardens, Bullen, Surrey. Was taken from River Murmur February 11th. Body been in the water some hours. Fully clothed. No hat.

Here followed details of the clothes with which Anthony, at the moment, was unconcerned.

Death from drowning. No signs of physical violence . . . body that of a man of middle age (subsequently stated by widow to be forty-two years of age), fair hair, blue eyes, small fair moustache, teeth even and regular . . . short-sighted (habitually wore glasses

*out of doors), two moles on chest, one and also vaccination mark
on left arm, five pock marks on chest. Probably from chicken-pox
when an infant. Height approx. 5 feet 10 ins., weight 12 st 11 lb.
Body healthy and in good condition considering man's age . . .*

Anthony read on—he wanted details and particulars that
belonged more to the personal life of the dead man. He eventually
came to what he desired.

*Deputy Treasurer of Tudor, Surrey. Appointed four years ago.
Entered Treasurer's Department at age of 18—24 years previously. Worked his way up. Popular amongst staff—on the whole.
No financial difficulties. Married, with one child—daughter, Frances, aged ten. Reputation and character both pretty good. Nothing
known against him. Query vices? None to speak of—according
to nearly all accounts. Expected home on day of death at about
seven o'clock in the evening—gathering of friends—social evening—card forty (see various statements in other dockets). Was
observed to leave his office at the Town Hall, Tudor, at approx.
5.5. p.m. Was also seen at Tudor station and afterwards on the
platform there at 5.17. Undoubtedly caught the train to Bullen
at 5.21 and almost certainly alighted at Bullen station. Porter at
Tudor station stated that Grant was seen to enter train. Porter's
name William Colton, 17 Burgess Avenue, Tudor. All effects left to
widow—including insurance (Meteor Insurance Society) amount-
ing to £1000. From survey of all facts brought to light concerning
Hubert Grant, suicide extremely unlikely. All appearances suggest
that Grant had assignation with a woman whom he met when he
left the train at Bullen station. The note found in the dead man's
pocket (see separate file) strongly supports this theory, which,
however, was vigorously denied by Grant's parents, Ralph and
Constance Grant. Mr. and Mrs. Grant senior, during interview,
and under stress of considerable emotion, expressed themselves
as absolutely convinced that there was no woman in their son's
life beyond his wife, Dorothy Grant . . .*

Anthony read on, searching for more details, but found nothing more that he regarded as having any real importance. He then

turned to one of the other dockets, containing a number of individual statements. The first which he read had been taken from

"Bernard Taylor Linklater, Borough Treasurer of Tudor." Confirmed that Grant had no worries or difficulties of any kind, as far as he knew. He was an able, efficient officer whose work never gave the slightest cause for dissatisfaction or complaint. He (Linklater) had said good night to Grant just before five o'clock. Scouted the idea of suicide and expressed himself as "amazed" that Grant could have had what Linklater described as "an illicit feminine influence in his life". As evidence in his faith in Grant's ability and integrity, Linklater stated "upon my approaching retirement on Superannuation, should have had no hesitation in recommending Hubert Grant to the Finance and General Purposes Sub-Committee as my successor".

Anthony smiled—he had met people of this type before. He continued his reading.

He was on excellent terms with Grant and had not had an angry word with him "all the time we have worked together as Chief and Deputy".

Again Anthony read on for a time, to find nothing further to interest him. He thereupon turned his attention to other statements.

Mrs. Dorothy Grant. Widow of Hubert Grant. Aged thirty-one. Has complete alibi for the whole of the evening when the tragedy took place. Friends with her from the early part of the afternoon and right the way through until the following morning (see various statements taken by the Police). Her character blameless and to all appearances beyond suspicion. No sign or suggestion of third party in the background—query a lover somewhere? No trace of anything or anybody likely to fill this bill. This—after exhaustive inquiries. Three women with Dorothy Grant during the afternoon. Maureen Townsend, Ethel Thornhill and Ella Fanshawe. All friends of both the Grants. None of these women could possibly have been the woman who presumably met Hubert Grant between Bullen station and his home. Other guests present later—Richard Fan-

shawe, Roy Thornhill. Respective husbands of the two women of these names. All these people interviewed subsequently and several statements taken—none of which threw any light on the fate of Hubert Grant. One guest who should have been present at the Grant's house that evening but who failed to put in an appearance— Gervaise Chard, a free-lance journalist of 19 Nathalie Gardens, Ealing. Chard 'phoned from his office to Mrs. Grant advising her that owing to unexpected circumstances he would not be able to keep his appointment.

Anthony paused here to think. Eventually he made certain notes and passed on. Amongst other things, he noted Chard's name, occupation and address. He then read the statements of Dorothy Grant, Maureen Townsend, Ella Fanshawe and Ethel Thornhill. He carefully noted that the widow made no accusation or suggestion of any kind against her husband's fidelity. This fact he considered as significant.

Anthony continued by reading the statements taken by the Police from Roy Thornhill and Richard Fanshawe. He noted (with some disappointment, let it be said) that the former was a motor engineer with a business in Tudor and the latter, a Local Government Officer. He would not have minded running against a certain connection with the coal trade. He smiled whimsically at the thought. But there was one thing which emerged from the various statements which could not be gainsaid. All the people in Grant's inner circle of friendship had unshakable alibis for the evening of his presumed murder. And not too-cleverly constructed alibis at that! Anthony checked them all as they had been presented to the Police. All—with the exception of this man, Gervaise Chard. There seemed to be no statement here from Chard. He would certainly have to look into that.

He then examined the file which contained the typewritten note which had been taken from Hubert Grant's overcoat pocket. He read this note carefully.

Wednesday morning. My darling Hubert, I simply must see you tonight. I will he waiting for you in the usual place and at the usual time. Yours always, V.

"The usual place" and "the usual time". Anthony stood by the fireplace and studied the phrases. They undoubtedly suggested an understanding of some duration between Hubert Grant and the writer. That is to say, if they were genuine. "V"! Who was "V"? He turned to Inspector Sim's report on this particular point.

No woman could he traced anywhere in the district who could, he reasonably associated with this note. "V", of course, might very well have stood for a nickname of some kind and not signified an appropriate Christian name. Every avenue of inquiry which the Police explored in this respect ended in a blank wall.

Anthony went back to his chair and thought things over. Returning to a perusal of the file after a time, he found further particulars and details with regard to Dorothy Grant which had evidently been added by the Police at a later date.

Mrs. Grant (widow of Hubert Grant) some short time after her husband's death secured position as cashier in Rose's, High Street, Tudor. This is a printers' and stationers'. About six months later, Mrs. Grant sold house in Bullen and removed from the district. New address at Simonstone, Essex. No suspicious circumstances attendant on this move of any kind.

Here the Police record ended. With the exception of the notes on the inquest proceedings to which Anthony referred last of all. These yielded him scarcely anything worthy of mention. Anthony noted that the Coroner was Dr. Dodd-Winstanley. From the various remarks and opinions he had interjected from time to time, Dr. Dodd-Winstanley appeared to be much more endowed with intelligence than most of his brethren. Eventually the jury had returned an open verdict. Anthony was not surprised at this fact. In view of the facts which had been put in front of them, any other decision could hardly have been expected. As MacMorran had indicated to him, when he had handed over the files, there was no hint or sign of Weston *anywhere*. On the other hand, if the killings of Weston and of his wife were actuated by revenge—surely the odds were that the revenge was for the murder of Hubert! In what direction was there any other motive? The woman "V" had never been found. If she had had a husband—here Anthony shook his head impatiently. He had become annoyed with himself. He was allowing his thoughts to be diverted into the most absurd and even ridiculous channels. Suddenly he made a resolve. He went to his telephone and rang Chief Inspector MacMorran at New Scotland Yard. The Inspector himself answered the 'phone.

"I want to ask you a question, Andrew. You shouldn't have any difficulty in answering it. What's the full name of the firm which employed Laurence Weston?"

"I can tell you that at once, Mr. Bathurst. It was a firm of accountants and auditors—Hatfield, Le Fleming and Co., near London Wall somewhere; I believe. You'll find 'em in the telephone directory. I didn't go there myself. Hemingway covered it. If it's any information to you, everything's all right at that end. They gave Weston a splendid name in every respect. Thought the world of him. According to the story Hemingway brought back with him, Weston was sitting pretty there. Would have finished up with a really 'posh' job with 'em."

"Right-o, Andrew. Many thanks for the information. I want to have just a couple of words with Messrs. Hatfield, Le Fleming and Co. Shan't detain 'em overlong."

MacMorran became immediately curious. "You sound to me as though you're on to something. Am I right?"

"Don't know yet, Andrew. Not sure. You'll have to restrain your inordinate curiosity for an hour or so. Adios."

Anthony rang off. His next job was to look for Hatfield, Le Fleming & Co., in the first edition of the current *London Telephone Directory*. When he had found the number, he got through at once and asked for the secretary. After some delay, a reedy-voiced man began to talk to him.

"This is Mr. Chester Marsden . . . Yes, secretary to Hatfield, Le Fleming and Co. . . . Yes . . . yes . . . yes. What is your inquiry, please?"

Anthony explained who he was and what it was that he wanted.

"I see," came the thin, querulous voice, "well, then, tell me *exactly* what you desire to know."

Anthony provided more details. Chester Marsden listened to him with what Anthony thought, at the other end of the line, must be seething impatience. At last the secretary, unable to contain himself any longer, broke in.

"I can answer that for you at once. The late Mr. Laurence Weston, as far as we, his employers, are concerned, had no connection with any firms or companies to do with fuel supplies. No, sir. None whatever! I trust that my information completely answers your inquiry."

Anthony intimated that it did but stated at the same time that he had one more favour to ask of Mr. Chester Marsden.

"What is that?"

Anthony made his second request plain.

"Certainly. I can do that for you with pleasure. I understand that you require a specimen of the late Mr. Laurence Weston's handwriting. Am I clear on that?"

"That's it, Mr. Marsden. Let me have anything you can spare. I'll tell you what you can do. You will probably feel more satisfied to do it in this way. Address it to Chief Inspector Andrew MacMorran at New Scotland Yard. As you probably know, that's the name of the gentleman who's in charge of the investigation into Mr. Weston's death. Thank you very much, and accept my apologies for taking up your valuable time. I'm extremely obliged to you."

Anthony hung up. He'd make arrangements for MacMorran to bring that over to him directly he got it. He then decided that he would interview one or two other people—including a certain Mr. Gervaise Chard.

CHAPTER VII

WHEN Anthony Lotherington Bathurst ascended the steps of the Town Hall and municipal offices at Tudor, he had gone there with the express intention of having a talk with Fanshawe. He had noted from the dossier he had been privileged to read, that Fanshawe was Chief Clerk in the Town Clerk's Department. When Anthony entered the Town Hall, he walked straight to the vestibule to make his inquiries of the hall-porter. The hall-porter was, naturally, not there. Anthony waited patiently for him to put in an appearance. After a time, during which the situation had not altered in any degree, Anthony stopped a weedy-looking youth who was lounging along smoking a cigarette and inquired as to where he could find Mr. Fanshawe. The youth stabbed with his cigarette in the direction of a room immediately to Anthony's right hand.

"Ver-tha," said the youth.

"Thank you," said Anthony. "I had hoped to find the hall-porter here, but he appears to have been superannuated."

"'E's gawn out," replied the youth, "tergettermiddie."

"Really?" said Anthony. "Many thanks for the information. It was a happy inspiration on my part when I decided to speak to you."

He turned and walked over to the room which the youth had indicated. Several typists carrying cups of tea looked at him through their nostrils as though he were something that had arrived as a result of a most unpleasant volcanic eruption. The room he entered was evidently a general office. A man was speaking on the 'phone.

"It's 'Browning' Avenue. I said 'Browning'! No. Let me spell it to you. Bee-har-ho-doubleyou-hen-heye-hen-gee! That's it! Now you put that down and don't forget it."

He replaced the receiver, turned and saw Anthony. "Wotcher-want?" he asked.

"A word with Mr. Fanshawe, if I may have it. Perhaps you wouldn't mind taking my card in to him." Anthony passed over his card.

"Not tryin' to sell anything, are you?" said the man with a suspicious look—"because if you are—I'll tell you straight off it's no good. You ain't got an earthly."

"No," returned Anthony, "you may dismiss any anxiety on that account—I have nothing to sell—not even good manners."

The man grinned—he was under the impression evidently that Anthony had paid him a compliment. Mr. Bathurst waited a few more minutes before the man reappeared. He was then conducted into an inner room. A man was sitting at a table in this room to whom Anthony took an instinctive liking at first sight. His dark hair was streaked with grey. His face was long and lean but creased with lines of good fellowship and good humour. Dick Fanshawe looked up. When he looked up, Anthony liked him even more.

"Sit down, Mr. Bathurst—there's a chair there, and let me know what I can do for you."

Anthony smiled. "Thanks. As you may have already guessed, I'm here in the matter of the Weston murders. Am I right? Did you guess?"

Fanshawe nodded. "I had half an idea." He put his pen down on the table and turned to Anthony in his swivel-chair. "Pretty ghastly business. I knew Mrs. Weston very well."

"That's why I'm here." Anthony looked round the room. "How about a beer somewhere? More conducive—don't you think?"

Fanshawe nodded with decision. "Great idea. Come with me. Just a minute, though." Fanshawe spoke on the internal telephone. Then he joined Anthony at the door. "We'll have one at the 'Lion'. Not a bad show and it won't be overfull at this time in the morning. It's not too far."

As they walked, Fanshawe talked. Anthony let him talk. He told Anthony of his relationship with Hubert Grant "and his missus". Told him of the night Hubert had failed to arrive home and of the part he himself had been called upon to play. Anthony listened without the hint of an interruption. They came to the "Lion" and entered the saloon bar.

Anthony ordered drinks. Fanshawe continued to talk. At last, Anthony presented a question.

"Now, Fanshawe—there's one question I must ask you. I'm asking you because I think you're as well qualified to answer it as anybody—if not better. Had Dorothy Weston made the acquaintance of Weston before Grant died?"

"Oh—no! You can take that from me. She met Weston over the other side of London—at a place called Simonstone, in Essex. As a matter of fact, my missus and I popped over to see her in the car—last Whit-Monday, I think it was. We heard all about it. Quite a romantic sort of business. She gave my missus all the details. My missus was full of it for days. You know what women are over anything like that." Anthony nodded. Fanshawe drank up and ordered a second round. "This recent business was a great shock to both of us. Who on earth could have wanted to harm either of the Westons fairly beats me. Weston himself struck me as a particularly decent chap and Dorothy—well, Dorothy was always one of the very best."

"It's strange," meditated Anthony aloud, "three violent deaths coming one on top of the other. Makes one wonder where the genesis of the crimes really lies."

"You're right. When you come to think of it, poor old Dorothy has had a raw deal in life and no mistake. First Hubert, then Frances, and now this double murder."

"Frances? Who was Frances? I haven't heard either of her or about her."

Anthony's statement was not strictly true.

"Frances was Dorothy's daughter by Hubert Grant. Didn't you know that?"

"No. What happened to her?"

"Oh—a perfectly ghastly business—the poor kid was run over and killed early in the year. Coming home from school one day. Hubert's father wrote and told me all about it. It nearly finished the old boy—and his missus. They're by way of being a marvellous old couple—getting on for eighty, both of 'em."

Anthony was still content to listen. "Nice little kid, Frances," continued Fanshawe; "my missus was terribly upset about it when she heard. That was rather peculiar, too—in a way. The Westons didn't tell us they'd moved from Simonstone to Sudmore. Nothing in it perhaps—may have slipped their memory—but considering how friendly we'd been with Dorothy, we thought it rather funny."

Fanshawe looked at the clock in the saloon bar. "Look here, I'll tell you what. I've an idea. Come home with me and have a bite of lunch and meet the missus. She'll tell you a darned sight more about everything than I can. Where's your car?"

"In your grounds at the Town Hall."

"Good. We'll stagger back and get it. You can drive me home. What do you say? On?"

Anthony smiled at Fanshawe's eagerness. "Right. I'll accept your invitation."

He felt that an interview with Mrs. Fanshawe would probably be more profitable to him than anything Fanshawe could give him. Ten minutes brought the car and them to the Fanshawe villa. Ella Fanshawe was, of course, delighted to meet him. Fanshawe introduced him and explained the situation to her. She responded by putting up a really excellent cold lunch. *Hors-d'oeuvres*, fresh salmon and a most delectable fruit flan. Anthony gradually worked round to the main purpose of his errand to Tudor. He let Fanshawe put many of the questions to his wife that he had put to Fanshawe. Eventually Fanshawe came to the question of Dorothy's first knowledge of Laurence Weston.

"I can tell you exactly how she met him," explained Ella Fanshawe. "She told me the whole story. It was like this. After Hubert died, she felt that she couldn't stay in Bullen or Tudor any longer. She had a job in the district, but she felt that she couldn't possibly keep on at it. She told Frances how she felt about things and decided to move somewhere right away. If possible and practicable, somewhere on the other side of London. She chose the Essex side, a little place called Simonstone. Quite nice—Dick and I went over there in the car—last Whitsun. Well, when she had been there some little time, she felt that she must take up something. You know what I mean—get an interest. Just about this time, she saw an advertisement in the local paper at Simonstone for players for an Amateur Dramatic Society. She had always had a hankering for this sort of thing—used to talk about it to me quite a lot when she lived here—and when she heard that these people needed new members, she applied, had an audition or whatever they call it, and was accepted. I'm not surprised. I should say from what I know of her that she was pretty good at all that sort of thing."

Ella Fanshawe paused—to take breath. Anthony seized the opportunity to nod his sympathy and interest. Ella took up the parable again.

"Well, there isn't much more for me to tell—she turned up to a rehearsal or something and met Laurence Weston. He happened to be a member of the Simonstone Dramatic Society. Naturally someone introduced them. As a matter of fact, poor Dorothy told me that he originally thought she was a *Miss* Grant. She looked frightfully young for her age. Well, they used to meet at rehearsals, they were attracted to each other and the upshot of it all was that Laurence

Weston asked her to marry him. That's the full story, Mr. Bathurst, as I had it from Dorothy's own lips."

"I see. Well, that's very clear, Mrs. Fanshawe. Thank you very much for the information." He looked in the direction of Fanshawe. "Perhaps you will forgive me if I strike yet another personal note?"

Fanshawe gestured his acceptance of the position.

"I'm going right back to the early stages. To Hubert Grant. You remember the typewritten note which was found in his overcoat pocket? Well, this is the question I'm going to ask you. You were a colleague of Grant's of several years' standing. In addition to that, you knew him as a friend. You visited his wife and him at their house and took your wife with you. You knew him, that is to say, both professionally and socially."

Fanshawe nodded.

"Well then, what were your primary reactions to Hubert's note signed 'V'? The Police questioned you, I've no doubt?" Fanshawe thought carefully before he replied. "At the time I was questioned by the Tudor Police, I hid nothing from them. I'll hide nothing from you now. I'll tell you what I thought about that note and what I still think. And that's this! It was 'hoo-ey'. If Hubert Grant went after a woman that night, it would be one of the greatest surprises that Life's ever handed out to me. You see—I knew Hubert Grant—as you've just pointed out. He was no 'wencher', believe me. He wasn't a saint—far from it—but that wasn't one of his vices. For one thing—let me put it like this—he hadn't the guts to risk his job for anything of that kind. Don't forget he had his eye fixed on becoming Borough Treasurer. Hubert Grant was a man who essentially always played for safety. He'd go 'solo' with an 'abundance' hand—that's the kind of bloke Hubert Grant was."

Dick Fanshawe stopped and then went on almost immediately.

"That's pretty well the gist of what I told the Police when they questioned me—and I'm sticking to it."

Anthony knew from what he had seen in the dossiers that what Fanshawe had just said was true. So he plied him with a further question. He looked at them so that his glance would embrace both Dick and Ella Fanshawe.

"Well, then, if that's the case—and I'll admit that I see no reason to doubt it—what did happen on the night that Hubert Grant went to his death?"

The Fanshawes looked at each other as though seeking mutual inspiration.

"I wish I knew," returned Dick. "You can guess the thousands of times I've thought about it. But I've got nowhere—absolutely nowhere."

"You can't make the slightest suggestion?"

"I cannot," replied Dick Fanshawe.

"What about you, Mrs. Fanshawe?" Anthony turned to Ella.

"To me," she said, "it's all a puzzle and a mystery. Just as these last two murders are." She leant forward towards Anthony. "Mr. Bathurst, do you think they're connected in any way with the death of Hubert?"

Anthony took some time before he replied to her. "Yes, Mrs. Fanshawe," he said at length, "I do: I'll tell you something. Something which will not be made public until the inquest on Mrs. Weston."

Ella Fanshawe's eyes were hard and brilliant as Anthony faced her. "What is that, Mr. Bathurst?"

"A piece of paper was found pinned to Mrs. Weston's frock as she lay dead on the floor."

As he made the announcement, the two Fanshawes stared at him in wonderment. Dick's eyes were wide open and Ella's lips were parted. It was she who eventually asked the inevitable question. "A piece of paper? What kind of paper?"

"A slip of paper with yet another typewritten message on it. Coincidence, isn't it? I'll tell you what this message was. I can remember it, I think, without any trouble.

"*Wishing you a happy landing on the other side of the Styx, where doubtless Hubert will arrange to meet you. I remain, sincerely yours, "Harry the Hangman".*"

He watched them both closely to see the effect of these last words. Fanshawe furrowed his brow and looked troubled.

"Don't get it," he remarked, "don't get it at all."

Ella shook her head rather helplessly.

"There's venom in it," said Anthony. "Venom and vindictiveness. Directed against Mrs. Weston. I find myself asking 'why'?"

"I can understand you. I feel much the same myself. But I can't find a reasonable answer that satisfies me." Fanshawe held out his case for Anthony to take a cigarette.

"You can't?"

"I most certainly can't. I haven't the slightest idea or theory about any one of the three murders. The whole business to me is just inexplicable."

"You know of nobody . . . who might have been venomous or vindictive towards Mrs. Grant, as she was, and who became Mrs. Weston?"

"Nobody. As far as I know, judging from the life she lived here, she hadn't an enemy in the world."

"You're not helping me much," said Anthony with a smile.

"I know we're not," replied Fanshawe ruefully. "I feel that we're both rather letting you down—but damn it all, I can't tell you what I don't know, can I?"

"Not very well," returned Mr. Bathurst—"anyhow, I'll ask you one more question. A rather peculiar one, too, you'll probably think, when you hear it. Did Mrs. Grant—I say 'Grant' advisedly—have any special interest in coal or coal merchants?"

Dick Fanshawe stared. "Haven't the foggiest, old man. Certainly I never heard that she had. But why—in the name of all that's wonderful?"

Before answering him, Anthony looked towards Ella Fanshawe. She was reacting differently. "Well, Mrs. Fanshawe, you look more promising than your husband does. What have you to tell me?"

Ella gestured to him as though she were about to utter a disclaimer. "Not very much of importance I'm afraid, Mr. Bathurst, but I've just remembered one thing. It was your reference to coal merchants that made me think of it. I can remember being at Dorothy's one afternoon, not so very long before Hubert died, when the postman came. He delivered no less than three of those coal merchant's cards to the house. I can remember seeing Dorothy bring them in with her from the front door after the postman had knocked. I saw the cards on the table afterwards. And I noticed something rather strange about them—at least I thought it was strange at the time."

"And what was that, Mrs. Fanshawe? I confess that you have me tremendously interested."

"Why—not one of these price cards that Dorothy had was from a local firm. They had all been sent to her from firms in London or thereabouts."

"How did Mrs. Grant receive these cards?"

"How do you mean, Mr. Bathurst?"

"Well—did she treat them as important or as nothing worth?"

"I don't think I noticed as much as that."

"Well—was she pleased, for instance? Or even annoyed?"

"No-o. But let me try to think. If anything, she became just a little absent-minded. That's as far as I can remember."

"H'm. Absent-minded. Might mean anything, I'm afraid. Still, never mind about that. You've cleared up one point for me. Oh, by the way, something's occurred to me. When you saw those cards on Mrs. Grant's table, which side of them did you see? Which side was uppermost? The price-list side, or the side where the address was?"

Ella considered. "The price-list side, I think."

"Bad luck again—still—can't be helped."

Anthony rose and held out his hand to her. "Many thanks—for both your help and your hospitality."

"Going?"

"Yes—must."

Ella Fanshawe smiled and shook hands with him. Anthony, as he held her hand, realized that it was not long since that she had been a distinctly attractive woman. Fanshawe came across to him questioningly.

"Tell me, Bathurst—before you leave us. I must know your opinion. Was Hubert Grant murdered?"

"I fear so, Fanshawe."

Fanshawe looked pale. "Was Weston murdered?"

"Yes. I think so."

"Was Dorothy herself murdered?"

"Oh—undoubtedly! Strangled from behind, my dear fellow. Nasty."

Fanshawe, paler than before, went and sat down. He clasped his knees between his hands.

"Oh," said Anthony Bathurst, "before I forget it. I want to have a word with Gervaise Chard. You know him, too, I think? What's the best place to find him these days?"

Ella Fanshawe assured him promptly. "At the *Daily Picture* offices, Fleet Street. But I don't think Gervaise can tell you as much as we have."

"You never know," returned Anthony. "And cheer-o till next time."

CHAPTER VIII

DIRECTLY he set out to interview Gervaise Chard, Anthony felt pretty certain that he knew where the interview would take place. He knew the district and he had begun to know this man. He 'phoned to the offices of the *Daily Picture*, only to be informed that Gervaise Chard was out.

"In which one am I likely to find him?" asked Anthony with uncanny prescience.

"Try the 'Dragon'," came the laconic response as the receiver was hung up.

Anthony put on his thinking cap. He had, of course, never actually met Chard and hadn't the slightest idea what he looked like. "I can but try," he said to himself, and at once made his way from the 'phone box he had just used, to the hostelry which had been nominated as the most likely for Chard's visiting. Once in the bar, he ordered a drink and, as he paid for it, whispered a direct inquiry to the barmaid who served him.

"In the far corner," she answered, "with the long cigarette-holder."

Anthony saw where she had indicated, took his beer, and walked over. The man who had been pointed out to him, was short and inclined to be fat. His face was plump and ruddy and unruly fair hair fell over his forehead.

"Mr. Gervaise Chard," said Anthony, "am I right?"

"You are," said Chard, "right or right beside. And I suggest that either's good enough. And what about you, sir?"

Anthony passed over his card as he had passed it over to Dick Fanshawe in Tudor not so many hours previously.

"H'm," said Chard as he took in the significance of the name, "the Weston murders, I presume?"

"You've said it," replied Anthony.

"From what angle?" Chard leant back in his seat.

"I'm afraid—the official. Why? Will it make any difference?"

Chard was slow in answering. "Seems to me it might. Without knowing any more than I do at the moment. I was a friend of Mrs. Weston's. And because of that friendship, I should hesitate to say anything that might afterwards be used conceivably for either her detriment or her hurt. You see, my friendship with her was rather real. I may say that I liked her immensely."

Anthony drew up his chair nearer to their table. "Let me order some more beer," he said, "and then let us talk. 'Us'—Chard, and that word 'us' means Gervaise Chard and Anthony Bathurst. Notice the well-defined limits."

Chard made no answer, but he nodded as though he understood. Anthony bought the beer. Chard drank. Anthony drank and said "listen to me." Chard folded his arms and put them on the table. Anthony talked. Chard listened intently. After a time he made his first interruption.

"Wait. I may have absurd ideas on the subject and I may even have got you all wrong—but here's telling you what I did on the evening of Hubert Grant's murder. You may as well know now as later. I had to cover a first night at the 'Excalibur' for the *Sunday Sunshine*. The job came along suddenly. I couldn't refuse it. What was the show, now? Just a minute and I shall remember it, I know. *The Proof of the Pudding*. That's where I was. I got a girl in the office to 'phone Dorothy at Bullen and tell her that pressure of work would prevent me going along to her 'do'. Put that down, will you? Before we go any further I shall have to assert myself—I can see that."

Anthony nodded and went on. Chard listened attentively to all that he had to say. He looked extremely mystified when Anthony came to the typed message from "Harry the Hangman", but Anthony noticed that he offered no contribution of opinion. Anthony came by stages to the end of what he intended to tell Chard. Chard nodded his appreciation of Anthony's narrative.

"Now," said the latter. "I want you to help me. In this way. Answer one or two questions for me. Yes?"

"All right," returned Chard guardedly, "but I reserve the right to refuse any of them."

"Well—we'll see about that when we come to them." Anthony asked about Hubert.

"In my opinion, for what it's worth, and I knew Hubert Grant pretty well, you must remember, he had no feminine entanglements. That letter which was found in his overcoat pocket, I regarded and still regard as 'phoney'. There's your first question answered."

Anthony asked about Laurence Weston. Chard looked at him suspiciously.

"I had never heard of Laurence Weston, had never heard his name mentioned until some time after Dorothy had married him, Take it from me, he was never in her life at Bullen."

"Was there any other man?" Anthony thrust the question at him sharply and fiercely.

"This is where I exercise my right of refusal," returned Gervaise Chard.

"De mortuis," murmured Anthony, *"nil nisi 'bunkum' est."*

Chard flushed. "That's unkind and uncalled for."

"I don't mean it like that. Why not help me to the truth if you possibly can?"

Chard remained silent. Anthony tried him again. "It can do no harm to her now. Whereas lies and falsehood may always hurt."

Chard still maintained his silence. This time Anthony was determined not to break it. Eventually Chard spoke.

"You've certainly got a way with you."

"I'm Irish," responded Anthony, "so what would you?"

"All right. I'll answer the question you ask me. After all, I don't suppose that I can do very much harm at this stage. Most of the harm, at least, seems to have been done already."

Anthony waited for him. Chard drank some beer and made a start.

"I used to go the Grants' place at Bullen fairly frequently. Little social gatherings, card parties—you know the kind of crush I mean."

Anthony nodded.

Chard continued. "I used to go every year at Christmas. Poor old Hubert used to fancy his Yuletide party no end. I'll say this for him—he always did us jolly well. Not exactly wizard—but very satisfactory, thank you. Mostly the same crowd of us used to pick up the invitations. Especially did this apply to the Christmas 'do'. There used to be, on the average, a dozen to twenty people there. We had good times. Intelligent people, neither too rich nor too poverty-stricken to enjoy the good things of Life. When we played games, they were more or less intelligent games—not just ridiculous assing about or playing the giddy ox. I liked Dorothy, as I told you just now, and I could put up with Hubert. I was invited there to the Christmas party just a month or two before Hubert handed in his dinner pail. When I got there, I found the usual mob in attendance. The Fanshawes, the Thornhills, Hubert's people—a wonderful old couple—a girl named Townsend and a doctor named Kennerley, with his sister. Kennerley himself was a bachelor. We all mixed in well together and the whole affair was going with a swing when I spotted something,"

Gervaise Chard paused in his story. Again, Anthony let him take his own time with regard to proceeding. Chard drank again and put down his glass.

"We had started to play 'Murder'. Or perhaps it would be truer to say that we were all waiting for the word 'go'. Frances, the little girl, simply revelled in it, so we nearly always played it first, if only to please her. I spotted something which took me back instantly to an incident which had occurred in the house earlier in the same day. As a matter of fact, very soon after I had staggered in. Now remember this again—I liked Dorothy Grant, in a 'pally' sort of way—and we understood each other well enough to be able to say most things to each other without risking offence—you know what I mean. We were having a cocktail together. Before sitting down to dinner. Dinner at the Grants' on Christmas Day was usually round about three o'clock. Having it later, meant breaking too much into the evening. Well—I said something to Dorothy, something pretty ordinary—I can't remember now exactly what it was and to my utter amazement, she rounded on me and properly tore me off a strip. Fact! When she had her say, I knew without the shadow of a doubt that there was a rift in the lute of Grant. Something was radically wrong between her and husband Hubert. *And*—rightly or wrongly—from the terms of what she had said to me, I deduced another man on the horizon. I knew her well, you see, knew her reactions and psychologies."

Chard leant over to take a cigarette from Anthony's proffered case. Anthony held a lighted match for him. Chard exhaled two or three wisps of smoke before he continued.

"Nothing more transpired. We had dinner and we came to the evening and Frances's star turn 'Murder'. I've already mentioned one of the guests—a Dr. Kennerley. And that he was there with his sister. As far as I know, he had never been to the Grants' house before. Certainly I had never met him there. He was a good-looker. Tall, dark, clean-shaven and with that 'come hither' look in the eyes that pleases most women and completely devastates some. A ladies' man all right, if ever there were one! Just after 'Murder' had started, I spotted Kennerley looking at Dorothy and Dorothy was a darned attractive woman, don't forget. She was thirty, I know, but had the knack of looking at least ten years younger. I saw his look and I recognized all the signs and symptoms—believe me! *And then I saw Hubert, of all people, watching Kennerley as he was watching Dorothy!* I didn't like the situation one little bit. To tell the truth, I scented trouble there and then. Here, however, my story begins to peter out. I *believe*, though, that when the players scattered in the dark for the game to begin in earnest, Kennerley followed Dorothy up to one of the bedrooms and that Hubert knew what his game was. They say that the spectator sees most of the game and I certainly saw plenty that night."

"What happened after that?"

"Ah—that's where my story peters out very definitely. I kept my eyes open. But nothing seemed to happen. Hubert looked sick. Dorothy looked pretty tense and keyed up with excitement. Kennerley looked like a man who was very much on his guard. Belligerent perhaps, but defensive at that. The atmosphere, though, which I knew had been created, lingered on. As far as I was concerned, the show, as a show, had most decidedly begun to flop. I never saw Hubert Grant again."

Anthony thought hard over what Gervaise Chard had just told him. From some points of view, this was the most effective contribution that he had so far received. There was something tangible here. Most of the other stuff had been nebulous.

"All this, of course, that you have told me, you kept from the Police when they approached you, after Hubert's death?"

"You bet I kept my mouth shut. I wasn't shopping Dorothy for a King's ransom. Not on your life. It's only because the poor girl's dead, that I've opened out to you. Had she been still alive, I shouldn't have breathed a syllable."

Anthony found himself beginning to wonder more and more. These were deep waters indeed. "What happened to this Dr. Kennerley—any idea?"

"He's still where he was, I believe. At Tudor, in the Local Government Service. Colleague of Hubert's—or was. Public Health Department—or something like that."

Anthony felt the thrill of the chase take hold of him. "I wish you had told me that before. What's the actual job that he holds down?"

"Let me see. Hubert did tell me." Chard wrinkled his brows. After a time his face cleared. "I've got it. It's come back to me. Assistant M.O.H. I remember Hubert telling me that he was sweating on the top line about getting the M.O.H.'s job. The present man's near his retiring age and Kennerley is hanging on there to get the job when it's going."

Anthony made mental notes.

"You know," said Chard reminiscently, "I've often found myself wondering what was the real reason why Hubert invited the Kennerleys for that Christmas Day dinner. As I said, nobody there seemed to know them."

"Except perhaps—Mrs. Grant?"

"Yes. I suppose that's about the size of it." Chard nodded in agreement.

Anthony felt that the time had come to play his trump card. "Let's get back for a bit to Weston," he said quietly. "The man who fell dead in the 'Greatorex' Restaurant the other day. Somehow, for myself, I always find myself coming back to him. When he married Mrs. Grant, they lived first of all at Simonstone in Essex. After a while, they moved farther out to Sudmore in the same county. Now, you have insisted to me that Weston and Mrs. Grant were unknown to each other at the time of Hubert Grant's death."

"I'd swear to that in a Court of Law."

"Good. I like people to have decided opinions. Now look at this, will you?"

Anthony produced an envelope upon which a name and address had been written. Chard took it from him and studied it.

"Well?" he said interrogatively.

"That," said Anthony, "is a specimen of Laurence Weston's hand-writing. Supplied to me, at my request, by the firm of accountants and auditors in whose service he had been for many years—right up to the day of his death."

"I've never seen it before," said Chard, "so it's no use your—"

Anthony cut in. "Just a minute, and you'll see to where I'm leading."

He rummaged in his pocket again, to produce other articles. "Now—cast your eye over these, my dear Chard."

Chard saw a number of postcards in front of him. Upon picking the top one up, he saw that it was the usual postcard issued by a coal merchant, advertising the prices of his various grades of coal. Turning it over, he saw, too, that it had been addressed to "Mrs. D. Grant, 'Red Roofs', Ridgway Gardens, Bullen, Surrey". "Notice the handwriting," observed Mr. Bathurst softly.

Chard had gone white. Anthony was not sure of the emotional quality which had caused this condition.

"Yes," replied Chard. His voice was just a little out of control. "I do, it's the same as the other. It's Weston's without a doubt." His breath came quickly.

"Exactly," remarked Anthony; "just my point." He waited.

Chard bit his lip.

"But just a minute," he said after a few seconds' interval, "before we jump too hastily to conclusions. Isn't it possible that these cards were sent off after Hubert had died?"

"I've thought of that, too," returned Anthony, "but look at the dates on the postmarks. I want you to. You know when Hubert Grant was drowned. I should hate you to be unconvinced."

Chard examined the various dates with close attention. "You're right," he said slowly. "Every one of these cards was posted to Dorothy while Hubert was alive. Honestly, Bathurst, I'm amazed!" He continued to look through the cards. "I say," he said, "this is damned funny. There are actually two here that were posted to her on the day preceding Hubert's death. I remember the date of that so well. They must have reached her on the morning of the very day he died. I don't know that I like that. I regard it as highly significant."

"I am in no mood to contradict you," replied Mr. Bathurst.

CHAPTER IX

ANTHONY sat in MacMorran's room at Scotland Yard. The Inspector was talking and Anthony was listening.

"I've been through the bungalow at Sudmore with Inspector Chetwode, as carefully as I know how. And believe me, Mr. Bathurst, I've picked up nothing. You can take it from me that there's nothing there that's likely to help us to a solution. Not a crumb. Not a sausage."

Anthony smiled at him. "And yet, Andrew, despite all you've just said, I hope to find a certain something when I go down there again. If I don't, I shall be surprised. Still—never mind—we'll wait and see." Anthony paced the room. "In some ways, Andrew, I regard this as the most remarkable case that has ever come my way. With such a sinister genesis behind it. I know who killed Hubert Grant, but I'm only just beginning to realize who murdered the Westons."

MacMorran looked at him with incredulity. "Eh—what's that?"

Anthony continued as though MacMorran had said nothing. "And when I reveal the truth to you, Andrew, I'm afraid you're going to have the biggest shock you've ever had in your career. That's what I'm thinking, Andrew. But I have one more call to make before I can reasonably feel certain of my ground, and I'm making that call today, my dear chap."

"In what part of the world are you making it? Sudmore?"

"No. I'm going to Tudor. I may have to go on to Sudmore later. I shall have the car. But I'll see first how I get on at Tudor." Anthony picked up his hat. "As a matter of fact, Andrew," he said, "I've already been to Tudor once this week and if I'd had any luck, I shouldn't have had to go again. I suppose you wouldn't care to come with me?"

"I would—but I can't! I've an appointment with the Commissioner at eleven o'clock on the 'Greatorex' restaurant end of the case. I'll tell him where you've gone and also of your roseate optimism." MacMorran grinned at his pleasantry.

"That's O.K. with me, Andrew. And I'll be round again tomorrow. Have the red carpet down, will you?"

Anthony waved his hand and departed. An hour and a half later he was in Tudor. He first sought out Fanshawe in the Town Clerk's Department at the Town Hall. Fanshawe was in and at once put up his "Engaged" sign when Anthony was shown into his room. Anthony got to business with him immediately.

"Why didn't you tell me about Kennerley?" he thrust.

Fanshawe didn't bat an eyelid. "What about Kennerley?"

"Incidents," grinned Anthony, "at the Grant dinner party on a certain Christmas Day."

"What the hell are you talking about?" continued Fanshawe.

"Don't you know?"

"No. Shouldn't suggest I didn't if I did. But don't beat about the bush. Come right over."

"All right. I'll tell you what Gervaise Chard told me. I ran him to earth up in Fleet Street in a saloon bar. This is the story of Gervaise."

Anthony told Fanshawe all that Gervaise Chard had said with regard to Dorothy Grant, Kennerley and Hubert. He concluded the narration by saying "well, Fanshawe, you've heard the yam, how much is there in it?"

"Again, as far as I'm concerned," answered Fanshawe, the essence of coolness, "nothing at all. If things were as Gervaise Chard hints—well, leave me out—because I didn't spot the slightest sign of 'em." Fanshawe leant back in his chair.

"Right-o. I'll accept you at face value. But do me a favour, will you? That's what I really came to ask you. Take me round to Dr. Kennerley's office and do the honours. By the way, is he M.O.H. yet?"

"No. Still Assistant. Dr. Nance hasn't retired yet. Early in the New Year, I believe. All right—I'll take you round to Kennerley. Now?"

"I think so. Why not?"

"Suits me. Come along then. The Public Health Department's on the other side of the building." Fanshawe looked at his watch. "We should catch him in just about now."

"Pal of yours?" queried Anthony.

"No. Not exactly. Why do you ask?"

"Oh—merely wondered. I always like to be fortified with as much knowledge as possible. It helps me to avoid making a mistake."

They walked round the side of the Tudor Town Hall, out through a small gate and came round to the other side.

"This is the Public Health Department," announced Fanshawe. "The first room on the left is the general office, the second belongs to Dr. Nance, and the third is Kennerley's. I sincerely hope you catch him in. He's by way of being an elusive bird."

Fanshawe approached the third door on the left and tapped on a glass panel.

"Come in," cried a voice.

Fanshawe stuck his head round the door. Then he jerked his head back again, turned and beckoned to Anthony Bathurst. "It's all right, Bathurst, Dr. Kennerley is in and disengaged. Come along."

They entered.

"Oh, Dr. Kennerley," opened Fanshawe, "may we have a private word with you?"

"Certainly—if you don't take too long. Sit down."

"Thanks. This is Anthony Bathurst. Dr. Kennerley, Dr. Julian Kennerley. I've taken the liberty of bringing Bathurst round to have a word with you. Hope you won't mind."

Kennerley frowned a little. "Bathurst? The name—"

"Oh, you know the connection. On this occasion with Dorothy Weston's affair. Bathurst has got the idea that you may be able to help him."

Anthony watched Kennerley's reception of this last statement. He saw that the frown on Kennerley's brow grew bigger.

"Why," he asked a trifle aggressively, "what on earth gives him that idea?"

Anthony turned to Dick Fanshawe. "Well, many thanks for bringing me round and introducing me to Dr. Kennerley. I'll drop in to your office and see you again before I go."

The hint was unmistakable. Fanshawe saw it and accepted it. "Right-o, Bathurst. I'll expect you then. In the meantime you and the doctor here can have a chat together."

Fanshawe rose from his chair and slid out of the room gracefully. Anthony took stock of Julian Kennerley's appearance. He was certainly a good-looking man. Tall, dark, well-cut features, dominating eyes, yet withal there was an expression on his face which Anthony instinctively disliked.

"Yes," he repeated to Anthony, "from where have you picked up the idea that I can help you over the Weston affair?"

Anthony's eyes met his and held them. "Dr. Kennerley, the Commissioner of Police has asked me to have a look at the case. One of the threads I've managed to pick up leads to you. To neglect that entirely would be incompetence on my part. That's the position between us at the moment."

"Incompetence and the Police wouldn't be strangers to each other so I don't see what you're worried about."

"Too true, I'm afraid." Anthony smiled sweetly. "Although I don't know that your profession can shout too loudly on that score."

There came a silence. Julian Kennerley fidgeted with a pen. "What do you want?" he asked sharply.

Anthony determined to strike at once. "What happened on the Christmas Day before Hubert Grant died?"

Kennerley looked superciliously across his table. At the same time he hesitated for half a second, perhaps, before he replied. "I'm afraid I don't follow."

"Surely—Dr. Kennerley. I refer, of course, to Mrs. Grant, as she was then."

"I don't understand you—and I fear that you're wasting my time."

Julian Kennerley picked up a small inkpot and toyed with it ostentatiously as he sat and faced Anthony on the opposite side of the table. Anthony chanced his arm.

"You were, I think, Dr. Kennerley, an admirer of Mrs. Grant's?"

Kennerley looked ugly. "I don't like your choice of words, also I hate to detain you." He continued to play with the inkpot.

Anthony rose.

"I'm sorry. If you *won't* help the course of justice. Doctor, well then—you won't. It must remain entirely your own affair. But there have been three murders—of Hubert Grant, of Laurence Weston and of Dorothy Weston."

"Question," declared Kennerley contemptuously.

"*No* question," replied Anthony with stern insistence, "can be entertained concerning Mrs. Weston's murder! Considering that a slip of paper was found pinned to her frock which presumably had been deliberately placed there by the murderer. That's something you may not have known. Dr. Kennerley."

"I certainly did *not* know it. What was it all about?" Kennerley spoke almost carelessly.

Anthony repeated the words of the note. He was amazed at the look of growing horror that showed in Kennerley's eyes. "This somewhat remarkable note," concluded Anthony, "was signed 'Harry the Hangman'."

As he spoke, the inkpot with which Kennerley had been toying, slipped from his fingers and fell with a crash upon the table.

CHAPTER X

ANTHONY knew half the truth in a single blinding instant. He stood there quietly and waited for Julian Kennerley partly to recover himself. After a time, Kennerley looked up at him.

"Careless of me. Inkpots are not the most convenient things to play with."

"They are not alone in that respect, I suggest, Dr. Kennerley."

Kennerley appeared to regain much of his ordinary composure. "What do you mean exactly by that?" he demanded.

"I should have thought that you would have known."

"How should I know? And what right have you to question me?" Kennerley grew truculent.

"None at all," replied Anthony. Before Kennerley could reply to this, Anthony went on. "Are you content then," he asked, "to leave it at that?"

Again Kennerley made no reply.

Anthony proceeded to hammer home his advantage. "Because if you are, I am quite sure that I am."

Kennerley's face twisted with emotion. Anthony waited for him. He made no sign. Anthony turned to make his exit. Kennerley's voice arrested his progress.

"What do you imagine you know?" he demanded aggressively.

"I quarrel with your word 'imagine'. What I know—I know. I assure you that I am not dependent for my knowledge on any flights of imagination. Good morning, Dr. Kennerley."

Kennerley bit his lip. "Look here," he said, "come back and sit down for a moment. The best thing we can do is to talk this matter over."

"As an intelligent man, Dr. Kennerley, which I am sure you are, I congratulate you on your change of attitude. Especially seeing the awkward position in which you find yourself placed."

Anthony walked back and sat in the chair again. But Kennerley still found powers of resistance.

"There is no awkwardness about my position that I can't deal with myself. You get that—right from the start. What I wanted to say to you and what I called you back for—"

Anthony struck. He realized that Kennerley must be made to understand. "Look here, Dr. Kennerley. You may as well be told now as later. The man who wrote those lines to the late Mrs. Weston, under the sobriquet of 'Harry the Hangman', will be arrested for her murder. Get that! And as you yourself happen to be that particular gentleman, you will see exactly how you stand in that respect."

It was plain to see from the colour of Julian Kennerley's face that Anthony had struck home. "You can't prove that," muttered Kennerley.

"Why, man," retorted Anthony contemptuously, "your face betrays you. And unless you've got an unshakable alibi for the morning that Mrs. Weston was murdered, I wouldn't give twopence for your chances with an average British jury."

Kennerley pulled nervously at his lower lip. "If you want to know," he said in a changed tone, "I was nowhere near Sudmore on the morning of the murder. So you can't put anything—"

"You'll have to prove it," interpolated Anthony, "and occasionally, proving where you were at a certain time isn't anything like the simple task it ought to be. If you take my advice, Kennerley, you'll tell the truth—and you'll tell it now."

Kennerley looked ugly. Anthony took a chance. "Listen to this. I rather fancy you'll be surprised." He leant across the table and spoke deliberately. "I'll start from the Christmas Day that preceded the death of Hubert Grant. Please correct me when or where I go wrong. You were a guest at the Grants' home on that Christmas Day. You were attracted by your hostess. It may have been but a temporary attraction—a mere passing fancy—but that there was this sentiment on your part, I am firmly convinced." Anthony began to speak more slowly. He desired to see the effect that his words were having on Julian Kennerley. What he saw pleased him. He continued. "Mrs. Grant did not respond to these attentions on your part. Although her husband suspected them. And because of her attitude, your *amour propre* was injured and you began to nourish a violent animosity towards her. This was the condition of your mind when Hubert Grant was drowned in the waters of the Murmur."

Kennerley made a gesture with his hand as though he were about to deny something. But no denial came from his lips. Anthony went on with his recital.

"Some time after the death of Hubert Grant, the widow moved away from the district. And I suggest that she might even have passed out of your mind had not something happened to revive your interest. Would you mind confirming that, Dr. Kennerley?"

Kennerley nodded. "That's quite true. I may as well be frank. I heard from Linklater, the Borough Treasurer, that Mrs. Grant had married again. He and his wife ran into her down in the West Country somewhere." He paused for a moment, and then seemed to make up his mind with regard to something which had evidently been troubling him for some time. "I may as well tell you the whole story seeing how far things have gone and bearing in mind what you already know. It occurred to me that I would like to try a practical joke on the newly wedded pair. I had just a suspicion that everything wasn't above-board in the matter of Hubert Grant's drowning. I argued to myself like this. If they were innocent, they would treat my efforts with contempt, but if, on the other hand, they *had* been guilty of any jiggery-pokery, my little reminders would bring them up to scratch a bit and serve them damn' well right into the bargain. I couldn't prove anything, of course, but they wouldn't know that. After all, 'the play was the thing by which Hamlet caught the conscience of the King'. You may think that I acted foolishly, but I saw things differently then."

Kennerley shifted in his chair. "My main difficulty was to find out their address. I hadn't the slightest idea as to where they had gone. I didn't even know the ex-Mrs. Grant's new name. I had almost given up my project when one of those strokes of Fate came along that one cannot explain. I have an old hospital colleague in practice at Simonstone in Essex. It's near the little market-town of Brant. He asked me over for a week-end. I arrived one Saturday afternoon. His kid sister was playing in an amateur dramatic show that evening in Simonstone and they insisted upon my turning up to it. I consented. It was *The Barretts of Wimpole Street* and who should be in the cast but the girl I had known in Bullen as Dorothy Grant. I recognized her and her voice directly she came on the stage."

Kennerley began to smile to himself. He appeared to be revelling in the savour of his thoughts.

"I was delighted! I felt that Fate had delivered her and her husband into my hands. Her name was on the programme as 'Dorothy Weston' and it was easy for me to make inquiries of my host's young sister and get hold of the Westons' address. The result was that I sent my first reminder to them, or rather to her, as I addressed it to her, to arrive on the Whit-Monday. I sent a copy of the famous *Thompson and Bywaters Trial* with a note which I signed 'Harry the Hangman'."

Kennerley noticed the look in Anthony's eye.

"Refined cruelty, you think, I suppose?" Kennerley sneered.

Anthony shrugged his shoulders.

Kennerley essayed a defence. "In my opinion they deserved all that I sent them. I continued to send them similar messages at holiday times. The next I forwarded the Saturday before the August Bank Holiday but between that date and the Christmas that followed, the Westons moved. I had the tip about this quite casually, as it happened, from my old colleague's sister in the Simonstone Amateur Dramatic Club. 'Your acquaintances, the Westons,' she said, 'have moved away. Quite suddenly. And nobody in Simonstone or district seems to know either why they went or where they have gone.'"

Kennerley paused and lit a cigarette. He did not offer his case to Anthony Bathurst. Kennerley started off again.

"This sudden bolt by the Westons made me suspect them more than ever. So I determined out of sheer obstinacy to do my best to discover where they had gone. I got my friends to make certain inquiries in the district and round about the area generally. After some time, the scent was picked up again for me at a furniture storage depot and I was able to discover that they had gone as far as Sudmore, on the coast. I was as pleased as possible to think that I could put them on the spot again. I found the correct address by inquiry at the Town Hall in Sudmore and when Christmas rolled round once more, I tickled them up again. Then it occurred to me that I should grow tired of keeping up this game of mischief indefinitely. So I decided to chuck it. I sent 'em a couple of more threats—at least I think it was a couple—and then I was going to turn my hand in. I reckoned I had done enough. On one occasion I witnessed a motor accident in Cleves, and gave Weston's name and address as my own. The last two threats were addressed to Mrs. W.—like all the others."

Kennerley paused a second or so before he uttered his concluding sentence. This sentence he spoke with the utmost deliberation.

"And the amazing part of it all is this. That note which you say was pinned on Mrs. Weston when she was found dead was the finish up of my last message to her. I can't swear to the exact words, but as far as I'm able to remember them they're near enough exact. To me the whole thing is not only incredible—it's entirely without explanation."

Julian Kennerley rose from his chair and faced Anthony Bathurst. His features were working convulsively. He looked both white and worried.

"I swear I didn't murder Mrs. Weston—or her husband. In point of fact I had never even clapped eyes on him. Except in the show. I may be in a spot of bother—but I can easily get out of it. I can prove my innocence. I'll do that now." Kennerley's eyes challenged Anthony's as he spoke. "Do you mind if I leave this room for a moment? I promise you I'll be back within two minutes."

Anthony decided to give him no chances. "Where do you want to go?"

"To consult my chief officer, Dr. Nance. His room is on the opposite side of the corridor."

"I would rather you requested him to come over here." Kennerley's brows wrinkled in an unspoken question. Anthony followed up his statement. "I leave it to you to explain the circumstances. Surely you can word your request so that Dr. Nance will understand?"

A flush of annoyance showed on Kennerley's face. For a moment Anthony thought he was going to refuse. But a wiser counsel prevailed.

"All right," he said and sat down. Anthony watched him spin the dial of the internal telephone. "Is that you, Dr. Nance? This is Kennerley . . . yes, I know. I should be extremely obliged if you'd be good enough to step over to my office for a couple of minutes. I know . . . I'm sorry to bother you, but it's rather important. I'll explain in greater detail later. If you would be so good . . . yes. Thank you very much, sir."

Kennerley replaced the receiver. He turned to Anthony with a set, sullen expression. "What was the day of the two murders? My asking you that should prove my innocence, if nothing else."

"Last Wednesday."

"Last Wednesday—you say! Good."

Kennerley said no more. They waited for the arrival of Dr. Nance, Medical Officer of Health for the Corporation of Tudor. Dr. Nance took his time. When he eventually did arrive, Anthony saw a stout, heavily built man who suggested in appearance that his age was in the early sixties. Pouches of unhealthy flesh hung from his cheeks, giving him the look of a grandmotherly bloodhound. His manner was fussy, suave and ingratiating. Anthony, directly he saw him, suffered from an almost irresistible inclination to address him as "madam"! Anthony wondered how Kennerley would tackle the matter.

"Dr. Nance," the latter opened, "this gentleman is a Mr. Bathurst. He's come down here to have a word with me concerning the death of Mrs. Weston. If you remember, sir, Mrs. Weston was Grant's widow—Grant—who was Linklater's deputy. You remember it all—of course."

Nance puffed out his cheeks and uttered unctuous sounds. "Oh yes . . . of course . . . of course."

"That's all right then, Dr. Nance—now this is what I want you to do for me. Last Wednesday morning—carry your mind back, will you please, Doctor, and tell this gentleman where I was."

The Medical Officer of Health for Tudor looked distinctly uncomfortable. For years now he had found it a complete impossibility to remember anything. Kennerley realized that it would be necessary to prompt him. Anthony remained silent. Kennerley spoke.

"The Ministry of Health inquiry, sir."

Nance's face cleared perceptibly and showed unmistakable signs of dawning intelligence. "Of course! Of course! The new extension wing at the Isolation Hospital. The inquiry here in the Town Hall under Sir Egbert Egham! I couldn't get there. I was on the dried milk report for the Committee. You attended for me. Of course! Of course!" Dr. Nance beamed in the raptures of unexpected remembrance. Kennerley's lip curled in triumph.

"Tell this gentleman, Dr. Nance, if you will be so good as to oblige me, how long the inquiry lasted."

Kennerley waited for his chief's reply.

"From ten o'clock in the morning until just on one o'clock, I believe," purred Dr. Nance.

"Thank you, sir." Kennerley turned to Anthony Bathurst. "There you are. You hear what the doctor says. Prior to the start of the inquiry, I was in this office collecting certain papers and documents which were necessary to me when I was called upon for my evidence. I was examined by Sir Egbert Egham for over twenty minutes."

"Thank you," returned Anthony.

"I trust," said Julian Kennerley, "that you are now convinced as to the truth of what I told you?"

"I will carefully note all that you have said, Dr. Kennerley. And many thanks for the interview."

Anthony bowed to Dr. Nance and walked to the door. As he let himself out he heard the Medical Officer of Health mumble something in which the opening phrase was "Madam Chairman".

Anthony 'phoned Chief Inspector Andrew MacMorran. "Any progress to report, Andrew, at either end?"

"Verra little, Mr. Bathurst. I was hopin' to hear that you'd been able to make some yourself."

Anthony laughed. MacMorran heard the laugh at the other end of the telephone. "You must discourage that quality of yours, Andrew, that we know as undue optimism. Still—I'm getting on. I'll tell you why I rang. I want you to come down to Sudmore again with me. To the Westons' bungalow. How will tomorrow morning suit you?"

MacMorran intimated that the suggested time was convenient.

"Good. That's all right then."

"How long will the job take?"

"Depends. Shouldn't take long. It's all a question of whether I find what I hope to find. If we strike lucky, I *think*—mind you, Andrew, I only say think—that I may be able to tell you who murdered the two Westons. I've had a theory for some time now which I feel must give me the true solution."

MacMorran heard Anthony Bathurst's statement with approval. "That's good news, Mr. Bathurst. Shall I pass it on to the Commissioner?"

"No—not yet. I have at least two matters which are still occasioning me considerable interest. That's why I want to run down to Sudmore again."

"What are they?"

"The radiogram at the bungalow and the nearest approach to a medicinal chest which I can find there."

MacMorran whistled. "You don't say?"

"I do, Andrew—and very deliberately at that. I'll pick you up at the 'Yard' at ten ack emma. Time suit you?"

"O.K.," replied Chief Inspector MacMorran.

CHAPTER XI

WHEN Anthony Bathurst entered MacMorran's room at the "Yard" in accordance with certain arrangements which he had previously made, he found that Julian Kennerley, Chard and Fanshawe had all arrived before him. Andrew MacMorran, expectant and flushed with the anticipation of coming triumph, sat on the Commissioner's other side. Sir Austin opened the proceedings with extreme brevity. He explained that the conference which they had been summoned to attend would deal with the murders of Hubert Grant, Laurence Weston and his wife, Dorothy Weston—with whom the three gentlemen invited to be present had all been acquainted. Sir Austin concluded his opening remarks by calling upon Anthony Bathurst to make a statement.

"Sir Austin Kemble," said Anthony, "instructed me to invite you three gentlemen to be present this afternoon. During the time we are here I hope to get at the truth of the Weston murders. I might say at this juncture, that Mr. and Mrs. Grant senior have also been asked to be present and are hopeful of being with us a little later on in the afternoon."

Anthony paused. Chard looked puzzled, Kennerley defensive and Fanshawe keenly interested.

"I will begin," said Anthony, "by giving you my own theory of the Grant-Weston murders. The fact that I am and shall be, unable to prove some of what I am about to relate, must, for the time being, be accepted and, as it were, shelved. In that respect I am compelled to place myself in your hands. Is that understood?"

There were murmurs of acceptance from the company. Anthony went on.

"Thank you. Here then is my story. I will begin with the murder of Hubert Grant. In effect the 'removal' of Hubert Grant. His murderer will never be hanged. It was Laurence Weston—one of the cleverest, most cunning and most cold-blooded murderers it has ever been my lot to encounter. Dorothy Grant, as she was then, was fully party to the crime and an accessory before the fact. I suggest that she and Weston were lovers, who by extreme care and assiduous calculation had kept their understanding not only unsuspected by Hubert Grant the husband, but from everybody else as well."

A quick movement came from Julian Kennerley.

"Weston knew that if he provided Dorothy with an absolutely unshakable alibi and could not himself be connected with the crime in any way at all, they were invulnerable. He laid his plans thus, accomplished his purpose, and waited an appreciable time before he 'met' Mrs. Grant again and married her! Here is my proof of Weston's proximity to Mrs. Grant before Grant's murder. You will remember that all the Police inquiries into Grant's death failed to come into touch with Laurence Weston. Look at these—will you, please? Exhibit A. A specimen of Weston's handwriting submitted to me a few days ago by the firm with whom he was employed."

Anthony passed round an envelope to all the occupants of the room.

"Now—Exhibit B. Please observe the various dates. All of them—I have checked them carefully—were posted to Mrs. Grant to her house in Bullen *prior* to Hubert Grant's murder." Anthony circulated the pack of coal "trade-cards" he had taken from the bedroom at Sudmore. "Those cards, I suggest, gentlemen, were 'code' messages to Dorothy Grant probably as to detailed arrangements for the evening and the manner of Grant's murder. In the cases where the address has been written, the handwriting is Weston's without the shadow of a doubt. Mrs. Weston, as she became, made the mistake of retaining them. Sentiment? Very probably, I think."

There were gasps of amazement and incredulity as the cards passed from hand to hand for examination.

"You will observe, gentlemen, I am convinced, that here is undoubted proof of Weston's presence in Mrs. Grant's life while she was still the wife of Hubert Grant."

Dick Fanshawe leant forward from the seat in which he was sitting. "How do you explain the note that was found in Grant's pocket? The one which was signed with the initial letter 'V'? I was with Mrs.

Grant on the night that Hubert Grant was murdered and I'm naturally, therefore, rather keenly interested in that particular matter."

"I think that I can answer that for you quite satisfactorily. That note was prepared by Weston and put into Grant's pocket by Weston. It would cloud the issue and direct suspicion as to marital infidelity from the wife and on to Hubert Grant himself."

Fanshawe nodded. "Thank you."

Anthony prepared to continue. "In time, the guilty pair came together again. Not too quickly. Weston was a strategist of the first water. There was no haste and no impatience. But they had reckoned, and I happen to be sure of this part of the story, without a singularly jealous and unusually vindictive man. This man half-suspected them, but of course he had no proof to bring against them. All he could do, and did, was to torture Mrs. Weston at cold-bloodedly regular intervals by correspondence. The rather frightening 'sobriquet' under which he chose to mask his identity was 'Harry the Hangman'."

As Anthony spoke these words there was a stir in the room from several of the occupants. He waited a second or so for quietude to be re-established so that he might go on again.

"I have had an interview with this gentleman and he has confessed to me of his participation in the matter in the manner that I have just described. At the same time, however, he has provided evidence which proves completely conclusively that he could not have been the murderer of either Laurence Weston or Dorothy Weston. At the same time again, he has assisted me considerably in discovering the identity of the murderer of Mrs. Weston. I will deal with the two Weston murders, with your permission, one at a time."

At that moment there came a tap on the door and Superintendent Hemingway ushered in an elderly man and woman. Anthony introduced himself to them and then announced their names to Sir Austin Kemble and the others.

"Mr. and Mrs. Grant—senior. You have arrived," he added turning to them, "at a most opportune time."

Ralph and Constance Grant sat in chairs which Hemingway placed for them.

"Please listen carefully," said Anthony, "because I can make my case in words only. I have but one more exhibit. Which I shall produce later. A message from 'Harry the Hangman' was found pinned to Mrs. Weston's clothing as she lay dead on the floor in the bungalow at Sudmore. *Three* people only were aware of the existence of this message! Get that point—it's vital to the solution of the problem. The names of those three people? The writer, Mrs. Weston—and Laurence Weston—to whom Mrs. Weston had naturally shown it. As the writer was miles away from Sudmore on that particular morning of the murder, it is obvious, therefore, that Dorothy Weston was murdered by Laurence Weston, her wedded husband."

Exclamations of incredulity came from Chard and Julian Kennerley.

"I *think*," said Anthony, "that I know how the crime was committed. Again it was clever in construction. Let me read you the report I have received from a radio expert on the condition of the radiogram which belonged to Laurence Weston." Anthony proceeded to read Victor Gosling's report. "Weston realized that he had in his possession a radiogram which owing to its particular defect virtually 'turned itself off'. After being switched on, it would broadcast for a time and then eventually 'fade-out' of its own accord. When he established his alibi with the postman, the radiogram was working. A woman was broadcasting. *Her* voice was 'Mrs. Weston's reply' which the postman 'heard'. At that moment Dorothy Weston was already dead. Weston walked to the station, caught his train, and at some future time in the morning the radiogram 'faded out'."

"Just a minute." The interruption came from MacMorran. "What about the time by Mrs. Weston's watch? Wasn't it ten minutes past ten?"

"Weston put the hands at that time to strengthen his alibi and then stopped the watch. Overwound it very likely. After he had strangled her. The message from 'Harry the Hangman' he had all ready, having cut it off the original."

Ralph Grant rose in his chair and asked a question. "You have written and told me how my unhappy son died, Mr. Bathurst. I am grateful to you. But will you kindly tell me *why* this man Weston murdered his wife—the woman who was once my daughter-in-law?"

"I would rather," returned Anthony, "leave the matter of motive until a little later. Before I come to it, I want to deal with the murder of Laurence Weston himself."

He paused and looked round the room. Ralph Grant had sat down. Chard leant forward eagerly, Kennerley's lips were curling much as usual. Fanshawe looked worried and anxious. Anthony took something from his breast-pocket. It was a small, flat tin.

"This is what I will describe as Exhibit C. It contains a certain number of capsules. I will show you one." Anthony held one up between thumb and forefinger. "This came from the Westons' bungalow at Sudmore. Its principal constituent is halibut oil. They're facts. I now approach conjecture. That its predecessor, which was taken by Laurence Weston after his lunch at the 'Greatorex' restaurant, had had inserted within it a certain amount of cyanide of potassium. In other words, Laurence Weston, having murdered his wife but a few hours previously, was on the same morning, almost, murdered by the wife whom he had murdered."

Nobody in the room spoke. Chard half rose to his feet but then sank back again to a sitting posture. Anthony waited for anything in the nature of a serious interruption. None came.

"In my opinion, Dorothy Weston, who had simple access to her husband's medicinal capsules, prepared the fatal dose and it was only a question of *when* he took the particular capsule in which she had placed the poison. I will now give you my conjectures as to the motives behind these coincident crimes. Their genesis lay in the giving way of Dorothy Weston's brain. Consider the position. The first attack came from the ammunition provided by 'Harry the Hangman'. Directed in the main against *her*. Think of her regular periods of mental torture. The sinister hints at the dreadful things that were to come. Then the death of the little girl on the eve of Mrs. Weston's confinement. Then the child born blind. These were the things 'that caught the conscience of the King'." Anthony deliberately glanced at Kennerley. "Is it to be wondered at that her brain gave way under the pressure of these influences? In addition, we don't know what other forces there were, engendered by her own conscience, that worked incessantly and insidiously. Haunted, perhaps, by the ghosts she had deposed, she struggled on until the object of her affection became the object of her hatred. Laurence Weston was the cause of her sufferings. Laurence Weston therefore must be punished. That is how I read that riddle."

Anthony looked round. He saw that many of the people to whom he spoke were showing signs of agreement with him. He continued with his story.

"The brain is an organ of such surpassing delicacy. And disease of the soul is an eerie matter. Even a gross physical cause, such as the fall of a spicule of bone from the inner table of the skull on to the surface of the membrane which covers the brain, may have the ultimate effect of transforming a hitherto noble-minded man or woman into an obscene creature, with every bestial attribute. Let alone the woman we are discussing. Which brings me to the motive of Laurence Weston for destroying his wife. What can I say? That she had ceased to charm? Or that her mental degeneration was becoming a potential danger to him? From the point of view of divulging the truth of the death of Hubert Grant? I think that each of these was a contributory cause, with the latter the predominant one. It has occurred to me that she may even have talked in her sleep." Anthony stood up. "Take it or leave it, gentlemen. It's the best that I can offer you. For myself, I harbour no doubts."

There was a buzz of conversation. MacMorran came with a question. "Where did Mrs. Weston obtain her supply of cyanide?"

Anthony shrugged his shoulders. "I think you will find that she had a certain interest in photography. It's an idea at least. But obtain it she did."

Sir Austin Kemble, MacMorran assisting him, talked with the others. Anthony listened. Occasionally he answered further questions.

Gradually, one by one, the visitors made their departures. The last to go were an old man and his wife. They looked fearlessly into a shrunken future. But a cloud had been lifted from above their heads and there was rejoicing in their spirits for their eyes had seen salvation. Anthony shook hands with them as they went out. Then he turned to MacMorran and quoted:

"God's own best will bide the Test
And God's own worst will fall
But Best or Worst or Last or First
He ordereth it all."

"Ay," replied Chief Inspector Andrew MacMorran, "that's verra true."

THE END